# TERMINAL FATES

# TERMINAL FATES

## CHOOSER OF THE SLAIN™ BOOK SEVEN

MICHAEL ANDERLE

DISRUPTIVE IMAGINATION®

LMBPN Publishing
PMB 196, 2540 South Maryland Pkwy
Las Vegas, NV 89109

Version 1.00, February 2023
eBook ISBN: 979-8-88878-164-7
Print ISBN: 979-8-88878-165-4

# THE TERMINAL FATES TEAM

## Thanks to the JIT Readers

Daryl McDaniel
Dave Hicks
Jim Caplan
Diane L. Smith
Jan Hunnicutt
Paul Westman
Kelly O'Donnell
John Ashmore
Jackey Hankard-Brodie
Christopher Gilliard

## Editor
The SkyFyre Editing Team

# CHAPTER ONE

**Manassas, Virginia**
**Shopping district**
**Saturday morning**
**Late December**

Valerie Kearie needed to cram in her yearly dose of holiday cheer before the shine fell off the apple. The heels of her boots clicked against the pavement as she strode through the first true snow flurry of the season. She clutched a cup of cinnamon-mocha hot chocolate to her chest. All around her, the store fronts glittered with holiday lights and fake glowing icicles. Across the two-lane street, young families and ambitiously charming teenagers skated on the temporary ice rink the city erected every year, along with the holly-bedecked gazebo where Santa held court nightly up until Christmas Eve. At this moment a speaker on Santa's red velvet throne piped *Winter Wonderland* into the park.

A *Second Helpings* shopping bag swung from the crook of Val's elbow as she lifted her chin to the wind and enjoyed the prickly cold snowflakes melting against her skin. It had been a fruitful morning. She'd been first through the door for the grand opening of Manassas' newest secondhand and curio shop and had come away with almost half of her Christmas shopping handled. Her bag was heavy, weighed down by a set of vintage crystal whiskey glasses for Dad, a hideously sequined skater jacket that Grams would unironically adore, and three vinyl records to feed her brother Hank's new turntable obsession. Also in the bag were the sneakers Val had worn into the store. The wedge-heeled boots with copper rivets currently adorning her feet had been too tempting to pass up.

*"The matter of gift-giving is well in hand,"* Reginleif complained from somewhere inside Val's skull. *"Now the time for sacrifices draws near. We must locate a goat."*

Valerie sighed and sipped her cocoa. She crossed the street, passing a Salvation Army bell-ringer outside the dollar store. They were passing into the historic downtown section of Manassas.

Val tried to reason with the Norse demigoddess with whom she shared a body. "We have a Yule log and the Christmas tree back at the apartment." Despite her choice of occupation, her extensive education in Scandinavian history, and her current living situation, Valerie was still a white-bread American at heart and no amount of reminding could re-brand the Douglas fir filling a quarter of her living room as a *Yule* tree instead of a *Christmas* tree in her mind. Thankfully she had been able to convince Reginleif that the pine monstrosity could do double duty.

"And I'm brewing a batch of holiday mead in my

pantry," she added. "That's at least three big traditions we're honoring. Do we *really* have to sacrifice a goat to the Allfather, too? I mean, he knows we're in his court, right? Maybe I can just ship a nice collection of exotic meat jerkies to Asgard instead?"

Reginleif responded with an indignant splutter.

Valerie was considering various arguments against the oldest—and most inconvenient—Yule tradition when motion in one of the nearby shop windows caught her eye.

The *Manassas First Credit Union* was a small stand-alone building wedged between the older brownstones that made up most of the historic district. Sunlight caught the tinted front window at just the right angle, allowing Val a vague glimpse into the shadowy office beyond. She couldn't make out any details, but there seemed to be quite a lot of rapid motion happening in there.

She waited for a break in traffic and crossed the road, drawing on Reginleif's keen eyesight to pierce through the tinted glass.

Normal everyday folk do not, as a rule, *expect* to casually stroll past a bank robbery in progress in the course of their normal, everyday lives. Despite the action and adventure of the last nine months of her life, Val still had a sliver of a *normal, everyday* woman buried somewhere inside her, so when she saw the man in jeans and a dark jacket standing on the teller counter she assumed she was witnessing the mental breakdown of some particularly desperate account holder. Then he pivoted, revealing both the three-holed balaclava covering his face and the machine pistol clutched in his gloved hand.

The sight of it made Val's heart drop to the pit of her

stomach and Reginleif pop to full, eager alertness, like a dozing cat that's spotted the mouse.

"Action." The Valkyrie was elated, as if the six weeks since the last time they'd been shot at had been for her nothing but a dreadfully boring purgatory.

"Civilians," Val groaned, seeing the terrified shapes huddled on the floor beneath the masked man's dais as he whirled, brandishing his pistol. She reached the hedge in front of the bank window and crouched on the snow-crusted mulch. She glanced over her shoulder. Behind her, traffic continued its busy circuit through the streets and pedestrians strolled by in their hats and gloves, cheerfully oblivious to the crime in progress behind the tinted window not thirty feet away. On the other side of the thick, presumably bullet-proof pane of glass, the masked man hopped off the desk as another robber emerged from the back room with a knife pressed to the throat of a terrified bank teller.

"*There is the door,*" Reginleif pressed impatiently, pulling Val's attention to the bank's front door a few feet to her left. "*Step through it. Take action.*"

Val hesitated, squinting into the darkness. The bank teller was already emptying her drawer into the robber's open sack. Val counted at least four customers crouching in the corners.

"No," Val decided, slipping around the side of the building. She ducked as she passed the drive-through window, not wanting to catch the attention of anyone inside. "At least, not *that* kind of action."

Again Reginleif spluttered, the way a fire splutters when one splashes oil onto the flames. "*What other kind of action matters when miscreants terrorize the people? Shall thou dial thy phone and summon* the police?"

Val peered around the back corner of the building into the tiny employee parking lot separating the credit union from the alley.

"Jeeze. I know you're bored, but there's no need to get *nasty* with me." She swallowed the last two gulps of her hot chocolate and shoved the cup into the deposit slot.

Two cars sat in the lot, a Buick SUV and a Chevy Malibu, each parked on the side of the credit union's heavy steel back door. Those, Val assumed, would belong to the bank tellers.

The white panel van idling in the alleyway with the side door hanging open probably belonged to Reginleif's so-called *miscreants*. A skinny young man was twitching in the driver's seat, his gaze fixed on the credit union.

Val slung her shopping bag over her shoulder and sidled into the alley. "Let's at least *try* to avoid getting into fights with armed chuckleheads where civilians can get hurt, okay?"

Val knocked on the driver's window and the young man jerked like he'd been caught doing something shameful. His head whipped around and he shot Val a baleful look. She gave him her best I'm-Just-A-Sheepish-Bystander-Here smile and waved, gesturing at the window between them.

The guy— no more than a kid in a knitted cap and Steelers hoodie—rolled down the window.

"Yeah, what do you want?" he growled. His head swiveled back and forth between her and the credit union's back door.

"You don't happen to know where I could find a goat this time of year, do you?"

The kid blinked, whipping his head around to stare at Val.

She punched him in the nose.

**On the streets**
**Manassas, Virginia**
**Saturday morning**

Mannie's brain was an inferno and all he cared about was tossing another log on the flames.

Pollo flung the two rucksacks into the back of the getaway van and threw himself in after, cackling like the chicken that was his namesake. Somehow, despite the primo Peruvian Lady currently skull-fucking Mannie into a state of delirium, he found it within himself to be an asshole.

"Shut the hell up, el pollo loco," he growled, heaving the sliding door shut as the van lurched into motion. "You tryin' to get us caught?" His head was a spinning top. He groped around the darkness of the van's interior, searching for the bindle he'd left somewhere amid the handyman tools. One more hit. Hand to God, he'd have one more hit to round off this baller of a morning then he'd take it easy for the rest of the day. Hell, for the rest of the weekend. Maybe he'd give up the blow altogether, if God was good and those rucksacks contained some fat stacks of Benjamins instead of the Jacksons they were used to ripping off from the mom-and-pops and streetwalkers.

The floor shifted beneath Mannie's feet as the van rolled into the street. Pollo was sitting on the filthy steel, his arms wrapped around his legs and his black mask dangling from his fingertips as he laughed and laughed and laughed.

"Did you see her face?" the man yammered. His head smacked into the door as Dom whipped the van around a corner. Pollo grunted, then laughed again, rubbing his bruised temple. "Did you see that piggy's *face* when I pulled the knife on her? She nearly shit herself!"

"Learn how to drive, Dom," Mannie growled to the kid slouched in the driver's seat. "The last thing we need now is to get pulled over by the 5-0. Just keep it in your pants until we get out of the city and then you can drive donuts in a field somewhere until your hair falls out."

Dominic was a skinny guy, barely more than a kid. All Mannie could see of him was the hunching slope of his shoulders and the knitted cap tugged down around his ears. He made a noncommittal sound as he turned the van onto the county highway, heading west out of the city.

Mannie grunted, groping beneath the tool rack. His hand fell across something hard and flat, and he remembered that they'd need to pull over and swap out the van's plates. He'd take care of that as soon as he found his bindle and took that last good hit. One more hit, a hard-earned reward for a job well done.

He cursed the bad lighting in this van. One of these days he'd make good on his word and fix the switch. He couldn't see for shit. He had to paw through the storage spaces, fingers searching for the little box where the white

7

lady lived. All he could feel was the step ladder, the set of loose socket wrenches, the... the...

He frowned as his fingers sank into something soft and warm.

"Ey, Dom!" Pollo pulled himself upright, laughing as the van rolled over a pothole. His face was flushed too, from the coke, from the money, from the thrill of a successful haul. "You took a wrong turn, ya jackass. We're supposed to be going *north*. Up to the farm, remember?"

Mannie grasped the warm thing and pulled. A couple of screwdrivers tumbled across the van floor with a clatter and clash, knocked loose as something large and heavy rolled into the open.

Mannie stared, uncomprehending. Inside his head, the coke buzzed and burned and fizzled.

Dominic gazed back up at him, his eyes clouded and hazy, blinking blearily over the wide swath of duct tape slapped across his mouth.

Mannie glanced up to the cab. He didn't recognize the warehouses and machine shops sliding past as the van rolled down some abandoned access road. Nor did he recognize the bright green eyes staring back at him from the rearview mirror.

Before he could gain some control over his dance with the Lady and consider the situation, the driver slammed on the brakes. Mannie and Pollo shot forward, crashing into the back of the two front seats. Distantly, Mannie was aware of the crunch in his nose, but that was a problem for later—once the coke had worn off and he had things back under control. That would be any second now, he told himself.

His vision swam, and when it resolved he saw the driver climbing out of the front seat and turning to face them. Long golden hair spilled onto her shoulders as she tugged off Dom's knitted cap and tossed it carelessly aside.

"Good mornin', shitheads." She grinned, showing teeth that glinted in the dim light. "I've got to be at a meeting in thirty minutes so let's just make this quick."

**Basement Suite**
**Viking, Inc., Business Division**
**Manassas, VA**
**Saturday Afternoon**

"Hey, did you look through these?" Jacob Pinkerton dropped a bankers box full of rejected case files onto the table at the center of the room. The old card table groaned beneath the weight.

Kat glanced up from his magazine, eyeing Jacob and the box over the rim of his glasses. He licked his fingertips and moved on to the next page. "Those are all Hawk's rejected jobs from the last eighteen months," he informed Jacob archly. "I promised myself long ago that I was never going to do that man's dirty laundry again."

Jacob rolled his eyes and settled into one of the folding chairs to browse the files. The jarls had agreed, in principle, to support Jacob and Val as they got their new quasi-independent black ops unit up and running, and for that Jacob was grateful. There was a bit of backhanded resentment, however, in the way they had oh-so-graciously offered this new unit its own office suite...in the furnace room of Viking's basement, between the storage closet and the armory. For Valerie, who had been working out of a re-purposed janitorial closet, it was at least a lateral step. For Jacob, who had enjoyed a second-floor office with his very own window overlooking the back alley, it was a bit of a disappointment. It was plenty big for their needs, but it was always cold and smelled musty, and they had to keep a news channel running 24/7 to drown out the constant clanks and burbles and groans of the old building settling.

To Sylvester 'Kat' Mulaney, the dingy, concrete-floored dungeon was simultaneously a taste of home and an excuse to complain about the accommodations, which made it perfect.

Kat shivered in the chilly air and pulled his sweater tighter over his shoulders. "Shall we add another shovel of coal to the boiler, Master Pinkerton?" he asked in a light cockney accent. "Just so I don't freeze off me fingers while we wait upon the good Miss Daisy?"

Jacob glanced at his watch with a frown. It was almost half past noon. Val was flirting with thirty minutes late. *Five more minutes and I'll give her a call,* he told himself.

He cranked the dial on the old space heater that was keeping the basement at a livable temperature.

Kat sighed and dropped the *Soldier of Fortune* magazine onto the steadily growing pile beside him. "Lord have mercy, but the quality of their writing has really *plummeted* in the last few years. Used to be you could find a few juicy leads in a pit like that but now it's all about alien conspiracies and dire warnings about the dangers of self-evolving AI."

Jacob rolled his eyes again. Kat called browsing through

a two-year backlog of tabloids *market research,* and though Jacob would admit that once in a while the rags happened upon real news by accident, he somehow doubted Kat's efforts to rustle up new clients were entirely sincere. "Why don't you let me have a turn at the hard copy." Jacob reached for the stack. "And you get back to combing the dark web. You know, like we're paying you to do."

Kat drew himself up proudly. "Any teenager can get himself into trouble on the dark web." He gestured to the magazines. "It takes real *talent* to find leads buried in that stack of libertarian wet-dream fanfiction—"

He was working up a full head of cheerfully indignant steam when the door at the top of the stairwell creaked open and Valerie jogged down the steps. Her face was flushed from the cold and a damp plastic bag swung from one arm. She was slightly out of breath. "Sorry I'm late." She slipped into the office and shut the door behind her, closing them off from the miniature gym that took up most of the building's basement. "Traffic was a nightmare."

"Oh, you're telling *me,*" Kat agreed. "I heard there was almost half an inch of snow on the roads this morning. Half an inch!" He gestured to the news playing quietly on a screen in the corner. "And they're calling for more!"

Val chuckled distractedly as she shoved her shopping bag into the cubby behind her Ikea-standard desk. "You'd better get used to it. This isn't the Carolinas. We get snow here, every year."

"Then shouldn't *you* be used to it, Miss Daisy?" Kat teased, twirling a finger in her direction.

"He's right," Jacob pointed out somberly, looking up from an article about Brazilian guerrillas fighting deforestation in the Amazon. "It sets a bad example when the new boss shows up late."

"Co-boss. I refuse to take on *full* responsibility for this little experiment." Val flung herself into the empty chair beside Jacob. Her eyes were bright, he noted. She was flushed, as if she'd come from a workout, but he doubted she'd been kickboxing in *those* boots. He cast her a curious look, which she ignored as she reached for the bankers box of rejected case files. "So what's on the docket?" she asked brightly. "Do we have any client leads?"

Jacob began, "The jarls asked us to follow up on some issues that Reggie's team ran into while they were doing a job in Singapore—"

"Hang on now." Kat interrupted by leaning across his table to punch the volume button on the television. A *Breaking News* marquee scrolled across the WKMZ local news channel.

**Credit Union Robbery Ends with Three Suspects in Custody.**

A news chopper feed displayed downtown Manassas all crusted with snow and a collection of police vehicles surrounding a little brick building.

"Isn't that right up the street?" Kat asked, incredulous.

"Oh yeah," Val replied blithely. "That's been clogging up the streets all morning. Part of why traffic was so bad."

Jacob shot her a hard look.

"*Witnesses say the suspects fled the scene in a white panel van around eleven thirty this morning,*" the reporter on the scene was saying. "*And just a few minutes ago, police received an anonymous tip about a van matching that description parked near an old rail station less than a mile away."*

The camera cut to a still shot of a dingy white panel van parked half in a ditch off the side of an access road. *"The three suspects were discovered inside, tied up with electrical cords..."*

Kat chuckled delightedly and turned the volume down once more as he faced his coworkers. "Someone already trussed up the ne'er-do-wells like a couple of holiday hams? How thoughtful."

"Probably some rival gang trying to snag their steal." Val shrugged as she flipped through the Singapore case file.

Kat clucked. "Oh, Miss Daisy, where's your sense of drama? Wouldn't you rather believe there's some mad vigilante running amok in town? Krampus come down early from the mountain to punish all the bad little children?"

Val did not look up from her file, but Jacob caught the ghost of a smirk on her lips. "You've been reading too many of those adventure magazines."

# CHAPTER TWO

**Basement Suite**
**Viking, Inc., Business Division**
**Manassas, VA**
**Saturday Afternoon**

Developing an independent black ops unit required a shocking amount of legwork, most of it mind-numbingly boring.

When Valerie and Jacob had gone to the Viking jarls with the VALKYRIE proposal, they had expected a great deal of pushback. They were, after all, proposing that Viking's most reliable, trustworthy, and capable field agent —Jacob Pinkerton—break away from the company to team up with their newest, most reckless rookie—Valerie—to handle some of the trickiest, most dangerous jobs in the industry. Rather than balk at this flagrant act of defiance, however, the jarls had surprised them by seriously considering the proposal for nearly a week before coming back with a well-structured counteroffer.

They would support the formation of VALKYRIE as an independent entity, one tailored specifically to tackle the sorts of high-risk jobs that might otherwise expose an up-and-coming consulting firm like Viking to a lot of negative press. They would give the fledgling unit space and resources to take over some of Viking's more niche clientèle. They would even pay VALKYRIE a modest operations retainer to help get her feet under her. In exchange, they had a few straightforward demands.

The first was that VALKYRIE would not take any jobs that would lead to competition or a conflict of interest with Viking's current client pool, and they would prioritize any jobs that Viking brokered for them. They would stand ready to step in if any of Viking's active jobs required their specialized sort of backup. Their new, slender operating budget would necessitate that each member of VALKYRIE take a hefty pay cut ('As much as we love to see our associates both current and former succeed,' Charlie Evans had explained graciously, 'That operating stipend has to come from *somewhere*').

And, of course, VALKYRIE had to take Kat.

"Thank God for that," Hawk had told Jacob in a rare moment of companionable confession. "Taggert's been talking about bringing the man on as a full employee, especially after Mira turned us down and went back to Colorado. It's like he wants me to lose whatever hair I have left. Hate to see you go, Pinkerton, but glad you're taking the liabilities with you."

*Liabilities.* That had irked Val when Jacob had recounted the conversation to her. She liked each of the Viking jarls, in a way. Taggert, despite a past pasted over with *classified* files and sealed documents, had proven himself to be a model of integrity, a rare beast in the world of paramilitary contractors. Evans was warm and convivial and always ready with a box of donuts or a pie to sweeten a sour day. Hawk was...Hawk. Ornery and rude and prone to bouts of pettiness, but steadfast and skilled and, most importantly, discreet.

Kat was a bombastic eccentric who enjoyed pushing Hawk's buttons, but he was far from a *liability*. No, Hawk had been referring to someone else.

"Evans didn't want to let us go," Jacob had explained that night after the final meeting when they'd gone out to celebrate their unexpected victory over burgers and milk-shakes. "She's worried about competition, yeah, but she also doesn't think there's enough collective experience between us to make this work."

"She thinks Kat and I will drag you down," Val had answered wryly, to which Jacob had shrugged and dipped his french fry into his chocolate malt.

"The *hiromenn* call her Momma Bear for a reason. Taggert voted to let us go because he knows that forcing us to stay with the company might lead to resentment, which is bad for operations. It was Hawk's deciding vote that surprised me."

They had both expected the head of IT to turn a petty hand and refuse to allow them to form a unit that might one day compete with Viking's interests. According to the company charter and their employment contracts, he would have been within his rights to do so.

"I've been thinking about it," Val confessed after glancing around to make sure there were no other diners in the nearby booths. "Maybe we shouldn't have been surprised. Hawk's been on to me from the beginning."

Jacob shifted his weight uncomfortably but nodded. "I think we have to assume he knows about you. He just doesn't know what to do *about* you, so he wants to keep you at arm's length."

The thought had turned Val's strawberry milkshake sour in her mouth. Hawk was a genius at surveillance and for months he had been dropping stray hints and asking casual but leading questions about Valerie's unconventional skills. Hawk breaking character to support the formation of VALKYRIE cemented the idea that he knew far more about Val than her short resume would suggest. *How* much more, she couldn't say.

She did not like this game of unknown unknowns. Especially not when she was playing it with someone who was ostensibly her ally.

That final meeting and celebratory dinner had been weeks ago, and the intervening time had been filled with so much damned paperwork that Val had barely had time to breathe, much less play mind games with the old man. Most nights, Val went to sleep brainstorming ways to find new clients, dreamed about insurance adjusters, and woke up worrying about how she was going to make payments on her new car on her shoestring budget.

"I motion that we pay a lawyer to fill out the international regulatory LLC forms and damn the cost." She pushed herself away from the card table at the center of their basement office. She threw a hand in the air. "All in favor say, Aye."

"*Aye*," Reginleif chimed in swiftly.

Jacob sighed and leaned back from his own stack of paperwork. "Nay. I warned you going into this that figuring out health insurance was going to be a bitch, but we're already more than halfway done. I've just got to fill out the last of these waivers and we'll be cleared for dangerous field work."

"Nay," Kat agreed, kicking his feet onto his desk as he flipped through another magazine. He was wearing thick red and white striped socks. "As much as I do love you, Miss Daisy, you know I'm not going to take another pay cut just to hire some pencil-pusher."

That was easy for Kat to say. One of the conditions of his employment within the new VALKYRIE unit was that he not be required to take up any work outside of his carefully defined role as head of intelligence and tech support.

"I think we could all go for a break, though," Jacob suggested with a glance at his watch. "It's about time for dinner. I'll run down to the deli—"

"You *absolutely* will not." Kat hopped up from his chair and bopped Jacob lightly on the head with a rolled-up magazine. "It's my turn to stretch the legs and you will not steal that from me."

After collecting cash and deli orders from his new comrades, Kat slung a bright blue parka over his shoulders, slipped his feet into some fur-lined moccasins, and disappeared up the stairs.

"He's in for a rough ride when it actually gets, you know, *cold* out," Val observed.

Jacob got up from his chair and sauntered into the gym area of the basement, pulling off his sweater to reveal a white undershirt. He snatched a couple of boxing gloves from beside the ring and tossed them over his shoulder to Val, who scrambled after him. After six hours of filing paperwork on a Saturday afternoon, she was ready to unwind by punching something repeatedly.

"Are we going to tell him about you?" Jacob asked without preamble as he ducked into the ring. "Or are we going to wait and wait until it becomes awkward like it is with Hawk?"

Val grimaced as she kicked off her new boots. "I'm gonna come clean with him eventually," she decided. "But there are implications to consider."

Jacob grunted as he threw a few warm-up punches.

"Beyond the obvious." Val unhooked her jangling sleigh bell earrings and hopped into the ring after Jacob.

"Beyond the obvious?" Jacob cocked an eyebrow. "Beyond 'hey, your new employer and co-founder happens to be an ancient Norse goddess'?"

"Well, yeah." Val limbered up with a series of kicks. "For example, right now when there's a question of overall operations, you, me, and Kat vote on it. Reginleif is cool with that—management isn't her bag. But if I reveal her to Kat, she's going to take more of an interest. She's going to want to have a vote on matters, too."

Jacob shook his head, incredulous, as he squared off with Val at the center of the ring. "I guess I understand."

"But will Kat?" Val threw a casual punch at Jacob's wide chest, which he deflected easily enough. "Frankly, I don't see them getting along very well. Kat's got a petty streak, too. He might see it as one person—" she waved, indicating herself "— getting two votes. It will just cause drama and hurt feelings. That's all assuming he can handle the truth at all and it doesn't just scare him back to Asheville."

Jacob feinted and Val ducked to the left in time to receive a nice thwack across her middle. She winced. "I don't want to rock the boat right now. Not while we're still in the crib. I just want to keep Kat happy, at least until everything is stable." She spun, throwing up her leg in one of those kicks that Jacob insisted were so dangerous. He ducked beneath her heel, but the violent motion threw him off balance and she took the opportunity to hop forward and pummel him. There was a brief pause in the conversation as they attempted to beat the snot out of each other. It ended with Valerie in a headlock beneath Jacob's sweaty arm.

"Pinned ya." He grinned. "You must be distracted."

"We *need* a reliable computer whiz and we're not going to find anyone else nearly as capable as Kat," she grunted, trying and failing to pry herself free from his rock-hard biceps. With Reginlief hovering close in Val's head she could think of at least a dozen ways to extract herself from the situation but the truth was she didn't want to. Her mind was on other things and it seemed wise not to thoroughly kick her partner's ass *every* time they sparred.

She liked the smell of him, all up close and personal. She wondered, suddenly, how long Kat was going to be gone. The whole reason the team agreed to work on Saturdays was to let them have the building to themselves...

"At least not on our budget," Jacob agreed, releasing his hold and going to the edge of the ring for his water bottle. "You make good points. We should hold off on dropping bombs until the situation is more stable." He turned to her, tilting his head back and squirting a stream of water into his mouth. "On that note, though…"

Val wiped a bead of sweat from her forehead. Jacob didn't need to finish his sentence. Now that the most essential of the startup paperwork was complete, VALKYRIE *needed* to pick up some cases. The jarls might have been supportive in spirit, but they weren't going to fund this little experiment forever.

"Any nibbles from Agent Wiley or the DEA?" she asked. It had been Jacob's job to reach out and inform their contacts in the federal government of the Viking structure change.

Jacob shook his head. "They assure me that we're on the shortlist to call if they have anything, but the FBI and the DEA like to stick with what they *know* works. I bet you a dollar that if we hear from them, it will be via the Viking channels."

This wasn't a *bad* thing, per se—Viking would still pass the job along to them—but it did rather kneecap their efforts to build a name as an independent organization.

"What about Reece and Interpol?" Jacob tossed his empty bottle aside and resumed his position at the center of the ring.

"Same," Val reported wistfully. "It looks like Forseti is laying low for now. Reece doesn't have any of *our* kinds of leads. Sam Friedman out in Hungary says one of his business partners is dealing with what might be some industrial espionage. He's recommended us."

That had been a few days ago, and she wasn't hopeful that they'd be getting an urgent call for help from Eastern Europe any time soon. "We might just have to go after some of those bounties and guns-for-hire jobs in Kat's magazines after all."

"Not exactly tasteful," Jacob agreed. "Or reliable. We need steady cash flow. Something to supplement our Viking funds and keep us afloat until we build up the right client base. Are we gonna go another round or just stand here yapping?"

Val squared off with her partner once more, only half paying attention. "I guess it doesn't necessarily have to be *this* kind of income stream," she mused, dodging the first flurry of blows.

"We could hold a bake sale." Jacob pressed forward, grinning as he tried to punch around Val's blocks. She hopped backward, dancing around the edge of the ring. Inspiration struck and she leapt forward, going for his exposed flank. "Not a bake sale." She thwacked him firmly in the ribs and rolled out of reach before he could turn on her. "A brew sale! The craft beer market is saturated but there's only one or two meaderies worth a damn on the whole Eastern Seaboard. We could do real old-fashioned brews. The hipsters will drink it up."

Jacob laughed. "After all the paperwork we've done, now you want to try applying for a liquor and brewing license, too?" He rounded on her, and three rapid, powerful socks to the gut convinced him she was serious. He heaved, startled by the force, and threw a hand up to concede the match before she could punch him again.

"Sorry." Her eyes were shining now. "We got a little amped up. I lost track of my strength." She offered a hand but he shook his head.

"Nah, we both know you can kick my ass six ways from

Sunday. I let my guard down. That's on me." He touched his tender gut. "But maybe I should get myself some body armor for sparring..."

She smiled sheepishly and peeled off her gloves. Her skin was glowing. The brief workout had done her good, or maybe it was the idea of mead filling her head with fuzzy dreams. "We'll get all of the honey locally sourced and stick to traditional recipes. If we start the first batch soon it should be ready for bottling in about six months. The budget will be tight until then but a good mead will sell out in days."

"I thought you wanted to be a secret agent," Jacob teased. "I was just thinking about ways to make a quick buck and your very first idea would require a time investment of at least six months before first payoff."

Val opened her mouth, to say what, she wasn't sure, but was cut short when the door at the top of the stairwell slammed open.

"Great." Jacob threw a towel over his shoulder and climbed out of the ring. "I was starting to wonder if Kat got lost on his way to the deli."

"Miss Daisy?" Kat called down the stairs. "Jake? Why don't you folks come up to the main offices for a minute? Jasper is here with a friend and they'd like to talk to you."

# CHAPTER THREE

**Conference Room**
**Viking, Inc, business division**
**Manassas, VA**
**Early Saturday evening**

Kat declared that he would sit this meeting out, and the reason why became immediately clear.

Val and Jacob walked into the AV conference room to find not only Taggert and his slender, olive-skinned guest sitting at the table, but Charlie Evans and Nathaniel Hawker as well. Something in the air put Val immediately on alert. Some little matter of paperwork or process wouldn't bring all three of the jarls into the office on a Saturday. There was real work to do. Kat normally jumped at the opportunity to irritate Hawk with the very fact of his existence. His excusing himself meant that he smelled *serious business* in the air as well.

Jacob sensed it also, seeming cautious and a little self-conscious as he draped his towel over his shoulders and settled into one of the empty chairs. "Sorry," he told the jarls. "I wasn't expecting a meeting, I would have washed up."

"It's a last-minute thing." Taggert waved the half-apology aside. His gray flat cap was crusted with snow and he was wearing a knitted brown scarf. Outside, the snow flurry had turned into a snow gale. Charlie had made herself at home, cozying up to the conference table with a big mug of steaming tea. She looked a little dreamy, as if she had been stealing an afternoon nap beside some crackling fireplace before the call had gone out.

Hawk was half-hunched behind his computers at the end of the table, looking as though he hadn't left his office since Friday morning, though Val knew for a fact he was supposed to be at a crypto conference in DC this weekend.

"Are you keeping up with the local news?" Hawk asked without preamble as Val settled into a chair beside Jacob. The harsh glow of the screens reflected off his pale eyes as he read an article. "Shakedown at the credit union this morning. Suspects in custody are saying they were assaulted by a gang of six angry women who fled the scene before police could catch up."

Val gave an honest, full-throated laugh. "Weird story. But I guess it's better than getting the snot beat out of you by *one* angry woman."

Charlie giggled into her tea.

"Kearie, Pinkerton." Taggert commanded the attention of the room by taking off his cap and shaking away the snowflakes before nestling it back onto his shiny pate. "I'd like you to meet Mateo Alvarez. He's the chief aide to Jorge Vargas, the first minority senator of Campeche in Mexico."

Val straightened, turning her most professional smile on the olive-skinned man in his tan suit jacket. "Bienvenidos, señor, but I'm afraid that's about the extent of my Spanish." She held out her hand, which he shook with a gracious nod.

Jacob, on the other hand, greeted Alvarez with a firm handshake and a long inquiry into what Val gathered was the current state of the Mexican football season, in fluent Spanish. This made the slender man crack a smile. He gave a modest response and settled back into his seat beside Taggert, relaxing visibly.

"It sounds like Hawk and Mister Alvarez were socializing at the conference when Alvarez learned of a problem back in his home office that we might be able to help with," Taggert explained. "Viking has done some work for the Mexican government before. Sounds like kismet to me." He nodded to Alvarez, who took up the mantle and continued speaking.

"Thank you for meeting with me on short notice." He spoke softly. His accent had a faint lisp, which surprised Val. She had thought that a mark of continental Spanish, not Mexican Spanish. "The senator's preferred security contractors backed out on us barely twenty-four hours before the fundraiser gala. It has caused quite an upset in our office. My colleagues and I have been scrambling to find suitable coverage. You can imagine my relief when Mister Hawker said he had a team ready for the job."

"Of course," Val agreed, shooting Hawk a questioning look. VALKYRIE was supposed to review jobs before signing on, but Alvarez was making it sound like the ink on the contract was already dry. Hawk was busy at his computer, immune to Val's stare. "But why don't we start from the top, señor? Tell us about the situation in your own words."

"Senator Vargas is a member of the Evolución Social party of Mexico," Alvarez began. "Two years ago, he became the first member of the party elected into the Mexican senate. Evolución Social is a young grassroots coalition of mostly leftists and social democrats, with a growing number of rural conservatives."

"Aren't those rather uneasy bedfellows?" Val drew on what she could recall of Mexican history. Whatever this job was, she supposed she would have to brush up on it quickly.

Alvarez smiled stiffly. "Sí. Our constituents are united behind a single issue. Breaking the hold that the drug cartels have over the everyday lives of Mexican citizens. We realize that no progress can be made on any other issues until we put Mexico back in the hands of its law-abiding citizens."

Val nodded her understanding. Nothing could unite a divided people like a common enemy.

"The senator has devoted the last five years of his life to eliminating the Tierra Roja cartel in our home state of Campeche," Alvarez went on. "Filling the resulting power void with respected, democratically elected community leaders. When he was raised to the Senate, he was appointed head of a task force devoted to eliminating Tierra Roja from the hemisphere completely."

"Making him target *uno* on the cartel's hit list," Jacob guessed.

"Not just the Tierra Roja hit list," Val added. "If he's

serious about standing up to the cartels and he's any good at it at all, every criminal organization in Mexico is going to want the man dead."

"Not just in Mexico," Alvarez agreed. "The senator has been on a diplomatic mission in the United States for the last several days. His goal has been twofold. First, to facilitate the extradition of a Roja kingpin known as Cascobel."

"Cascobel." Jacob frowned, turning the word over. He shot Val a puzzled look. "...Jingle bell?"

Alvarez let out a dry chuckle. "Not quite so merry, I'm afraid. The name is a reference to the serpent's tail."

"Oh." Understanding dawned on Jacob's face. "*Rattlesnake.*"

Alvarez nodded.

Taggert cut into the conversation for the first time. "I've heard about this brouhaha. There was a joint operation in Florida a few weeks ago. The DEA, FBI, and Mexican special forces raided a drug den near Miami. They took this man into custody. He's been in high-security lockup ever since."

"While our governments argue over what to do with him," Alvarez confirmed. "Thankfully Senator Vargas has convinced your government that he ought to be returned to Mexico to stand trial."

"That seems like the obvious thing to do, if he's a Mexican national," Charlie put in. "I mean, he's not an American citizen, is he?"

"No." Alvarez shifted his weight uneasily. "Legally, yes, the course of action is clear. On the ground, however, there have been...misgivings, about handing him over to our government."

"There is the perception that the cartels still have a lot of say in the courts of Mexico," Val ventured, choosing her words carefully. She didn't know how easily Alvarez might be offended. "Perhaps the DEA didn't want to hand this guy over if they believed there was a good chance some corrupt judge would just turn around and set him free."

"Our office has poured our blood into convincing the United States federal government that Cascobel will be safe in our custody." Alvarez nodded, bluntly accepting the poor reputation of his government without protest or reproach. "And that he will face proper justice in Mexico."

Jacob let out a low whistle. "So Senator Vargas is already on the cartel's shortlist for execution, and now he's in charge of escorting a powerful gang leader across international borders."

"Let's hope the man's will is up to date," Hawk muttered darkly. "I'm struggling to think of a more dangerous situation for an up-and-coming politician to be in."

"The senator's usual security contractors for this side of the border have suddenly come down with a mysterious illness." Alvarez opened his palms out to the jarls. "Leaving our office in something of a difficult situation."

"This mystery illness." Charlie clutched her mug close to her chest and sipped her chai. "Do we think it's caused by a sudden influx of *cash* or perhaps *threats* from certain unnamed criminal organizations?"

Alvarez shrugged. "Probably. You understand, señora, that I don't have the manpower to look into the betrayal right now. The senator has a slew of events scheduled over the next week before we return home."

"Events." Val straightened in her chair. "Right. You said

the senator was in the States for two reasons. The first is to bring Cascobel safely back to Mexico."

"The second is to fundraise for Evolución Social. Rally support for our cause from the Mexican American communities. In light of recent events, I have tried to convince the senator to cancel the events."

"No go?" Charlie asked.

Alvarez shook his head. "There was something of a row in our office," he admitted sheepishly. "Us Mexicans, we can become passionate."

Val tried to imagine this demure, soft-spoken man red in the face and shouting at his boss. She could not.

"The senator insists that the events shall continue as planned," Alvarez finished. "Despite the threats and the security problems. He says we cannot be seen changing our plans due to cartel threats."

"*One must not show weakness to one's enemies,*" Reginleif agreed.

Valerie sighed. Regin, who had no understanding of modern politics and little desire to learn, usually slept through meetings like this. Of course she would rouse herself to voice her favor for stubborn pride. She was right, of course, as was the senator, but sticking to a busy social calendar would mean a huge headache for all the people trying to keep him alive.

Ah, well. That's what VALKYRIE was getting paid for.

All things considered, Val was happy that the job was in service of a man trying to clean up corruption in his community. It probably wouldn't pay well, but you couldn't put a price on integrity. She could forgive Hawk for volunteering them.

"The senator's next public event is a fundraiser gala tomorrow night," Alvarez went on. "We would be most obliged if Viking could provide event security while my office works on a more permanent solution to our contractor problem."

Taggert studied Val and Jacob across the table. Val didn't need to look at her partner to gauge his interest in the job. She could sense it in the alert-but-calm set of his shoulders. She nodded.

Taggert gave Alvarez a smile that was both sharp and utterly sincere. "No problemo, Mateo. Like I said, kismet. You have a need and we have the means. The VALKYRIE team will head out to Houston ASAP to cover the event. I'm sure we can all work out some kind of long-term arrangement for your security needs as well."

Alvarez relaxed as if a huge weight had been lifted off his shoulders, leaving his somewhat oversized and heavily starched jacket sitting stiffly upright as the man within slumped with relief.

"Excellent." Charlie snapped upright, her tone and posture all business as this talk of a case passed from hypothetical into concrete. She grabbed her laptop from her bag and unfolded it. "Mister Alvarez and I will get the ball rolling on the paperwork. There's some diplomatic stuff we need to settle where national borders are concerned."

"That leaves the rest of us polishing boots." Taggert pushed himself up from his chair and gestured for Hawk, Val, and Jacob to follow. With a polite excuse, they joined the head of Viking in his office.

Showing a not-entirely-surprising degree of prescience, Kat was already sitting at one of the chairs in front of

Taggert's wide desk, eating a chicken salad wrap with one hand and flipping through half a dozen browser tabs on his laptop with the other. Val caught sight of a few Spanish news headlines before Kat turned the laptop away and wiped his fingers on a paper napkin branded after the midtown deli.

"Been doing a little reading up on Senator Vargas," he confessed. "You know. Just out of curiosity. He's a handsome devil but I must say he's got 'tragedy-in-waiting' written all over him."

"He better not," Val retorted. "Not if we're the ones protecting him."

Kat put his wrap back in its clamshell to make room for the others. Taggert sat behind his desk and Val and Jacob squeezed into the seats. Hawk lingered in the doorway with his arms crossed over his chest.

"He's got a point," the head of Viking admitted in a low voice. "Vargas is in deep. There's good reason his office is having a hard time finding reliable, capable contractors to keep that man safe."

"That reason is *irony*," Hawk sniffed. "It's hard to pay for quality contractors on a public servant's budget when your whole spiel is that you *don't* take bribes from the cartels."

Val shot a questioning look to Taggert, who grimaced but nodded. "He's got a six-mile-wide target on his back and can't afford the sort of protection I would normally recommend for a man in his position."

"Oh, come now, Colonel," Kat chided jovially. "It's Christmas! Where's your generous spirit?"

Behind them, Hawk snorted.

"It'll be a huge blow to the Evolución Social cause if

something fatal happens to Vargas just as he's about to win a big victory for his party," Val reasoned. She glanced over her shoulder, eyeing the skinny man lurking in the doorway. "You *volunteered* us for the job."

Hawk's thin lips quirked into something that might have been a smile or a grimace. "Chickadee's got to leave the nest eventually. If you want to run your own operation, Kearie, you need to grab it by the reins and ride. You get no more freebies from me."

"Oh, don't listen to him." Kat rolled his eyes. "He hooked up this blind date right out of the goodness of his cold, dead heart."

Hawk opened his mouth but Taggert stepped in and deftly changed the subject before the bickering could escalate. "VALKYRIE doesn't yet have the resources to operate event security on this scale." He studied a glossy pamphlet on his desk. "I know this because I sign off on your budget." He turned the pamphlet over, revealing the name of the senator's next fundraising event: the Association for Mexican American Entrepreneurs' third annual Fiesta Navidad, in Houston, Texas. The picture on the front featured a four-foot ice sculpture of a cowboy on a bucking reindeer.

Kat snatched the pamphlet from Taggert's hand with a little coo of delight. "Oh, my stars, I haven't been to a proper ballroom since my cotillion days!" His expression turned sly as he flipped open the pamphlet. He shook his head with a soft *tsk*. "Expected to be over nine hundred people in attendance. There are only three of us. Looks to me like we're going to need to break a couple of those new

AI surveillance kits you're so proud of out of the box if we want eyes on the whole shindig."

Hawk went rigid, his face losing what little color it had.

An absent frown tugged at the corner of Taggert's mouth. "Nate, how does the temp help know about our experimental surveillance tech?"

"Oh, don't blame him." Kat graciously handed the pamphlet back to Taggert. "I'm just a nosy little stinker. But let's not be stingy with the gear, Colonel. It's half the reason I decided to stay on with your outfit."

"The AI gear isn't ready for field use." Hawk's tone implied that even if it *was* field-ready, Hawk wouldn't have lent it to Kat if the whole world was on fire and the box was the only thing that could carry water.

Jacob held up a questioning finger and gave voice to Val's confusion. "What's this about new surveillance gear?" he asked mildly.

"I said it's not ready!" the spindly older man snapped, making Jacob flinch. "Now if you'll excuse me, I have TPS reports to run." With that goodbye, he turned and vanished behind the door to his own office.

There was a beat of contemplative silence in Taggert's office.

"No AI then," Kat lamented. "Ah well. Maybe next time." He gathered up his computer and sandwich. "I suppose we'll want to pack out as soon as possible?" He glanced at Val and Jacob.

Jacob nodded. "Pack your sunscreen. Houston's sunny all year round." He cast a glance at Taggert. "Permission to phone Ash and tell her to gas up the Gulfstream IV?"

"Denied." Taggert scribbled a few notes onto a pad

behind his computer. "Sorry," he added with a glance at the VALKYRIE team. "We've got a team in Bern that needs the jet on standby. You're going to have to arrange for transportation to Texas with Mister Alvarez."

Kat's face fell as Val and Jacob got to their feet. "We're taking a *standard* airliner?"

"Hey." Val gave the man a gently teasing smile as they returned to the basement to pack. "We warned you from the beginning the job might not be glamorous. At least we're not sailing across the North Sea in a longboat."

"*A noxious journey indeed,*" Reginleif added sleepily.

Kat was disconcerted. "Mister Alvarez probably travels in business class at least, right? Right?"

# CHAPTER FOUR

**Washington Dulles International Airport**
**Terminal C, Gate 17**
**Saturday night, late**

Kat took one look at their boarding passes and decided that *basic economy* would never do. With a huff and his nose turned into the air, he declared that he would return momentarily, and vanished into the duty-free shop.

"I hope we'll be able to accommodate your associate." Alvarez ground a knuckle into his eyes, trying to rub away the fatigue tugging at the corners of his eyelids. "I see he is accustomed to a certain...standard of travel."

"Don't mind him." Val nervously turned away from Kat's retreat. She hoped Kat wouldn't embarrass her on their first field mission as an independent unit. She liked the strangely eccentric man but had to admit that Hawk had a point. He could be a lot to handle in large doses.

The terminal was largely empty on a Saturday night. Alvarez was scheduled to meet up with the senator and the rest of his staff in Houston and had been able to snatch a few extra seats on the domestic flight at the last minute. They made an awkward party, the tired, beleaguered little Alvarez and his three-man escort. Jacob lounged in a chair near their gate, idly reading over the Fiesta Navidad itinerary as he studied the thin crowd. Not that they expected to run into any trouble on this leg of the journey. He was guarding a stack of carry-on bags: Val's compact black suitcase, his own casually stuffed gym duffel bag, Kat's flower-print briefcase, and as many overstuffed personal items as the gate attendant would allow them to take onto the plane. Nobody wanted to bother with checking a bag at this stage in the game.

Kat returned from the shop a few minutes later carrying a golden gift basket under one arm. Val frowned, noting the fat stacks of gourmet chocolate truffles filling the basket. She opened her mouth to speak but Kat brushed past her, his jaw set at a determined angle, and marched straight for the gate attendant. She was a haggard-looking middle-aged woman in a company uniform and her waves of platinum-dyed hair were held in place by a festive red and green band.

"Good evening, sugar," he offered in his sweetest, most wheedling southern drawl. "That hairband is just adorable, I must say. Is that hand knitted?"

Alvarez leaned in close to Val and spoke under his breath. "What is he doing?"

Val frowned. Miracle of miracles, the tired-looking gate attendant's eyes lit up at the compliment and she giggled. She exchanged a few pleasantries with Kat before the man set the gift basket on the desk between them and slid it in her direction.

"I see that our flight's a bit thin tonight, Miss Delilah. And I was wondering if there were any empty seats available closer to the *front* of the plane for me and my friends. The big lug behind me tends to get airsick if he's got to sit behind the wings."

Delilah checked her computer and smiled again, and when Kat returned to the rest of the team he was short one chocolate-filled gift basket, but up four free upgrades to first class.

He dropped Val a wink. "It's amazing what you can get out of people if you just ask nicely."

**En Route to Houston**
**Delta Airlines Flight 4766**
**Saturday night, late**

The flight was indeed thin, and the four of them had nearly half of the first-class cabin all to themselves. It wasn't quite as nice as zipping around the hemisphere in Viking's private plane, but the complimentary roasted almonds and champagne were a nice touch.

"Mead would be a nicer touch," Val had suggested to Jacob when they boarded. "I bet we could sell it to airlines by the barrel full."

Jacob had rolled his eyes, as if Val were making a bad joke.

The moment they boarded, Kat apologized for his forthcoming motion sickness and abruptly knocked himself out with several tabs of Benadryl, leaving Val and Jacob alone with Alvarez to discuss the gala.

"The Association for Mexican American Entrepreneurs is just what it says on the box," Alvarez explained once they had reached cruising altitude and he could let go of his rosary safe in the assumption that the plane was not going to crash and burn. "Immigrants who went hunting the American Dream and actually caught it, you know? Upper-middle class members and above—general contractors, business owners, community leaders. Fiesta Navidad is their biggest event of the year. Everyone gets together to celebrate the shared heritage and rub elbows and make connections."

"Sounds like a place where a guy like Vargas can pull on a few heartstrings," Jacob mused. "Remind all the good folks where they came from and how much better their support could make the homeland." He seemed to remember too late that Vargas' right-hand man was sitting directly beside him and flushed faintly. "Uh, no offense."

Alvarez shrugged. "No politician can afford to be naive, Mister Pinkerton. You're right. Vargas goes to these events to ask for money. He's pretty good at getting it, too. Most of the association members worked very, very hard to get where they are. Their whole lives have been full of empty promises about how Mexico is going to get better under this government or that. Yet somehow Jorge smiles, and their purse strings all go loose. Our party is small and we come from a poor district. Most of our funding comes from people like the ones that will be there tomorrow night."

"Which explains why Vargas won't be put off," Val

reasoned. She flipped through the Fiesta Navidad pamphlet, taking in the sweeping ballroom of the Sunrise Ranch country club where the dinner was being held.

Alvarez nodded unhappily. "Twelve hundred," he muttered. "I just got an update from the events coordinator. They're expecting twelve hundred guests tomorrow."

Jacob forced a whistle through his teeth. "But it's invitation only, right?"

"Invitation only," Alvarez agreed with a sigh. "And every invitation gets a plus-one."

"We're less than eighteen hours from doors open. It's far too late in the game now to try vetting the guest list anyway." Val tried not to sound disheartened. "We need to remember. We're not going out there to *catch* any bad guys that might be out to hurt the senator. We're just going to keep him safe."

"Defense is an easier game." Jacob sipped his beer with a nod. "You're right. There's no problem with the senator having an additional plus-two, is there, Alvarez?"

The little Mexican man shook his head. "We've already accounted for the security detail. The one that dropped out. We had planned for four guards." His brow furrowed. "But you say there will be only two of you?" He cast a questioning glance at Kat, who was snoring softly behind his lavender sleeping mask.

"We'll have to sweep the country club first to be sure, but we'll likely have Kat staying behind-the-scenes to monitor the security cameras for any unusual activity." Val flipped open her laptop, nibbling on an almond as she considered the different ways a highly motivated cartel hitman might try to snuff out a troublesome senator.

Across from her, Alvarez stifled a yawn. "If you'll excuse me," he apologized. "I've had a very long day and tomorrow looks to be even more busy."

"Oh, of course." Val waved vaguely to the sea of empty seats surrounding them. "By all means, get some sleep. We'll be right here doing what we do."

Alvarez took up her invitation. The flight attendant brought him a pillow and blanket and he dozed off in a nearby recliner.

"I could use a nap too," Jacob confessed in a low voice. "Been up since six. I'll think better with a little sleep."

Val nodded, lost in her thoughts. The next thing she knew, she was all alone in this little quadrant of the plane, surrounded by softly snoring men.

She turned off the overhead reading light and let her eyes adjust to the darkness. The plane engines hummed beneath her. Outside, thin wisps of cloud slid past the windows.

She was not surprised to turn her head and see Reginleif looking back at her. The reflection was murky and vague, but over the last few months, Val had gotten used to looking in mirrors to see her other half looking back at her, horns and all.

"*Is this all?*" Reginleif asked incredulously.

Val cocked her head and drank the last of her complimentary champagne. When she spoke, her voice was a barely audible whisper, lost beneath the sounds of the plane, but it was more than loud enough for Reginleif to hear.

"Is what all?"

"*Our task. Oh, yes. Guarding the chieftain while he is*

*surrounded by enemies is a worthy cause, but...is it worthy of us?"*

Val's mouth quirked into a tired smile. Yes, after hunting down international cyber-criminals and leading private armies into battle against paramilitary zealots, the assignment in front of them felt like something of a step down. "It kind of doesn't matter right now. This is the job. We don't exactly have the UN knocking on our door asking us to go topple dictatorships in central Asia."

In the hazy reflection, Reginleif crossed her arms. *"And why must one have an invitation to seek out evildoers?"*

Val cocked an eyebrow. "The world is a bit more complicated now than what it was back in your day, dear. I suppose we could get on a flight to Rio right now and go put a violent end to the deforestation of the rainforest, but I don't have nearly a big enough ego to assume that I know how to handle the kind of fallout that would come after that. Maybe I create a power vacuum and even bigger badder guys step in to fill it. Maybe I just leave chaos behind that winds up hurting more people than it helps. I don't *know*. I'm just one person. I just look at the jobs that are offered to me and I decide which of them does the most good in the world while still paying the bills."

She expected Reginleif to push back against this line of reasoning, to call it weak-willed or naive or perhaps cowardly. She did not expect Regin to tilt her head thoughtfully to the side and give it the full weight of her consideration.

*"I take thy point. One must consider the implications of one's actions. Such decisions do lie in the hands of a chief or a king,"* she conceded.

Val blinked. "Not to look a gift horse in the mouth—you're right, of course—but I'm kind of surprised to hear you say that. I thought you wanted us to be our own chief."

*"Aye. Yes. But throughout my long life, even I have always bowed to the will of my superiors. At some times it was our eldest sister Brynhildr who commanded my spear, and at others, my orders came from the lips of the Allfather himself. But Brynhildr now sleeps, and the Allfather is presumably preoccupied with other matters. I...confess, I haven't much practice at being my own chieftain. I would not expect thee to charge headlong and recklessly into our new course."*

"Unlike you." Val smiled.

Reginleif had the grace not to deny it. *"Still, little sister, I wonder."*

Giving up on making notes for the night, Val closed her computer and slipped it into the seat pocket in front of her. She curled up in her recliner, turning her face to the cold surface of the window. In the darkness, stars and clouds slipped past. "You wonder what?"

*"This Tierra Roja clan,"* Reginleif murmured. *"Or, cartel, I believe the word was. They are criminals, aye? By definition?"*

"Yeah, the drug cartels are pretty bad dudes. I'm pretty confident on that one."

*"And they are the ones threatening the senator."*

"Well, there are a lot of people and groups who want men like Vargas dead, but I'm guessing Tierra Roja is at the top of the list, yeah." Val's eyelids were growing heavy. Jacob had the right of it, she decided. It was best to catch a few winks now, before they landed and the real work began.

*"As I thought. A defensive strategy has no endgame, Valkyrie.*

*Thou might protect the senator for as long as thou wishes, but so long as the enemy draws breath,* thou cannot win the battle. *Thou can only pray not to lose it."*

## George Bush Intercontinental Airport
## Houston, Texas
## Sunday morning, early

Val was shuffling off the jet bridge behind Jacob and ahead of a sleep-hungover Kat when her phone rang. Her first bleary, jetlagged thought was that *Ride the Lightning* was a weird choice for the airline to be piping over its gates at four a.m. on a Sunday morning. Then she remembered that she had recently rearranged the ringtones on her contacts list.

"I gotta take this." Hoping to force some energy into her groggy circulatory system, she slipped to the edge of the terminal and answered her phone while Alvarez and the rest of the red-eyed passengers from their flight staggered into the restrooms.

"Puck?" she asked anxiously. "You okay?" It was a measly 5 a.m. back at Puck's apartment in Manassas. The Kearie family had always been full of early risers, but they usually didn't call one another outside of normal visiting hours unless something had gone terribly wrong. Images flashed through her head. Puck, smiling at her from a Polaroid picture, burnt holes where his eyes should be. Puck, crumpled like roadkill at the bottom of a canyon, hundreds of miles from the nearest hospital.

Puck, fighting every hour of every day for the last five months to regain his ability to walk.

"Hey, Valley Girl." Val's brother sounded tired, but not angry or panicky. A good start. "I didn't wake you up, did I?"

"No." There was a roar from somewhere behind her as multiple toilets flushed in quick succession. "No, I'm just getting off a plane in Houston. We got a last-minute job working some event security this weekend."

"You playing rent-a-cop now?" Puck sounded vaguely incredulous. "What happened to the business consulting?"

Val felt her lips tighten into an awkward smile. She hadn't been forthright with her family about her new career ambitions over these last few weeks. "It's a quick thing." She crossed her fingers behind her back. "No big deal. I'll tell you all about it when I get home. What's going on with you? Why did you call?"

"Ah." Puck's tone turned sour. "Yeah. Um. I just got my final medical evaluation. Dropped in my email inbox a few hours ago." He gave a hollow laugh. "Gotta feel for the low man on the totem pole stuck doling out medical evaluation results on a Saturday night, right?"

Val's heart sank. Puck's recovery from injuries gained in the kidnapping incident in Algeria had been remarkable—borderline superhuman. The way he had fought through a dire spinal cord injury, Val might have suspected he was hiding a little Norse secret of his own. The doctors had told the Kearie family not to count on Puck ever walking without a cane again. Puck, in response, had told the doctors where they could put that cane. Now, he wasn't just walking to the mailbox every morning, he was back to jogging his weekly 10k.

"What did the medical eval say?" Val dreaded the answer.

"Well. There are some very nice notes congratulating me on the speed of my recovery."

"Puck…"

"It's my liver, Val. Functioning is still impaired, and the doctors say the damage is likely permanent. Not nearly bad enough to get me on any lists for transplants, but bad enough to get me out of active duty. Permanently." He laughed again, but it was a harsh, bitter sound. "Shit, man, all that partying I did in high school and in college, and my liver got me through it all unscathed. But you fall off one cliff in Algeria and crush one important valve or duct or whatever and suddenly Uncle Sam gets all scared about your enzyme levels or some shit and wants you out of the service."

Val slumped against the wall, suddenly not quite able to support all of her own weight. She felt like she'd been punched in the gut, and she could only imagine how much worse it was for Puck. "I'm so sorry," she whispered.

"Don't you apologize, Valley Girl. You might have pulled me out of that canyon but you didn't put me there."

Val closed her eyes, remembering the anonymous letter full of defaced photographs. Cleopatra—Claudia Moreno—might have kidnapped Puck and started the chain of events that led to his injuries and the collapse of his career, but she did it specifically to strike at Val.

For as long as Val could remember, Puck had wanted to be a soldier and a hero. Just like Dad, just like Hank.

"I wanted to tell you first." Puck's tone turned businesslike, but she thought she heard the cracking in his voice. "There's a letter of commendation here from my CO, too. Thank you for your service and all that. They're giving me an honorable discharge. I can start to make use of all those juicy VA benefits right away."

Val felt a shift in the air currents and opened her eyes to see Jacob standing in front of her with a look of deep concern etched on his face. She shook her head, trying to tell him without words that while the news was bad, it was nothing code-red.

Jacob's frown deepened. Shouldering his bags, he went to be the first in line as the Starbucks opened up across the terminal.

"Are you going to be okay?" Val asked into her phone. It wasn't every day you get fired from your dream career for reasons utterly beyond your control. Reasons that were deeply, deeply unfair.

"Yeah. Carol's coming over in a couple of hours. We're going to that music festival down in Richmond. It'll help keep my mind off things for today at least. I guess tomorrow I'll phone Dad and let him know. Then I'll start brushing up my resume. I think they're hiring stockers down at the Shop-N-Go."

Val sighed. "Promise me you won't do anything stupid before I get home."

"Stupid like what?"

"Like blowing all your money on an RV and declaring that you're going to live the nomad life while you *find yourself*. Or applying for a job as a cashier at a freaking grocery store. Your life's not over yet, man."

Puck chuckled dryly. "I guess we'll see about that. All right, Valley Girl. I'll try to hold off on my midlife crisis until after you get home. Just don't keep me waiting too long."

Val pulled herself upright, feeling a little better. Jacob had returned from the coffee counter and he was offering her an extra-large cup. He hadn't been gone long enough for the sleepy baristas to put together anything particularly fancy, but if she knew Jacob, he had loaded the thing down with cream and sugar, just for her.

"I'll do my best," she promised her brother as she took the cup. "So now I've got to get moving. Have fun at the festival. Win me a stuffed animal."

# CHAPTER FIVE

**Conference Room**
**Holiday Inn Express**
**Houston, TX**
**Sunday morning**

Alvarez hadn't been joking about the senator's tight budget, or his taste for modesty when he was traveling on the taxpayer's dime. Val tried to imagine any American senator staying at a hotel as common as a Holiday Inn while on an international trip and simply could not.

She supposed it wasn't really Texas if there wasn't a five-foot-wide set of longhorns mounted over the door to every room, but she would have expected a bit more corporate-enforced restraint from a national hotel chain.

"Admirable rack," Reginleif observed as they stepped into the little conference room.

It took all of Val's self-control not to burst out laughing into the dregs of her airport coffee. A half-dozen people in business suits loitered around the conference table.

Sloshing coffee over her blouse first thing would not have supported the air of professionalism she was going for.

"Miss Kearie. Mister Pinkerton. Mister Mulaney." Alvarez broke ahead to introduce them to the man at the head of the table. "This is Senator Vargas."

The senator smiled widely and stood to shake their hands. He was the only person in the room—besides Kat, who insisted that a button-down Hawaiian shirt was professional despite multiple assurances that it was *not*—not wearing business casual attire. Instead, a tight *Texas U* shirt stretched across the senator's muscular chest, spotted in places with sweat. A thin white hotel towel was draped across his shoulders, and when Val shook his hand she caught a faint whiff of deodorant and sweat above the smell of coffee. He had come from the fitness center, it seemed. An early bird.

Jorge Vargas had a wide, charming smile that made him look impossibly young. Val supposed that a few more years in the Mexican senate would wipe the youthful charm right off his handsome face and that would be a shame, but probably better than the alternative.

"Good morning." The senator spoke English without the faintest hint of an accent as if it were his first language. "Thank you for coming on such short notice. I hope you managed to catch some decent sleep on the plane because we've got a big day ahead of us. If not—" Grinning, he gestured to the carafe at the side of the room. "Help yourself to a churro. I was just discussing tonight's gala with these fine gentlemen. Mister Adams is in charge of security for the country club."

"Happy to do it, and glad to meet you." Jacob side-stepped the question of *good sleep* and, at the senator's gesture, took one of the empty seats at the table as Val went to refill her empty coffee cup, half a step behind Kat. "I'm glad to see you found some security staff after all."

"Oh, my boys and I were always part of the deal," Adams said generously. He was a broad-chested man with a receding hairline. Though he was wearing a perfectly mundane button-down shirt and jeans, Val couldn't help but think that was because it was too early in the morning for him to slap on his cowboy hat and tassels. "We run security for every large event at the club. Just to keep away any party crashers, you know."

"But they have been kind enough to step up after my own security detail fell apart yesterday," Vargas added.

Adams nodded. "We'll do the best we can for you, Senator. It'll go off without a hitch, I'm sure of it." His words had a careless quality, almost patronizing. It was as if he didn't expect trouble at the banquet. Or if he did, he was confident down to the core of his bones that he and his little posse of self-deputized cowboys could handle it.

"Still, it's always good to have a fresh set of eyes on the situation." Alvarez slid into the empty chair beside Vargas. The sleepy, demure little man had inexplicably vanished somewhere on the ride from the airport. Now back at Vargas' side, he was bright-eyed and intense. He studied Val and her crew with fresh intensity. "Fiesta Navidad has been on the senator's event calendar for months, which means the cartels have had a very long time to scope out the location and make plans. With our regular security detail falling apart at the last minute, they have the perfect chance to strike."

Vargas leaned carelessly back in his chair. "Fiesta Navidad is a high-profile event," he noted. "It's going to be packed to the brim with rich civilians and pillars of the Mexican American community. Tierra Roja wouldn't dare cause a scene. It would only rally the community further against them."

Alvarez sighed and cast Val an imploring, *do you see what I have to work with* look. "There are other cartels active in the region, Jorge," he pointed out softly. "Let's not forget that Tierra Roja is in disarray. Some ambitious young gangster looking to step up, make a name for himself, might decide that taking you out is worth the risk of making a scene."

Vargas shrugged. "Some tired old biddy might try to assassinate me by sneezing on me and passing along the flu, eh? We can't live in fear, Mateo." He cast a glance at Val's team.

Alvarez scowled, snapping out a line of rapid Spanish. Val didn't catch a single word of it, but she noted Jacob sitting up straighter beside her, on alert.

Alvarez finished his tirade in English for the benefit of the assembled Americans. "*You* are the face of Evolución Social, Jorge. Nobody else has been able to unite the constituents like you have. Nobody else has been elected to high office. If something happens to you, the whole movement falls apart."

Tense silence filled the room. Adams looked down, fiddling with the stirring stick in his coffee. The only person unaffected was Kat, who sat beside Val happily munching on a churro from the sideboard.

Finally, the senator lifted his gaze to Jacob. "What do our Viking friends think?"

Jacob and Val exchanged glances. Val nodded her assent. They were partners in this venture, but as progressive as Vargas might have been, he was still Mexican, and machismo ran bone-deep in his culture. He'd take advice better from a big beefy man.

Jacob sat up straight, cracking his knuckles as he leaned over the table. "It's VALKYRIE, actually. You're paying us to be paranoiacs, Senator. Mister Alvarez has a point. I believe this fundraiser represents a significant opportunity for your enemies to strike at you."

A hard glint crept into the senator's eye. "Would you also have me cancel, too?"

Jacob hesitated, considering his answer carefully. "On the one hand, it would be the safest course of action. On the other hand, it would put us out of a job."

Vargas tipped his head back and laughed. "Alvarez, I think you found some good people. But that's enough bickering for one morning, my friends. We have a party to prepare for."

# CHAPTER SIX

**Val's room**
**Holiday Inn Express**
**Houston, TX**
**Sunday morning**

After a light smattering of complaints about the *good ole boy posse*, Kat rode back to the country club with Adams and his men to start his analysis of the security cameras and make whatever last-minute upgrades he could manage. Jacob integrated himself into the senator's inner ring and spent the morning at Vargas' side, playing bodyguard as he familiarized himself with the man's habits and expectations. That left Val alone in the hotel room to research the senator and his long, long list of enemies. She hadn't crammed so hard since her second year of college when she had forgotten about her upcoming Statistical Methods midterm until the night before.

The more research she did, and the more case files and law enforcement reports she read, the more worried she became. If the professional bad guys of North America had a Most Wanted list, Jorge Vargas would have been in the top ten. Alvarez was correct. With Cascobel in custody, Tierra Roja might be in disarray, but plenty of other gangs and cartels in the region were looking to fill the power void.

"You see what I mean?" she muttered to Reginleif around midday when room service arrived with her omelet and hash browns. "When you strike out at the bad guys, sometimes even the professionals don't always know what the fallout will be."

*"Then one ought proceed with caution,"* Reginleif allowed. *"But one* must *proceed."*

Val felt somewhat adrift in the task. Jacob had been correct. Fiesta Navidad was a Big Deal. Under normal circumstances, Hawk would have had two or three of his interns back at HQ running background checks on every one of the hundreds of guests and waiters and caterers expected to brush elbows with the senator tonight. These weren't normal circumstances, though. Or rather, this was the *new* normal. The training wheels had come off the bike. VALKYRIE needed to learn how to fly solo.

Aware that they were three people doing what should have been the job of a dozen, Val could do nothing but plow ahead and put her faith in her partners and herself.

**Val's room**
**Holiday Inn Express**
**Houston, TX**
**Sunday afternoon**

Before she knew it, the clock had turned over and the second, even more exciting, half of the day had begun. Val wouldn't have expected a hotel like this to have much in the way of concierge service, so she was surprised when the lady from the front desk knocked on her door to present her with an emerald evening gown in a dry-cleaning bag.

"From the senator's office," the receptionist explained, who *also* sounded surprised to learn that her hotel provided concierge service. She had a second bag slung over her shoulder containing a rented tux from the nearest Big and Tall Men's Wearhouse. "He said to give you this as well."

Val took the dress and the folded card with a polite thank-you and waited until the door was firmly shut to read the note.

*I know you and your associates did not have time to pack anything formal before we left DC. I had to guess at your size, but my wife always told me that this style of dress is very forgiving. Thank you for looking after Jorge tonight. He is very important to us.*

*—Alvarez*

The dress bag included a pretty pearl necklace and two golden hairpins. Val checked everything over carefully before deciding that Alvarez was a sincere, if shy, sweetheart, and not some creepshow trying to tell the hired help what they had to wear.

Even if he was, he had selected a wrap-style gown, which was perfect for hiding a thigh holster and a couple of knives.

Thirty minutes later, she stepped into the hotel lobby to

find a ridiculously good-looking, broad-shouldered beast of a man in a tuxedo affixing a communicator to his ear as he discussed some last-minute issue with Adams' rent-a-cops. When the men in the stiff black security uniforms nodded and departed through the hotel's front doors, Jacob turned to see Val leaning on a nearby marble column.

He stared.

She smiled faintly. "It's not totally my style," she admitted, running her fingers over the fabric at her neckline, "but it's pretty good for a rent-a-dress." She held out her hand and wiggled her fingers. "You got one of those earpieces for me?"

Jacob flushed and hustled toward her, pulling the device from an inner pocket. He brushed a strand of loose hair from her cheek and fitted the little black lump into her ear with all the tenderness of a man presenting his date with a new set of diamond studs. He coughed. "Pretty good. Yeah."

He glanced down and she noted the way his eyes brushed over her chest and hips before landing on her feet. "You, uh, gonna be able to work okay in heels?"

Val chuckled. "I'll kick them off if things get exciting. It's a high-society event, and I'm going as a senator's guest." She brushed her toe against the hem of his trousers to expose his sturdy, all-business athletic shoes. "Us girls can't exactly get away with wearing combat boots to the ball." She gave him a grin. "You look good."

"*You* look good," he echoed, eyes downcast. Gods, she liked the way this battle-hardened warrior turned into a mumbling teddy bear when there were no hired assassins around to shoot. He was too much fun to tease. She was about to ask if that was a Kevlar wrap and holster under his jacket *or if he was just happy to see her* when the nearest elevator doors slid open and the senator stepped into the lobby.

If Jorge Vargas was handsome in his post-workout clothes, he was devastating in his black tux. Even Reginleif, who preferred her men big and hairy and bestial, roused from her rest to admire the slender, smiling fellow adjusting his cufflinks. Alvarez was at his elbow, his flyaway hair artfully messy as he struggled to keep up with his young and vital boss.

Two more of Adams' rent-a-cops tailed the senator and his aide as they approached the doors.

"You look excellent," Vargas declared, pausing to take in Val and Jacob. "Perfect. You'll fit right in." He held out a hand to Val. "Señorita." A dazzling, playful smile flirted across his lips as he took her hand and planted a dry kiss on her knuckles. "Since my beloved wife is unable to join us, would you do me the honor of being my date to the ball tonight?" He straightened and dropped her a wink.

Val let out a breathless titter. "The *esposa* wouldn't mind?"

"I don't think so." His smile turned mischievous. "Her Google Calendar says she's having *tapas* with the gardener tonight. She wouldn't pay us any mind at all."

Beside Vargas, Alvarez rolled his eyes but looked neither surprised nor upset. The two rent-a-cops behind them chuckled.

For the first time in quite a while, Val was speechless. Before she could decide if Vargas' flirting was affectation or sincere Latino ardor, the man drew himself up and became a professional statesman once more. "Will you ride in the limo with us?"

She was relieved that his tone had returned to one of pure business-oriented curiosity. "No." She glanced at Alvarez and the guards. "Jacob and I will tail you in the SUV. He's already looked the cars over for tampering. I need to make some final arrangements and preparations with my team. I'll join your party at the country club."

Vargas' smile returned, and it crackled up to his dark eyes. "I'll be honored. I hope you're comfortable doing a salsa in that dress, señorita. It's not a real Latino holiday party without dancing."

**In the trailing SUV**
**En Route to Fiesta Navidad**
**Houston, Texas**
**Sunday evening**

"All right." Val flopped into the back seat, pressing up close to Jacob's warm bulk as she fiddled with her earpiece. She thumbed the tiny dial, familiarizing herself with the different channels. Jacob touched his ear, tuning into the same frequency.

"We're t-minus ten minutes," Val reported. "Kat? Any news?"

A brief blurt of static was followed by a slightly breathless laugh. "Well, Miss Daisy, it seems Sunrise Ranch is the kind of place that keeps loaner suits on hand for guests who don't meet the dress code."

"You mean the maître d' wasn't going to let you wear cargo shorts to the ball?" Jacob asked dryly.

"Sadly no, not even the caterers or hired help can get away with dressing like common folk. It's not all bad, though. I do believe I am allergic to the fabric softener they use here. On the bright side, the young man in the coat room was *very accommodating.*"

Val sighed.

"Don't you worry, Miss Daisy." Kat switched to an all-business tone before she had to prod him back on topic. "Security here is as buttoned up as it can be, with such short notice. We've got all the cameras secure and working. They're covering about ninety-three percent of the grounds, and I've assigned one of Adam's men to patrol the restrooms and the hallway and back alley blind spots every ten minutes."

"How do we feel about Adams' rent-a-cops?" Val cast Jacob a sideways glance.

He cracked his knuckles, settling into the plush leather. It was one of those rent-a-cops driving the SUV, though he was behind a soundproof privacy screen. "Not bad," Jacob admitted. "Adams has a good reputation in the area. I ran background checks on all eight of the guards he had on duty tonight. Seven checked out clean as a whistle. There were some irregularities with the last guy."

"Irregularities?" Val asked sharply. Ahead of them, the senator's limo turned onto the highway and their SUV followed.

Jacob shrugged. "He's new to the business. Doesn't have much of a record or work history to consult. Adams says he was a new hire. A second cousin who needed some direction after graduating from high school. Not a problem, though. As soon as I brought it up, Adams offered to send the kid home tonight with standby pay. No muss, no fuss."

Val was gratified, if a little surprised, that a man like Adams was so willing to bench a family member on the word of some outside contractors. Perhaps she had misjudged him.

"I had a bit of free time once the cameras were settled," Kat remarked. "So I thought I'd see what we're up against."

Val nodded, though he couldn't have seen it. She'd been doing opposition research all morning. "Tierra Roja might be a bit of a mess since the feds took Cascobel into custody, but they've still got a pretty extensive network in the States. I pegged a couple of lieutenants that might try to shore up their authority by going on the offensive." She consulted some notes on her phone. "A Miami gangster known as Octavio, and Cascobel's nephew—"

"Hector Aurora," Kat finished. His voice turned grim. "His name came up in my research too, Miss Daisy. Sources suggest Octavio is holed up in Miami doing what drug lords do, but Hector has been below the radar since the feds took his uncle into custody."

Val winced. You needed to worry about where a man might be if Kat couldn't find him.

Kat had more. "Tierra Roja's stateside assets might be frozen, but cartels like this always keep a good portion of their funds liquid. If anyone knew where Cascobel was hiding some big bags of cash, it would have been Hector."

"Send any recent pictures you have of him to my

phone," Jacob suggested. "And tell Adams' men to keep an eye out for anyone matching the description."

"You think he'd risk showing his face in a place like this?" Val had her doubts.

Jacob nodded. "These cartels aren't like Forseti. If Hector is watching the Tierra Roja throne, then he's going to want all of his rivals to *know* he's responsible for the senator's demise. If he's got anything planned for tonight then I'd bet on him showing up to do it in person."

Their phones vibrated at the same time as a new file came through from Kat. Val glanced down to see a family photo of three Mexican men embracing around a table laden with tamales. According to the text, Hector was the fellow on the left, the one holding aloft a half-empty bottle of tequila. She studied his young face, committing his blunt nose and heavy brow to memory.

A few minutes later, the limo and SUV turned onto a country road just outside of the city limits. Val saw Sunrise Ranch looming on a low hill. It was a two-story stone and brick structure modeled after European castles of old, holding vigil over a pristine golf course worthy of any PGA tour. The fields in front of the ranch property were already scattered with cars and news vans, and paparazzi lined the red carpet leading up to the ranch's wrought iron gates. As they approached the drop-off line, Val saw a man in a cowboy hat and tassels step out of a Humvee, arm-in-arm with a stunning young woman in an ivory evening gown. Cameras flashed as the journalists and lookie-loos clamored up to the velvet rope without quite breaching the symbolic barrier.

Val caught glimpses of three humorless, dark-suited

men moving through the crowd, watching the scene intently.

"Everyone who made it as far as that gate has a press pass," Jacob assured Val, noticing her concerned look. "They're mostly reporters from the local Spanish-language newspapers. Everybody beyond the gate has an official invitation. The whole point of the thing is to draw attention to Vargas' cause, so we can't keep them away entirely."

Val nodded her understanding, if not approval, as the limo ahead of them slowed and pulled to the side of the road to allow the SUV to go ahead. The next thing Val knew, they were parked in front of the red carpet.

"That's your cue," Jacob teased, poking Val gently as he opened his door. "Break a leg."

Val swallowed, staring out at the dozens of photographers and reporters waiting to see who emerged from the SUV. That was easy for Jacob to say. He could slip out the back way and begin his patrol of the grounds while avoiding the limelight. Val did not relish the idea of standing beneath the unblinking eye of all those cameras alone.

"*Thou art not alone*," Reginleif offered.

Val sighed and grabbed the door handle. "Technically," she muttered. "But let's not try explaining that to the paparazzi."

She emerged from the SUV and took two steps toward the wrought iron gate, doing her best to ignore the flashes and the curious clamor of the crowd. A few people shouted questions in her direction, some in English and some in Spanish. Behind her, the SUV rolled away to be replaced by the senator's limo. She turned her back to the people as

Jorge Vargas stepped onto the carpet. The noise swelled as the journalists forgot all about this curious, lonely white lady, throwing a barrage of questions at the smiling senator instead. Val caught a few words. *Cascobel. Tierra Roja. Cartel.*

Jorge didn't seem to see the reporters and photographers. His gaze was set on Val like she was the only thing in the world. Smiling, he held an arm out to her. "Señorita?"

Val's stomach did an odd little flip. He had good cheekbones. Nice and sharp and high. When he took her arm and strutted down the carpet, casting smiles and polite, canned answers to the reporters, somehow he made Val feel like she was nine feet tall. He was a natural crowd-pleaser, with his easygoing charm and the throwaway compliments he tossed into the crowd. He was a king of the stage, and by extension he made Val and even the two rent-a-cops trailing them temporary royalty as well.

The stretch of red carpet leading up to the ranch's iron gate was about twenty feet long but crossing it felt like a dizzying, heady quest of hours, and was not unpleasant. Val bathed in a sea of camera flashes and questions as if she were pleasantly drunk, twirling her fingers and smiling at the throng. By the time they reached the security guards at the end of the line and the senator made a show of fishing into his jacket for his ivory-white laminated invitation, she was flush with excitement, panting slightly and deliciously lightheaded.

"Miss!" A middle-aged woman with a beehive hairdo and a knee-length pencil skirt leaned over the velvet rope, waving for Val's attention as the gate guards checked

Vargas' invitation against the man, his date, and their two bodyguards. It was all a show for the sake of the watchers. They were all Adams' men.

The press badge clipped to the woman's breast pocket read *Estrella de Houston.* Val cast her a polite, if absent, smile as the woman craned forward, holding out a small audio recorder. "Miss, I'm from the Star of Houston. Can I get your name for my article please?" The woman's small dark eyes glittered as she spoke.

"It's Kate." Val was relieved to know that even drunk on the adulation of the crowd as she was, she reverted easily enough to the alias she occasionally used for undercover jobs. "Kate Weiss."

"How do you know the senator, Miss Weiss?"

Val wasn't sure what answer she could have given, but by that point, the nearby reporters realized that the Star woman had a source on the hook and they fell on Val like a pack of dogs. They shoved recorders and mics into her face until they all blurred into one incomprehensible jumble.

"Are you friends with the senator's wife, Sofia Vargas?"

*"Estás consciente de...?"*

"How would you characterize your relationship to the senator, Miss Weiss?"

*"¿Te quedarás...?"*

"Are you concerned about the growing number of threats on the senator's life, Miss Weiss?"

All at once those weren't lamps or camera flashes or streetlights spinning around Val. They were candle flames, flickering in a dusty haze. Swirling and blurring together as she spun in a lonely black dungeon beneath the bowels of the earth. Dancing. Dancing in a gyre of sand and black feathers, fighting to stay upright as her head tilted and whirled. Fighting to keep her balance. Her boots scraped through the sand, shuffling around a pair of light, bare feet, swirling, swirling.

"*Hold on to your wits.*" Reginleif's groan sounded distant, unreal.

Something brushed Val's elbow and she whirled, her heart leaping into her throat. Adrenaline seared through her like lightning, turning her skin into a landscape of goosebumps, making wings swell against the inside of her shoulder blades. There. He was *there*, except—

Except he wasn't a slender, barefooted man in a knee-length duster. He didn't have long, silky black hair or blank, drug-clouded eyes above a manic smile or a fistful of glittering needles clutched in his fist.

He was tall and olive-skinned and handsome, with lovely high cheekbones and short brown hair.

Val gasped, fiercely yanking her horns back into her skull before they could slide out of her hair and expose her to the crowd. She felt her wings swell beneath the back of her dress, fighting for freedom and she recalled those, too. Reality reset itself. She was on the red carpet in Houston, not in the bomb shelter of McCormack Army Depot.

She grimaced, wiping her expression of horror into what she hoped was a passable nervous smile. She opened her mouth but Jorge brushed past her, gracing the crowd with his smile.

"Miss Weiss has been an invaluable aide to my office on this diplomatic trip," he told the microphones and cameras. "I've invited her to the fiesta as a thank-you for all her hard work. Let's not scare the poor lady off, *ai?*"

He nudged her gently, directing her through the gates and away from the crowd.

Val's senses returned to her as soon as she stepped through the gate and into the comparatively quiet, peaceful front lawn of the Sunrise Ranch, where the air was cool and quiet.

She felt her cheeks redden at once.

"I'm sorry about that," she muttered as they strolled up to the front doors to the country club. Strings of softly glowing tea lights were strung across the hedges lining the path. Somewhere in the cavernous halls of the faux castle, a mariachi band played a four-man rendition of *Mi Burrito Sabanero*. Val scanned the shadows as she walked, searching the bushes for hired assassins or cartel goons. She couldn't afford to be caught off guard again.

Vargas chuckled softly. "No problemo. The spotlight takes some getting used to. It's not for everybody. You looked like a deer in headlights."

Val fiddled with her earpiece, flipping restlessly through the limited channels. Her brain was a jumble of disorganized thoughts and emotions.

"*I am here, little sister,*" Reginleif whispered in the back of her mind. That was all the ancient one said, all she could say. Val sensed her drawing somehow closer as if to embrace her from within, warming her with her fiery, immortal presence. They were close, and Val was not alone in the darkness. Clinging on to that understanding, she found the strength to turn her mind back to the job.

"I'll stay by your side in all public spaces," Val told the senator as they mounted the steps to the entrance hall, where a throng of well-dressed ladies and gentlemen mingled and sipped flutes of champagne. "But try to give me as much warning as you can if you have business in any, uh, private place. Jacob will take over those."

"Of course." Vargas chuckled again, ever jovial and oblivious to his companion's inner struggle. "The journalists who make it all the way into Fiesta Navidad may pretend to rise above, but I imagine they'll gossip too if they notice you following me into the restroom."

Val was glad it was dim out here in the yard. It hid the second flush that crept into her cheeks. She was used to handling one or two interested parties every time she took herself out to a bar or club on a Saturday night, but something about strutting up a red-carpet arm-in-arm with a senator—and a charming, attractive one at that— just hit different.

Or maybe that was the fading whiff of adrenaline talking, distracting her.

*"Thou needn't be unmoored by any man,"* Reginleif proclaimed. *"Flirt back with him, Valkyrie! Beat him at his own game."*

Val relaxed a little, imagining the world the way Reginleif saw it: a never-ending series of battles and competitions and contests, only a few of which needed to be violent or even unfriendly.

She tightened her grip on Vargas' arm, held her head high, and strode into the Sunset Ranch's grand entryway.

# CHAPTER SEVEN

**Fiesta Navidad**
**Sunrise Ranch**
**Houston, Texas**
**Sunday evening**

The tapas were exquisite. Caterers flitted through the grand entryway, bearing plates of deviled prawns and little fried tortilla cups stuffed with roasted corn and topped with crumbles of spicy cheese. A server in a black tux slid past Val and Vargas, and flutes of sparkling champagne sprouted in their hands like crystal flowers. Men in bolo ties and embroidered jackets strutted over the marble floors, smiling and laughing and gregarious as they greeted each other like old friends. The women, too, were a sight, decked out in billowing scarlet and blue gowns embroidered with poinsettias and sunflowers. In the hotel, Val had considered her borrowed gown nicely captivating but now she felt downright drab compared to these colorful birds.

She sipped from her flute, craning her head back to

take in the wide chandelier hanging over the roped-off grand staircase. Someone had taken this austere, grand castle with its marble floors and gold filigree and the tastefully subtle evergreen boughs coiled around the banister, and made it undeniably *ethnic*. Ropes of colorful ornaments draped from the crystal chandelier down to the edges of the room, spinning like tiny dancers. Glowing six-pointed stars hung at the center of every archway and entrance. In a little alcove between the entryway and the ballroom, someone had pushed the grand piano to the side to make room for the mariachi quartet. Everywhere Val looked, she caught sight of little Christmas dolls tucked into the eaves and peering at the party from inside the twelve-foot Douglas fir at the center of the entryway.

Val glided through the crowd, the senator's shadow as he embraced old friends and shook hands with new acquaintances. Where courtesy demanded it, he introduced Val to this state representative or that union director, and she smiled and nodded and murmured a few brief Spanish greetings she had rehearsed in the car. As far as the other guests were concerned, she was the senator's arm candy for the evening and the two men in dark suits tailing them were the real security. That was fine by her. It left her free to study the crowd as her date schmoozed.

A gray silk photo screen stood beside the tree where a professional photographer with an official pass clipped to his jacket knelt and snapped pictures of every guest and couple that passed. Many people wanted their picture taken with the dashing Mexican senator, and Val spent most of the cocktail hour in the shelter of the tree, watching as Jorge posed and chatted. The women loved him almost as much as he loved them, she noted ruefully. Whatever tacit understanding Vargas had with his wife, Val hoped she wasn't going to have to protect the man from some sexy honeypot later this evening.

They were about thirty minutes into cocktail hour when Val noticed movement in a dark corner beneath the grand stairway. A pocket door in the wood slid to the side and Jacob emerged from the shadows. He latched the door firmly shut behind him and mingled easily into the crowd, wandering in Val's direction. He carried a chilled highball glass full of creamy brown liquid.

"No sniper nests in the belfry," he reported, passing the glass to Val. "Espresso and cream. I figured you could use a pick-me-up without the buzz."

Val set her nearly empty champagne flute onto the tray of a passing caterer and sipped the glass. Honey and cinnamon, not just espresso and cream. She gave Jacob an appreciative nod. "It's a good thing." She hesitated, debating telling him about her flashback on the red carpet before deciding that the touchy-feely talk would have to wait until the job was over. "I'm pretty sure I saw a few bottles of Amigos Perdidos behind the bar."

Jacob shuffled closer to her side as a cluster of high-society ladies strutted up to the photo booth. "What's that?"

Val smiled absently into her glass. The senator had hopped aside, making room for the new cluster of debutantes. The photographer fell into a rapid, excited Spanish tirade as he arranged the pretty young women into the most flattering poses. He was a bit handsy, taking brusque liberties in moving the women's shoulders and chins and hips, but they giggled, taking no offense. He was a professional, after all. He was wearing gloves, as if he were handling delicate porcelain instead of flesh.

Val pulled her attention back to Jacob's question. "Amigos Perdidos is a Mexican meadery that prides itself on its history. They claim their premium line recipe hasn't changed from the days of the Aztecs."

"Oh boy." Jacob straightened. The concern that crossed his face made Val smile.

"We're on duty," she assured him, taking another sip. "Coffee is going to have to suffice for now." Under her breath, she added, "Though it wouldn't be any great tragedy if one of those bottles went missing before the upper crust suck them all dry."

Jacob pretended he hadn't heard. Val watched as the senator fell into animated conversation with a broad-shouldered ox of a man with the sort of waxed mustache one expected to find on caricature portraits. Beside her, the photographer shooed the flock of young women onward to make room for an elderly couple. The air in the hallway was chilly, but the intense lighting had put a sheen of sweat on his brow. When he wasn't fiddling with his lenses, he fussed at his gloves.

"How's Kat handling himself?" Val hadn't touched her earpiece in several minutes, preferring to focus on the senator's flock of admirers.

"Pretty good. A little sullen that he couldn't enjoy the party, but stick him behind the screens with a Tom Collins and a plate of tamales and he's happy enough." Jacob checked his watch. "There was a bit of a mix-up with the catering company," he admitted. "They're running late."

"They are?" Val glanced around, noting the half-dozen

waiters whisking through the crowds with their plates of escamol and ceviche bites. "Could have fooled me."

"The *dinner* caterers," Jacob corrected himself. "Appetizers and drinks are supplied by the Sunrise Ranch. Dinner's coming in from a Mexican caterer in the city. The truck is pulling up to the kitchens now to start unloading."

"I wish them luck," Val muttered. "Dinner starts in twenty minutes. Delivering entrées for a crowd this size is no mean feat."

"Especially when they have to deal with security checks," Jacob said brightly. "Do you want to go frisk the caterers or should I?"

Val grimaced and drained the last of her coffee. She was doing fine out here, babysitting the senator. It kept her busy and distracted. No need to rock the boat. "You go ahead." She set the empty glass on an empty high-top table and followed her laughing charge into the crowd. "I've got it covered in here."

**Fiesta Navidad**
**Sunrise Ranch**
**Houston, Texas**
**Sunday evening**

The Sunrise Ranch management was remarkably skilled at keeping the upper crust separate from the hoi polloi. On one side of any given inner door: marble floors and wooden panels and soft lighting over plush carpets. On the other side: fluorescent lights, musty-smelling hallways lined with yellowed drywall, and haggard-looking waitstaff returning from their coveted cigarette breaks.

Jacob moved through the back hallways, bypassing the ranch's modest but bustling kitchen as he approached the delivery doors on the western edge of the building. Someone had propped the double doors open, and one of Adams' rent-a-cops stood outside the back door, looking on as a cluster of vaguely panicked delivery men argued with the ranch manager in the space between the dumpster and the half-dozen box trucks filling the service lot.

"They're arguing about where to take the hotboxes," the rent-a-cop reported. "The caterer says they need to go straight to the dining room before the food gets cold, but the manager is saying that their contract demands the ranch re-plate all entrées onto their branded flatware before serving."

Despite his functional grasp of Spanish, Jacob was having a hard time squeezing the details from the shouted argument and appreciated the guard's synopsis, even if he didn't appreciate the nature of the argument.

"You gotta be kidding me. We got enough shit on our plate without playing mediator, too." Growling, he stepped into the service lot and strode toward the two shouting men. "*No pelear. No pelear!*"

The manager and the caterer might have happily ignored Jacob's slightly clumsy Spanish, but they glanced over and saw the big, glowering man behind the words and thought better of it. The manager, a tall, midfifties man in a blue suit, sniffed contemptuously and rounded on the skinny little caterer.

"Take the dishes to the dining hall," he snapped as a few

of the waitstaff rushed forward to unload the tall steel cabinets from the back of the truck. "But we will reconsider any future contracts with your business, because apparently you people don't know how to read a goddamned clock!"

Jacob sighed. Movement at the edge of the lot caught his attention and he turned. While most of the Sunrise Ranch employees were busy loading rice and beans onto trolleys, one scruffy young man in a dishwasher's apron was moving along the darkened edge of the lot, hauling a large duffel bag over his shoulder.

The lot was full of inert service vehicles—branded panel vans for the florist and mariachi band and box trucks with labels like *United Liquor Distributors LLC* and *Party Time Rentals.*

Under normal circumstances, Jacob would have assumed that the dishwasher was sneaking away to steal another cigarette break behind the dumpster, or perhaps he was walking off the job entirely.

Except that Fiesta Navidad didn't constitute a 'normal' circumstance, and Jacob was getting paid to see boogeymen in every shadow. Besides, that bag the kid was carrying looked like it had some weight to it, and Jacob was familiar with all the interesting, dangerous toys one could hide in a good duffel.

Leaving the manager and caterer to work out their difference under the supervision of one bored rent-a-cop, Jacob stepped out of the halo of light by the ranch's back door. He stepped lightly over the crumbling asphalt, sticking to the deepest shadows as he tailed the kid to the edge of the service lot.

The kid dropped his bag near the back of a mid-sized freight truck. The brand on the side of the truck read *Southwest Hospitality Group*, which was the name of the company that owned the Sunrise Ranch.

Jacob watched with interest as the kid unlatched the truck's freight door and set one foot on the ladder leading up to the cargo box. He huffed and grumbled, adjusting the shoulder strap of his bag before heaving himself into the darkness. The door snapped shut behind him.

Jacob touched his ear, opening his commendations channel to Kat. "Suspicious activity in the western corner of the service lot," he murmured. "You got eyes back here, right?"

There was a pause on the other end of the line as Kat checked his cameras. "Sorry, sugar. That's one of the blind spots I have Adams checking every ten minutes."

Jacob rubbed his temples. Suspicious activity in a camera blind spot. Of course. "Run the plate. Number..." He leaned out to see the back of the truck. "ANG-176. It's got the Hospitality Group logo but it never hurts to check. I'm going in for a closer look."

"On it, sweetiepie. Don't get into any trouble."

Jacob muted his comms channel and slunk closer to the truck, slipping one hand beneath his jacket to loosen his holster. Holding his breath, he pressed his ear to the steel panel. Yes, that was movement on the other side. Thumps and shuffles and grumbling. It took him a moment to start picking meaning out of the mingled Spanish and English.

"Dios mío. These things smell like vinegar..."

"It's the industrial detergent they use. It's fine."

"These pants are too tight. They're cutting off circulation to my cojones. Carlo, swap me."

"Vete a la mierda. I like this one."

"Will you stop bitching? Just put on the fucking uniform. I'm on the phone. Ai, ai. Sí, señor. La tendremos muerta en menos de diez minutos."

*We'll have the pig dead in less than ten minutes.*

Jacob figured it a little late in the evening to start spitting a hog to roast. His comms channel beeped. Kat had an update for him.

"I'm afraid that plate's registered to an old Chevy Tahoe belonging to an unlicensed plumber from Dallas, sugar. Nothing in the Hospitality Group's fleet even close to it."

Jacob was not surprised. Sucking in the chilly night air, he slipped around the back of the truck. The rear door was dangling open by the tiniest fraction of an inch, but he dared not peer into the compartment.

"Put the word out," he whispered as he reached for the steel latch. "We've got hostiles in the parking lot. Anywhere between four and a dozen."

He stepped onto the truck's bumper, yanking the door shut and pulling the exterior latch shut in one motion. The steel wailed as it slammed into place.

A chorus of shouting rose as dozens of feet raced to the back of the truck. The door groaned on its track but held fast.

"On it." Kat's tone turned instantly businesslike. "They armed, Pinkerton?"

Jacob backed away from the truck, drawing his Beretta as he watched the door jump and rattle beneath the pounding of angry fists. "Oh, I think it's safe to assume they are."

A deafening *pop* accompanied a dime-sized hole in the door. The bullet sank into the windshield of a nearby panel van and the wailing of its auto alarm filled the night.

Not that Jacob could hear much of it, because the group of hostiles had decided the fastest way out of the shipping container was to turn it into swiss cheese.

"Scratch that," he shouted as he dove for cover. All around him, the air filled with gunshots and the stinking scent of sulfur. "Definitely armed!"

# CHAPTER EIGHT

**Fiesta Navidad**
**Sunrise Ranch**
**Houston, Texas**
**Sunday evening**

Cocktail hour was coming to a close. The guests had begun to file out of the entryway and into the ballroom where a fresh batch of caterers were setting out the water glasses.

"Señorita Weiss!" Jorge Vargas took Val by the arm, gesturing animatedly to a pair of reporters, a man and a woman wearing matching and well-tailored black suits. "Let me introduce you to my friends Anita and Leon. They're journalists from *Time Magazine*. They're working on a story about the fall of Tierra Roja in the United States."

"*Time?*" Val's eyebrows shot up and she shook the proffered hands. After watching the senator chat with everyone from the caterers to the Attorney General of Texas for the last hour, she shouldn't have been surprised to see that his connections ran that far up the media ladder.

"That's right." Anita's face split into a wide smile. Her bottom teeth were crooked, as if they'd been rearranged in some drag-out brawl in her recent past. "Don't worry, it's not going to be a cover story or anything but the chief figures the apprehension of Cascobel on American soil is worth at least a ten-page run."

"Not a cover story?" Vargas groaned melodramatically. "Come on, tell me the collapse of one of the oldest Mexican cartels isn't worth at least a feature!"

Anita smiled playfully. Leon hovered over her shoulder, silent and blank-faced. "I'll believe you've put Tierra Roja to bed for good when Cascobel is safety behind bars in a high-security prison." She raised her half-empty cocktail glass in salute. "*Then* I promise, I'll do everything in my power to get your face on the cover. So long as you give me an interesting story, of course."

Vargas chuckled. To Val, he said, "Every time we meet, Miss Anita asks to shadow me. A reporter on the front lines of the drug war. I always tell her that if she can get a reasonable security budget worked out with her office, I'd be happy to add her to the entourage. Until then, my home state can be an unfriendly place for a journalist who asks too many questions."

"Reporters go into dangerous situations every day," Anita shot back. "It's all part of the job. We do what needs to be done, for the greater good." Her gaze shifted to Val, who realized with a jolt why Vargas had dragged her into this conversation. He wanted the reporter off his case.

She painted on her best I'm-just-a-girl-in-over-her-head look. "Then you're a braver woman than I am. God, I've had to close down all of my social media since I started working with the senator. The number of death threats in my inbox has gone through the *roof*. Lots of angry young men out in the world, all of them looking for payback."

Anita's give-em-hell grin flickered, but only a little. "I'm sorry to hear that, Miss Weiss. People like us are always going to get more than our share of death threats from angry young men."

"Then there were the brake lines." Val cast a nervous glance at Vargas, who nodded wisely.

"The brake lines," he agreed, picking up her improv ball and running with it. "When we were coming to Houston from Miami, my driver picked us up in a rented auto. We were on a busy highway when the lines gave out. Barely got off the side of the road before plowing into some poor family in a minivan. Tierra Roja may be dead as an organization, Anita, but the men who survived it are all out for revenge. They have connections all over the place."

This seemed to put Anita's hopeful attitude to bed. She drained the last of her glass as the four of them passed beneath the grand arch leading into the ballroom. "I see we'll have to save the discussion on shadowing you for another day. Tell me about your situation in Mexico, Senator. I understand there wasn't much enthusiasm for this trip among your colleagues."

The corners of Vargas' mouth tugged downward. "The people, especially the politicians, have given up hope. They have accepted the cartel's power over our everyday lives as an inevitable fact. They see what I'm doing as upsetting the apple cart. They think—"

A distant *pop* rattled the glassware on the western edge of the dining hall. Heads turned curiously as a second *pop* followed the first.

"Did someone break out the firecrackers?" Anita asked.

Val's earpiece beeped with an urgent message from Kat.

"Looks like there's excitement in the service lot, Miss Daisy. Some party crashers snuck in through the back gate."

Before Kat had finished his sentence, several more *pops* floated up from the maze of back hallways. People murmured uneasily as the crowd started to realize what *else* that sound might be.

Val's pistol was out of its thigh holster and in her fist. Out of the corner of her eye, she saw Anita's face stiffen with shock and Leon draw a tiny pea-shooter from beneath his coat. More pops turned into a long rattle of gunfire, followed by the first distant, agonized scream of the evening.

"Jorge!" Kicking smartly out of her emerald-green pumps, Val grabbed the senator with her free hand and shoved him back toward the entryway. Around them, the crowd was dissolving into a restless, uneasy mob.

To the senator's credit, he did not freeze or stiffen under Val's guiding hand. Indeed he flowed gracefully in the direction she indicated, as if he had been secretly training for the emergency-evacuation dance for months before the big show. Gripping him tightly by the arm, Val pushed between two big, confused-looking men in cowboy suits. She glanced over her shoulder to scan the dining hall. It had turned into a disturbed ant hill. She saw no sign of Adams' black-suited rent-a-cops among the crowd.

She faced forward, pushing Vargas' head down to minimize his profile as they turned the corner out of the ballroom. She whacked her earpiece with her wrist. "Where is the rest of the security team? Give me an update, Kat!"

Chaos swelled on the comms line, and then a painfully loud blurt of static as someone fired a gun too close to a mic.

"Adams just left CnC and he's headed toward the service lot to back up Jacob," Kat shouted. "We're trying to organize the rest of his men but it's—"

"—a mess," Val finished the sentence. Adams might have taken his job as hired security seriously enough, but even if his men held the same high ideals, it was clear that their experience was more theoretical than practical.

*At the first sound of gunfire, the rookies forget all their training.*

As part of their pre-dinner prep, Val and Jacob had planned a couple of getaway routes in case the senator needed to be quickly evacuated. Obviously, the path through the service lot was a no-go, and one glance out of the ranch's yawning front door told her that there was too much chaos in the courtyard.

It would have to be option three: the servant's corridors.

"This way," she ordered, steering her charge toward the Christmas tree. They shuffled past the photo screen, where the photographer was kneeling and rummaging through his gear bags.

"Grab your shit and get outta here," Val snapped as they passed. "You can—"

The photographer straightened and she glimpsed the

startling dark glare plastered across his face. He held something long and cylindrical in his gloved hands.

She let out a wordless shout and shoved Jorge to the floor. The first bullet whizzed past her head and shattered several ornaments on the Christmas tree, and a dusting of impossibly thin colored glass rained over the marble floor.

"Go!" She waved Jorge toward the hidden door beneath the staircase. The senator ducked his head, locked his fingers around his skull, and rolled beneath the boughs of the tree.

With her body pressed to the cold floor, Val twisted to see the photo booth. Little bits of broken glass snagged at her dress and raked bloody scratches against her chest. The photographer had climbed, trembling, to his feet. The revolver clutched between his hands was about the biggest Val had ever seen. In a shadowy environment, a lax security guard might have mistaken the barrel for a specialized camera lens.

Val raised her pistol and aimed, but the photographer lurched forward, scanning the messy boughs of the tree as a flood of panicking aristocrats spilled out of the ballroom behind him. Val snarled and scrambled to her feet. Her shot was ruined. Even if she hit the assassin dead-center, there was a good chance the bullet would clear his body and hit some background innocent.

The little sweaty man in the gloves found what he was looking for in the dark spaces behind the tree and raised his revolver. There was no more time for waffling.

"Take cover!" Val screamed into the crowd as she pushed her way between two señoras in frilly ball gowns. She thrust her pistol toward the photographer's exposed back and squeezed the trigger. She hit him—or at least she thought she did. The photographer fell to his knees, and the sound of a gunshot triggered an all-out riot. People screamed. Some panicking wannabe matador slammed into Val's side, almost sending her sprawling before she caught her balance and flung herself clear of the budding stampede and into the photo booth.

Her focus landed on the clean bullet-sized hole ripped through the photo screen.

*I missed?* Val thought dumbly. *At fifteen feet?*

She looked down to see the hale and hearty photographer glaring up at her from the floor. His arms swung up.

She moved without thinking—or rather, Reginleif moved within her. Shooting was more Val's bag, but when it came to hand-to-hand combat there was no fiercer foe than Reginleif Stormrider.

She twisted her hips and kicked. The fleshy arch of her foot connected smoothly around the barrel of the gun with a stunning *smack* and knocked it clean out of the assassin's hand. The revolver spun through the air, vanishing into the stream of people flowing from the ballroom to the front courtyard.

"*Kate!*"

Val's head whipped around. Jorge Vargas had made it to the pocket door beneath the staircase, but instead of vanishing safely into the hidden maze of servants' corridors, he had turned to wait for her.

He caught her attention and waved, gesticulating wildly toward the upper balcony.

Val twisted, looking over her shoulder as another blast of gunfire rattled the ornaments and sent the crystal chandelier rocking on its chain. That bullet could have flown six feet over her head or missed her carotid artery by a centimeter. She would never know. A man in a waiter's uniform stood on the staircase landing, aiming an automatic pistol toward the sheltered pocket door. It was only unfortunate happenstance that Val was in the line of fire. The man didn't seem to see her as he aimed.

She shot him. This time she saw the hole appear in his shoulder before the man staggered backward and collapsed on the polished stairs.

Beneath her, the photographer twisted, reaching into his lens case.

Val brought the butt of her pistol down on the top of his head with enough force to split a watermelon. He slumped and moved no more.

The marble floor between the photo booth and the hidden door was littered with blasted pine boughs and shattered ornaments, and Val, to her chagrin, was barefooted.

*New rule*, she decided as she went up on her tiptoes and sprinted across the treacherous minefield. *We wear proper shoes on the job. I don't care how bad it looks. We find a way to make it work.*

By the time she reached the huddling senator, she was bleeding from dozens of tiny cuts across her feet, shoulders, and chest. Her toes were freezing, and the back lacing of her dress was coming undone.

"What are you waiting around here for?" She snatched Jorge by the shoulder and dragged him away from the chaos. "The ball's over, señor. It's time to get you to the after-party."

**Fiesta Navidad**
**Sunrise Ranch**
**Houston, Texas**
**Sunday evening**

Shooting one's way out of a locked room only worked if one could create a hole big enough to reach through and manually undo the lock. To Jacob's surprise and relief, it seemed as if this particular hit squad had only brought small-caliber guns to the show. Good for hiding in uniform pockets, bad for blasting through steel paneling.

Still powerful enough to fuck up whatever unfortunate soul happened to be on the other side of the wall, though.

Jacob crouched behind a van parked beside the counterfeit Hospitality Group truck as the trapped gangsters filled the night with the ear-splitting din of close-quarters gunfire. A loose round skipped off the asphalt at Jacob's feet, sending a sharp spray of debris across his chest and face. He gasped, shuffling farther back behind his cover.

"Kat, where the *fuck* is my backup?" he snarled into his earpiece.

The man at the other end of the line sounded strained, far from his usual chatty southern cheek. "Uh, um—oh dear. It looks like most of Adams' men have decided they're not getting paid enough to deal with this. The ones I can see are making a show of pushing the guests to evacuate. That's something, I guess. Right?"

Jacob groaned. Kat might have been a genius, but in

moments like this Jacob missed Hawk's cutthroat, ice-cold professionalism.

"That's something that doesn't do *me* much good." He rose a few centimeters and tilted his head back to peer over the nose of the van. "Tell me there's backup on the way, Kat."

"Oh, right. Police have been called. ETA five minutes. Miss Daisy is getting the senator to safety and Adams just left CnC, heading your way."

Jacob doubted the old cowboy would be enough backup for this job, even if he got here at warp speed. It was probably taking the gangsters more time and bullets than they would have liked, but the area around the back panel latch was dissolving. It wouldn't be long before they busted free. Jacob's partner might have been reckless—and durable— enough to take on at least half a dozen hitmen in a head-on fight, but Jacob Pinkerton was not. At least, not without the aid of a couple of grenades.

Too bad they hadn't fit under his dinner jacket.

He was about to army crawl away from the warzone when he noticed a ghost of movement in the truck's driver-side mirror. The door cracked open. Back in the shooting gallery, the guns went silent, as if the trapped gangsters had gotten their shit together and realized there was a smarter way out of this trap. Why waste your bullets when you can just shout at old Juan the Delivery Man to get off his ass and *open the damn door?*

Jacob saw the opportunity and lunged for it. He sprinted around the tail of the van. There was a person in the cab, and if the gods were good, he was the same guy who had driven this fraud of a truck into the service lot.

The middle-aged Latino man leaned out of the driver's door. Gripping a pistol in one hand and a set of heavy, jangling keys in the other, he scanned the darkness between the parked vehicles before he dropped to the ground.

He took one step toward the rear of the truck and Jacob barreled out of the shadows and sank his shoulder into the dangling cab door. The man cried out as the slamming door caught his shoulder and ripped a bloody gash down his arm. Jacob shoved and sent the man sprawling to the ground. Gun and keys spilled from his hand with a clatter.

Inside the shipping container, the men began to shout once more.

Jacob crouched to snatch the dropped pistol and keyring before stepping over the stunned and bleeding driver and dropping into the driver's seat with a heavy *thud*. He flung the gun onto the passenger seat, rammed the key into the ignition, and cranked it. Beneath him, the engine rumbled to life.

Back in the shipping container, the gangsters had decided they couldn't trust Delivery Juan to get the job done after all, and began shooting once more. Juan himself rolled over on the asphalt, groaning and protesting piteously as he stared up into his hijacked cab.

"*Será mejor que muevas el culo,*" Jacob roared as he shifted the truck into gear. He was grateful to the weaselly little driver for one thing: the man had parked this truck at the edge of the service lot, so there was nothing between Jacob and the darkened countryside but a flimsy stretch of chain-link fence.

Jacob hit the gas and the truck surged forward. A heavy

*bang* came from the shipping container, but he had no time to worry about that now. Jacob had an urgent anti-delivery to make.

The chain link crumpled like tissue paper beneath the truck's grill. The cab rattled manically over the uneven, unincorporated prairie land west of the Sunrise's tournament-worthy golf course. Jacob cranked the wheel, bringing the truck parallel to the service road leading up to the castle. In the rearview, a line of glittering chaos was spilling out of the far end of the building. He could already see red and blue cop cars broaching the dark horizon.

Jacob hit the gas, pushing the speedometer well into the fifties as the truck ripped across the uneven ground. If the assholes in the back managed to get that damned door open, hopefully they'd think twice about jumping ship at these speeds.

Jacob tapped his earpiece, shouting to make himself heard over the unholy rattle. "KAT! Tell the cops on the highway I'm coming to meet them, and I'm bringing a truckload of angry gangsters."

**Fiesta Navidad**
**Sunrise Ranch**
**Houston, Texas**
**Sunday evening**

The ranch's security office was a small, sweltering windowless room that smelled like a sweaty gym sock. It contained a bank of security monitors, two cramped desks, a stack of ancient dining chairs with stained upholstery that someone had clearly forgotten about, a gun safe, and, most importantly, a reinforced steel door.

In other words, it was a panic room that the kitchen staff had been using to store a bunch of old junk, but it did its job well enough.

Val, Kat, and Jorge watched on the security monitors as squads of police surrounded the ranch, shepherding the panicked guests away from the crime scene and sweeping the area in equal measure.

"Jacob's reporting in from up the highway," Kat reported, touching his headset. "He says he and the police have taken six armed men into custody about a mile to the west of here. He left the driver behind in the parking lot."

Val sucked in a breath, scanning the bank of monitors. She found Adams, the big security cowboy sans his fair-weather posse, hustling in from the service lot with a handcuffed, limping man in tow.

She wanted to be out of this claustrophobic, sweltering room. She wanted to be roaming the grounds for assassins, cleaning up the mess they had made. The air in here smelled like old fryer oil and didn't sit well in her stomach after the rich appetizers.

The name of the job was *protection*, though, and as much as she valued Kat's technical expertise, she didn't trust the pudgy middle-aged man to put up a stellar defense if a few stray hitmen came looking for the senator. So she stayed, pacing the tiny room as Jacob and Adams and the police secured the rest of the property.

Jorge touched her arm. Sometime in the last half hour, crows' feet had spread from the corners of his eyes, but his smile was still warm and charming. "You know what I'm hearing from this?" He gestured to Kat, who was gnawing on the straw of his empty Tom Collins glass as he stared at the screens. For lack of anything better to do, Kat had been anxiously updating them on the outside status every two minutes.

"What's that?" Val asked.

"*Minimal casualties.*" Jorge's smile widened until Val couldn't help but fall into its gravitational pull. He was like a force of nature. "Ambulance on the scene already and no one reported dead except for the hit man you shot on the staircase. Eight more of them in custody."

"Stroke of luck." Val's attempt at modesty was feeble beneath his warm gaze. Her uneasy stomach settled. Her pulse slowed. She allowed herself to give Jorge a tiny smile in return. "But we should be glad for that, I guess."

Jorge found the least-stained chair in the stack and set it on the floor. "You should sit down and let us take care of those cuts on your feet. The floor is filthy. We don't want you to get an infection."

Only a little self-conscious, she sat and allowed Jorge to kneel before her and rummage through an old first-aid kit Kat pulled from beneath the desk. "Not so many cuts as I thought," he noted, turning her ankle over in his fingers. "Your skin is tougher than it looks."

In a few minutes, Reginleif's healing factor would render this little aid entirely unnecessary, but it gave Val and Jorge something different to focus on while the police cleared the scene. He had good hands, Val thought. Strong and warm.

"*Uncalloused, though,*" Reginleif observed with a hint of disappointment. "*Not the hands of a warrior.*"

"We're not in the market for a *warrior*," Val reminded her companion. "We've already got ourselves a damned good one. Also, he's married."

That would never stop someone like Reginleif from reaching for what she desired. Nor, it seemed, did the senator or his wife hold the bonds of marriage utterly sacred.

"You called me Kate," Val blurted, feeling the need to yank her mind away from this line of thought.

"Of course," Jorge murmured as he applied a thick bandage to an already-healing cut on the heel of her foot. "It's your alias."

"I mean, even while you were being shot at. You kept cover." She remembered the way he had moved so easily, once the shooting started. "You're used to this."

Jorge shrugged. "Don't tell Alvarez," he teased. "But my family and I *do* take our security practice drills seriously."

Val noticed Kat staring at them from behind Jorge's shoulder. The computer guru met Val's gaze and drew one finely-shaped eyebrow up to his receding hairline. He sucked on his straw, making the ice at the bottom of the glass gurgle.

Val rolled her eyes. Her earpiece beeped.

"Area is secure," Jacob reported, drawing Val's attention back to the here and now. "It's safe enough to come out. Let's get the senator the hell outta here."

**Fiesta Navidad**
**Sunrise Ranch**
**Houston, Texas**

## Sunday evening

They had Jorge nearly back to the security detail's black SUV when things went askew.

The yard and roundabout in front of the castle had been cleared of all the unwashed masses. Gone were the reporters and paparazzi that hadn't been able to land an invitation. Someone had rolled up the red carpet, revealing a pathway rather in need of re-paving. Most of the displaced guests in all their formal finery had been bundled up and bustled back to the city, but a few lingered behind the yellow tape strung across the ranch's visitor parking lot. The SUV that had brought Val and Jacob to the party was parked inside the line, and Jacob had already checked it for any sabotage. They wouldn't need a driver. After tonight, they didn't exactly trust Adams' drivers.

Jorge was about to duck into the back seat beside Jacob when he glanced over and froze. Val followed his gaze to a police car about twenty yards away. Despite the sound thrashing she had given him, the photographer hitman had regained his senses and was being shuffled toward the car by two uniformed cops.

"Ai…" Jorge turned and strode across the empty asphalt, lifting his hand to catch the cops' attention. "Ai, one moment, please. I'd like to ask our friend a question before you take him away."

"Crap." Val spun away from the SUV and followed her charge. She'd put her shoes back on, and the heels caught and stuck in the patchy pavement, making her wobble.

Jorge reached the cuffed photographer, brushing aside the weak protests of the policemen. The photographer's eyes went wide as Jorge stepped up so close that their noses nearly touched.

"*¿Tienes hijos, hermano?*" Jorge's voice was high, tight. His face glowed with intent. He spoke so rapidly that Val couldn't pick out a single word. "*¿Sobrinos? ¿Eh? ¿Es este el mundo en el que quieres que crezcan?*"

"*Vamos!*" The photographer snarled and lashed out, snapping his teeth in Jorge's face.

"Enough, enough!"

Val caught her balance and reached the fray as the police pushed themselves between the two men. She put a hand on Jorge's shoulder, and for half a second she thought he would back down. Then the photographer screamed something over the officer's shoulder as they tried to wrestle him into the back of the car.

"*Mandaré a mis sobrinos a la Isla de las Flores a violar a tu hijita!*"

Val didn't know the full nature of the insult, but the deep loathing in the man's voice was a universal language all its own. All the color ran from Jorge's face. With an animal shriek, he surged forward, breaking free of Val's grasp. He elbowed one of the shocked policemen aside, punching and kicking as the photographer scrambled backward into the car.

"*Vamos!*" Val cried, pulling one of the flailing officers aside. She could have broken any of these men in half but at that moment all she wanted to do was get everyone away without any further injuries. "Oh, for fuck's sake, *stop it!*"

To her surprise, it was Jacob who managed to reach into the back of the cruiser and grab Jorge by his collar.

The big man had left the SUV and joined the fray. He hauled the kicking, breathless senator backward, and the police leaned into the cruiser to check on the photographer. He wasn't moving.

*"No puedes proteger a tu hija iniciando peleas callejeras!"* Jacob bellowed, shaking the senator by the lapels. Jorge gave one or two more useless thrashes before going still. Eyeing the man warily, Jacob busied himself straightening Jorge's disheveled coat.

"Make sure you're on your guard at the jailhouse tonight," Jorge told the two officers. All the warmth had run out of his voice. "You're hosting some very dangerous men." He glanced at Val. "Let's go."

Jacob fell into step beside Val and they followed the ashen senator back to the SUV.

"The cameraman made some specific threats against Vargas' daughter," Jacob whispered.

Val's stomach turned a funny loop. She had a brief flash of memory: a photo, falling out of an envelope. It was a picture of her twin nieces, Emmie and Allie, playing in a swimming pool. Claudia Moreno had burned their eyes out with the lit end of a cigarette. "I didn't know the senator had a daughter."

The look on Jacob's face suggested that this was news to him, as well. "He probably doesn't like to talk about it when there are dozens of cartel assassins trying to bring him down."

Val swallowed and nodded. They reached the SUV and she opened the driver's door. "Because of course the bad guys always bring kids into it."

## In SUV
## En Route to the hotel
## Houston, Texas
## Sunday night

"I'm sorry you saw me like that."

Val glanced into the rearview mirror. She had lowered the privacy screen that normally separated the driver from passengers. Vargas stared out of the window as the lights of Houston came into view, his expression blank. Despite Jacob's efforts, his jacket and shirt were still a mess, and Val saw a crust of dried blood on his knuckles.

It was the first thing he had said since she'd started the engine.

Beside the senator, Jacob shifted his weight. "I'd have done the same thing if he'd said a goddamned word about my family."

Jorge nodded, his gaze still locked on the cityscape outside the window.

Val licked her lips. Now that they were talking again, it was time to get back to business. "Kat sent me an update about Alvarez a minute ago." She shifted out of the passing lane. "He made it safely back to the hotel with the others. They'll meet us there."

"I don't want to go back to the hotel." Jorge looked away from the window for the first time and met Val's gaze in the mirror. She saw a smoldering hell behind his dark eyes. It made both her and Reginleif shiver.

"Take us to the station where they're holding the assassins," Jorge requested. "I have work to do."

"This isn't Tijuana, Senator." Jacob scratched his chin. "Diplomatic immunity will only protect you so far."

Jorge only grunted.

"This *isn't* Mexico," Val added gently. "The police and local FBI office are on full alert. Nobody's getting to those prisoners tonight." She had plenty of fair criticisms to level at the American penal system, but that much was true. Not that she didn't sympathize—like Jacob, she'd have been rabid if it was her family the gangs were going after—but as she kept reminding herself, *stopping the bad guys* wasn't her job tonight.

Her job was keeping this one very angry man safe.

"You're right," Jorge conceded after a long and ugly silence. "You're...right." He drew in a deep breath and let it all out in a great exhausted sigh.

"The man said your daughter was on Flower Island," Jacob prodded. "Is that...?"

Jorge grunted. "*Isla de las Flores.* Sí. A little island off the coast. Passed down through my wife's family. We've tried to keep our home there a secret but rumors get out."

"But you don't think he was just spouting rumors to get a rise out of you," Jacob suggested.

Jorge shook his head. "Maybe. Maybe not. Maybe he was just trying to scare me out of the States. Send me running to hide back in Mexico, leave the cartels alone for a bit while I take care of my family."

"*A clear-eyed man,*" Reginleif observed. "*At least, once the first flames of passion die out. Perhaps a warrior after all.*"

*Not all warriors have calluses,* Val agreed silently. Following the instructions on the dash, she turned left at the next four-way intersection. They were in the downtown district now, a few minutes from the hotel.

Jacob hesitated, starting and stopping several sentences before settling on one simple question. "What will you do now, Senator?"

"I would bet my favorite fishing rod that Hector Aurora is behind this attack. These gangsters think they're going to make me choose between my mission and protecting my family." Jorge shook his head firmly. "No. I will do both. I must. News of the shootout will be tomorrow's headline. I cannot show fear. I will not retreat."

"You're going to continue on with your diplomatic tour?" Jacob was visibly startled. "After everything that just happened?"

"It's only another seven days." Jorge gave him a wan smile. "Just three more fundraisers. Tonight's attack must have taken weeks of planning on their part. No way they have a backup plan in place to strike at me while I'm talking to the North American Avocado Growers Association, right?"

Val let out a low whistle. "Ballsy," she admired. "I'll clear my schedule. Pinky, would you drop a line to the jarls? It looks like we're in for a busy week."

"Sí, señorita," Jorge agreed as Val pulled into the hotel parking lot. "But maybe not in the way you think."

"What do you mean?"

"Your team did very well tonight. With almost no preparation you handled the job of a dozen men. You stuck by me when my longtime detail and the ranch security staff ran away. Loyalty like that is hard to find. It's even harder to purchase, on a budget like mine."

"Right." Val drummed her fingers on the steering wheel impatiently. Rather than pull up to the hotel's front door to drop the senator off, she parked in the nearest open spot and turned to face the men. "Which is why we need to get to work on the rest of your tour. We can work out the billing details later, Jorge. I believe in your fight. I want to keep working with you."

Beside the senator, Jacob cocked his head. "'*Jorge*'?" he mouthed curiously.

Val ignored him. She'd saved the senator's life tonight. That earned her the right to be on a first-name basis with him.

Jorge was shaking his head again. "You misunderstand. Now that their big attempt at assassination has failed, I think the most dangerous part of this trip is behind me. It's not my life I'm most worried about, señorita. I want you to go to Isla de las Flores and protect my family."

# CHAPTER NINE

**Val's room**
**Holiday Inn Express**
**Houston, TX**
**Monday morning**

"...Except it's not just going to be while the senator finishes up his diplomatic tour of the States," Val admitted. "Cascobel's trial begins immediately after that. He intends to be present throughout the whole thing."

Val's laptop screen was split into five windows. Jasper Taggert, the man in the upper left, rocked back in his chair and folded his fingers behind his shiny scalp. "That could go on for weeks."

In the window directly below him, Hawk grunted and typed something into his computer. The downward angle of his webcam accentuated the sharp hook of his beaklike nose. "Projected to be four weeks," he confirmed. "By the most liberal of forecasters."

"That'll take you well into the New Year." Charlie Evans

nibbled her bottom lip. She was twirling a crazy pen through her long fingers. Val wondered if she knew her background was set to an underwater theme.

"Oh no," Jacob muttered. He filled the fourth window, though he was less than five feet from Val, right on the other side of the wall. "Four weeks on a tropical island…it's going to be terrible."

Hawk shrugged, glancing up at the webcam as if he could shoot them a *significant gaze* through the beady black camera. "Everyone knows the best time to take a vacation is when you're trying to get a new business up and running."

"It's not a vacation," Val protested irritably. She hadn't been too happy herself when Jorge had explained the full extent of his plan, but in the early hours of the morning, he had managed to convince her that it probably was for the best if she and Jacob were actively guarding his family instead of tailing him through the rest of his tour and the trial. It would put his mind at ease. He'd be less likely to overlook anything vital.

Besides, he'd been blunt about his lack of faith in their normal bodyguards. Four weeks was plenty of time for someone like Hector Aurora to arrange for a few bribes and a kidnapping.

"If this is how you want to spend the next month, I don't see why not." Charlie frowned, studying some ledger sheet in front of her. A cartoon shark swam past her head. "We don't currently have any other jobs available for you. The downside is, of course, if something more exciting or high-profile pops up we'll have to assign it to one of our own teams. You can't very well jet off in the middle of guard duty."

"I wouldn't worry too much about what might be." Kat was in the fifth and final window. His video conference background had been set to a mundane starscape. The feed from his camera hiccuped and burped every few seconds. "A bird in the hand is worth two in the bush, Mama always said. I'd be lying if I said I wasn't disappointed with the payment for this little job but there are certain—" A blur of static clouded his face and then cleared "—perks to consider."

"Where are you right now, anyway?" Taggert asked Kat, giving voice to Val's unspoken curiosity.

"I am down at the police precinct." Kat's eyes narrowed behind his horn-rimmed glasses. "Spending long hours and very *un*pleasant nights sifting through all kinds of trash on these gangsters' phones. Their own mamas must be—" *sssshkshs* "—ashamed."

"Find anything interesting?" Hawk leaned back and covered a huge yawn as if to spite Kat's exhaustion. Kat's lips pressed into a puckered little prune.

"Three new types of porn I wish I didn't know about. Looks like the phones were new acquisitions. Burners, really. No hints on the current whereabouts of Hector Aurora, if that's what you're asking, but a few snippets about our El Águila. That's what they call Hector south of the border." He tsk'd and shook his head. "These tough guys really do love their nicknames, don't they?"

"What do they say about El Águila, *Kat?*" Hawk asked pointedly.

"Just enough to make me think our little faux-tographer

wasn't bluffing." Kat sighed. "Some chatter about a possible kidnapping. It does look like the remnants of Tierra Roja might be plotting to move against the senator's wife and daughter after all."

This was why Kat had ultimately voted to accept the job despite its low pay. He didn't like to see innocents in the line of fire any more than Val did.

"Do they call him El Águila for any particular reason?" Jacob sounded thoughtful as he sipped his hotel-lobby coffee. "The eagle is the symbol on the Mexican national flag. Is he a self-styled patriot? A nationalist?"

Val knew her partner well enough to know that what he was *really* asking was whether Hector was an ideological zealot, and not just another criminal looking to make bank off the drug trafficking industry.

Thankfully, Kat shook his head. "Doesn't look like it. They say he's very observant and ruthless, but I think they call him that because he's just got one crazy big honker. Like someone else I could—" *shhhhk* "—mention."

"What the hell is wrong with your webcam, Kat?" Taggert finally demanded.

"It's nothing," Hawk began. "Don't worry about it—"

When the next wave of static cleared, Kat was sitting upright and alert, eyes all aglitter. "Why, I am so glad you asked, Mister Taggert! What is *wrong* with my—" *shhhkkkk* "—webcam is that it's the piece of junk default hardware that came with the piece of junk laptop I'm using." There was half a second of lag to buffer them all for the tirade that came next.

"…And I'm afraid that between the ball last night and the investigations this morning, I just haven't had time to pop down to the nearest Best Buy to pick up a half-decent computer!" *shhkkksssh* "—have to settle with the dinosaur model supplied to me by Viking. Did you know this OS is—" *shhkkk* "—generations behind, Mister Taggert? And it's not even a *good* old operating system. Why, it's as if someone in the office over there is trying to cripple our operations by saddling us with useless equipment!"

"*So maybe next time you'll bother filling out the correct requisition form instead of just assuming you can waltz into my storage closet and take whatever the hell you want!*" Hawk shouted.

About twenty seconds of dead air passed before anyone spoke again. Val wondered if Taggert and Charlie were deeply regretting their decision not to cough up more dough when they'd been trying to negotiate employment terms with Mira Hargrove.

Taggert cleared his throat. "There, uh, is some better gear available for contractor use in our stores, Kat. That is, assuming it's not already being used by our in-house teams. Just…make sure you go through the correct channels. We can't afford to lose track of some of this stuff."

"Last in line for the functioning equipment. That's just dandy." Acid oozed from Kat's voice, topped with a healthy dose of sugar from his heavy southern drawl. "I suppose I should have bargained a little harder at the negotiating table."

"So, yeah." Val checked her schedule in a desperate bid to change the topic. "We'll be flying down to Campeche with the senator in a couple of hours. He wasn't scheduled to make a detour back home but after last night he wants to make sure his family is settled and safe before he gets back to the grind."

"Sounds good," Hawk said brusquely. "A month is a long job. Are you going to need any more gear, Pinkerton? I'd be happy to overnight a shipment if you send me an address."

In his little corner of the screen, Kat spluttered.

Jacob shook his head. "Vargas made it sound like his house on the island is pretty well stocked, and we agreed to travel light. I'll let you know if that changes."

"Copy that," Hawk answered. "Now if you'll excuse me, I have to get back to planning the Lakeland Christmas party."

"That doesn't sound like your cup of tea," Val noted lightly.

Hawk grunted. "I drew the short straw this year." His window went dark.

"We'll wrap it up then, if there's nothing else," Taggert proposed.

Val thought about asking Charlie to clean out her mailbox while they were gone but decided she'd have her building superintendent do it.

"Nothing else for me," she replied. "Just stay on the line a minute if you would, Kat?"

The others said their goodbyes and one by one, the screens went dark. Val was left staring at the grainy man on her screen.

Kat took off his glasses and rubbed grit from the corners of his eyes. "Remind me to grab some extra Benadryl before our flight out. How can I help you, Miss Daisy?"

"I was wondering if you had any leads on Hector Aurora's movements or locations."

Kat adjusted his glasses and gave her a slow, sly smile. "You looking to raise some hell?"

Val remained expressionless. "I'm looking to stay informed."

Kat nodded. "I suppose we all need our hobbies, don't we? I'll see what I can dig up for you."

"I'm counting on you." Val leaned forward and killed the call.

Her eyes fluttered shut. Dawn light was glowing around the edges of the heavy blackout curtains drawn across her window. It had been a long night, and she'd gotten through it by the grace of two stolen catnaps. Not nearly enough time to settle down and think about some things she'd been putting off. She felt those worries bubbling to the surface of her mind now, popping and bursting like a sea of camera flashes.

There was a knock on her door. "Val," Jacob called. "Alvarez wants to meet up and debrief in ten. Have you had breakfast yet?"

Val sucked in a deep breath and pushed to her feet.

The self-reflection stuff would have to wait. If all went according to plan, she was going to have a whole bunch of free time over the next few weeks.

**Private airstrip**
**Outside of Houston, Texas**
**Monday, noon**

A Cessna Citation was gassed and waiting by the time they made it to the private tarmac.

"Have we checked the pilot?" Val asked Jacob when her eyes landed on the jet.

"It's a trusted private charter," Jorge assured her. "He's flown my family and members of the *Evolución Social* many times."

"All the same," Jacob pressed as the car stopped. "I'd like to chat with him before we take off."

"You are more than welcome to do so, of course." Jorge stepped out of the vehicle and grabbed a small travel suitcase from the trunk. The senator was in a much better mood this morning, but if it was due to an improved outlook on life or that they were going to see his family, Val couldn't tell.

"Tell him Perrito said you were ok," Jorge added. "He'll get a laugh out of that."

"Perrito?" Kat stepped out of the back of the SUV and adjusted his sunglasses. "Doesn't that mean *puppy*?"

"It does, Señor Gato," Jorge teased. "The pilot, you see, is my older brother."

The plane was tiny.

"*Cozy,*" Kat suggested hopefully, settling into one of four seats in the cabin and fussing around in his bag until he found his sleeping mask. "But at least there's room to recline, right?"

He popped two pink pills, dropped the mask over his eyes, and said no more.

If Val hadn't known any better, she would have guessed that Jorge and Gabriel were twins, not just brothers. When he came out of the cockpit to introduce himself and submit to Jacob's security inspection, he kissed Val's hand much as Jorge had done the night before.

"*His hands are calloused indeed,*" Reginleif noted coyly. "*I see three very attractive men on this plane, Valkyrie. Now is the time to make thy move.*"

Val snatched the seat across from Kat so neither Jacob nor Jorge had a good, unobstructed view of her blush. She was no prude, but some things were beyond the pale. "What exactly are you suggesting?" she hissed. "A mile-high orgy in a cramped cockpit? Don't you think Kat would find that a little annoying?"

"*Only if we don't invite him,*" Reginleif dismissed. She was ambivalent toward their tech guy, but Val had to admit she had his number.

Jorge settled into the seat across the aisle from her, and a minute or two later the plane began its long sprint down the runway. Having completed his check of the storage compartment and lavatory to his satisfaction, Jacob took the only remaining seat in the cabin.

The space was small indeed.

"Tell me about your family," Val blurted, turning to Jorge. "Your daughter. How old is she?"

The senator blinked but pulled out his phone and leaned across the narrow aisle to show her the screen. "My Ana." He opened up his picture gallery and swiped through a few files until he found the one he was looking for. A young girl, about eight or nine, appeared on the screen. She was olive-skinned and smiling, with an indigenous flat nose and wide brow. She was wearing a red dress and had her arm wrapped around the neck of a bemused-looking baby goat. Jorge swiped and the girl was a few years older, feeding seeds to a scarlet macaw in some rich green jungle.

"My Ana. She turned twelve over the summer. She was so scared to graduate into junior high and start at a new school. My wife had the idea that we should take her on a safari, you know? Take her out to see the jungle, the old Mayan temples at Chichén Itzá. Boost her confidence. Make her excited to see the world."

Up until this point, Jorge might have sprinkled a few "señoritas" or "amigos" into casual conversation, but his impeccable American accent had never wavered. Now, though, as he spoke about his family, a distinct Mexican cadence slipped into his words. Val found she liked his accent more than his perfect English.

"Did it work?" Val asked.

Jorge chuckled and nodded. "I've never seen her so excited. Ever since we got back she's had her heart set on becoming an archaeologist. She said she wants to spend every summer now exploring the old ruins."

Val felt herself smile. "That's the dream."

"You like history, too?"

Across from Jorge, Jacob chuckled into his laptop. "You know, Viking wasn't sure about hiring Val at first because we thought she'd be too much of a nerd."

"I have a degree." Val allowed herself to preen a little on this topic. "My focus was Europe and Scandinavia specifically, but everything old is fascinating."

Jorge nodded as if he had expected no less. "You will like my daughter," he decided. "And I think she will like you very much. You and Jacob, don't be intimidated, all right? She has a big personality, once you get to know her.

She doesn't just love ancient ruins. She loves action heroes, too."

"Good lord." Jacob shot Val an amused expression. "I'm not sure I can handle *another* one like you."

Val grinned. "Kid after my own heart. Let's just hope that her Christmas break is more "ancient ruins" and less "action hero.""

"If it's not," Jacob added under his breath, "the kid's in for quite a show."

# CHAPTER TEN

**Isla de las Flores**
**Off the coast of Campeche, Mexico**
**Monday Evening**

Val had only to lay eyes on the two of them reunited to understand that, all flirting and teasing aside, Jorge Vargas and his wife Sofia were madly, ridiculously, irredeemably in love.

"Like something out of a fairy tale." Kat sighed and fanned himself with a shiny jungle tour brochure he had picked up somewhere between the tiny private airstrip where the Cessna had landed and the short ride on the forty-foot fishing boat that had brought them out to this little slice of tropical paradise. Jorge himself had driven the boat as if he'd been born on the sea.

"I feel a tiny bit redundant," Val agreed under her breath. "We're supposed to be protecting Jorge but he's the one at the head of the line with a machete and sailing the ship, you know?"

They'd arrived at their final destination, a sprawling villa on its own private island nestled in the warm sapphire waters of the Gulf of Mexico, an hour or two before sunset. A welcoming party of nine people—house staff, family servants, and a thirty-something woman every bit as beautiful as Jorge was handsome—had been at the docks to greet them.

Jorge had thrown himself into the little crowd like the prodigal son returning home, leaving Val, Jacob, and Kat to unload their scant baggage and stand around on the docks, waiting to be introduced.

It had taken a good thirty minutes, but the little crowd mostly dispersed. The maids rushed off to prepare supper, the groundskeeper wandered back into the dense vegetation, and the gnarled old man with a walking stick—Val wasn't sure what his role on the island was—shuffled down the docks to stare out over the shimmering waters.

Val, Kat, and Jacob found themselves on a wide patio overlooking the island's pristine cove, sipping glasses of chilled coconut water and pretending that Jorge and his wife weren't a mere six feet away on the other side of the big bay window, making out like teenagers who had discovered the joys of French kissing.

Jacob leaned against the rail with his back to the display, taking notes on his tablet as he studied the land sloping away beneath them. Isla de las Flores was three-quarters of a mile long and about half as wide, and bursting with verdant foliage. Wild jungle pressed up against the villa walls, which hugged a half-acre garden of carefully cultivated fruit trees. Aside from the main house, the only buildings on the island were the garden and utility sheds, the boathouse, and a tiny defunct weather station on the eastern shore.

"Maybe we should borrow a couple of night-vision headsets from Hawk after all," Jacob mused as Val joined him at the balcony rail. "According to Jorge, there are only seven people living on the island and they're all longtime family servants."

"It's not a very big island," Val observed, letting her eye roam across the foliage sprawled beneath them. "But I guess it would be easy to hide out in the jungle." She glanced over her shoulder to confirm that Kat was out of earshot. The man had settled himself onto a lounge chair and was already fiddling around on his computer.

"We won't need night-vision or thermal goggles to confirm there aren't any unauthorized hermits squatting out in those trees," she murmured. "We'll just do a thorough sweep of the island after lights-out tonight. Just to confirm there's nothing bigger than a wild pig out there."

"We will?" Jacob rubbed the back of his neck. He'd acquired his first bug bite of the trip. "I'm not too familiar with the terrain and in the dark—" He saw the look on Val's face and understanding dawned on his face. "Ah. Okay. *You* will."

"*I look forward to it,*" Reginleif declared. Val could feel the other woman stretching out, like a cat shaking off her daytime nap and preparing for the night's hunt. "*It is warmer here than back in our home forests, but that should be no matter. It has been too long since we've hunted by starlight and felt moonlight on our bare skin.*"

"Our next order of business is to investigate the known inhabitants of Flower Island." Val didn't need to tell Jacob this, but it didn't hurt to clearly define their objectives. "Once we confirm that everyone is safe and accounted for, all we really need to do is make sure nobody else gets to the island. Boom, family secure. I mean. Right?"

"Here's to hoping." Jacob shrugged. "Security details are always a kind of gamble. All you can do is stay sharp and hope the ball doesn't fall on black."

"I don't like it," Val admitted. "Just playing defense. The best way to protect these people isn't to hide them on some secret island. It's to get out in the world and *stop* the people who want to hurt them."

Part of her dreaded the prospect of sitting still for weeks while they waited for Cascobel's trial to conclude. It felt like an invitation for nightmares.

She was going to have to deal with them eventually, she knew.

As soon as the job was over.

"Going out into the world and stopping the bad guys is exactly what Jorge is trying to do." Jacob graced her with one of his rare, genuine smiles. "He's just fighting the battle in the courts instead of the streets. Since he's the one signing our paychecks, that means we're fighting the good fight too. Just in a more passive way than you're used to." He rolled his shoulders, drawing in a bone-deep breath of fragrant tropical air. Down here on the gulf, you'd never guess it was almost Christmas. Only the ornaments strung across the guava trees in the garden hinted that a holiday was fast approaching.

*"Perhaps we shall find a proper goat in these woods,"* Regin-

leif speculated.

"We're not sacrificing a goat." Val had repeated the phrase so many times in the last two weeks that it had become a mantra.

*"We abandoned the Yule log and the evergreen tree back in thine apartment,"* Reginleif protested. *"And with no suitable replacements to be found in this strange land. Thou must make some concessions to tradition, Valkyrie!"*

Jacob went on, oblivious to Val's inner argument, "In the meantime, someone does need to protect the innocent. We can't just lock them in big iron boxes until the trial's over."

"Can't we? Have we actually ruled out the *big iron box* strategy?" Val glanced over her shoulder. The villa's big bay windows afforded a clear view into the living room. Jorge and Sofia were nowhere to be seen, but Val noted that one of the doors in the hallway was hanging open.

The senator and his wife must have snuck off for a few minutes of pre-supper privacy.

Val was about to turn her attention back to Jacob when she noticed Ana standing in the doorway between the patio and living room. The girl had been at the docks with the rest of the staff to greet them but had shyly refused to say more than one or two words when her father introduced her.

Now, realizing that she had been spotted, Ana Vargas let out a little gasp and jerked backward.

"It's fine," Val called. "You can come out here, Ana. We don't bite." She thought a moment before correcting herself. "Well, we do. But we only bite bad guys."

Flushing darkly, the girl emerged from the doorway.

.  .  .

Val couldn't help but smile. Her twin nieces were both blonde-haired, blue-eyed girls with *volleyball stars* and *sorority sisters* all but rubber-stamped into their DNA, very different from this round-faced child with keen and wary eyes. A universal self-consciousness ran through all preteen girls, though. If Val tried hard enough, she could almost remember it, herself.

"Hola," she offered earnestly, trying to put the girl at ease. "Your papa talked about you on the trip here. He is very proud of you."

Ana's flush darkened, but she stepped onto the patio like a shy deer who, despite all her instincts, was dying from curiosity.

"Hola," she murmured. "*¿Habla español?*"

"He does," Val admitted, jerking her thumb at Jacob. "But me, not so much, sorry. I speak other languages."

The spark of curiosity in Ana's dark eyes kindled. "What other languages?" Her English was clear and softened with a warm central Mexican accent.

Val smiled. "German and Dutch." For some inexplicable reason, she added, "Old English, too, and Old Norse." It took all of her willpower not to add *Asgardian,* though she wasn't entirely sure what language the old gods kept.

"*Those are not thy tongues,*" Reginleif teased. "*Dost thou pine for a child's admiration?*"

"Come on. Be a sister and back me up here," Val protested.

"Are you from Germany?" Ana asked. Caution and curiosity had duked it out within her, and curiosity carried the evening. She approached boldly now. Val noted, however, the way the little girl angled her steps to avoid coming too close to Jacob.

"No. We're both from Virginia." Val settled onto one of the lounge chairs, putting her closer to eye level with the girl. "You know where that is?"

Ana cocked her head, frowning as she struggled with some past geography lesson. "Somewhere in eastern America," she ventured.

Val nodded, impressed. She wouldn't have expected a ten-year-old non-American to have a grasp of the general arrangement of US states any more than she would have expected a ten-year-old American to name the Canadian territories.

"Yep. But it looks like we're going to be staying with you on Isla de las Flores for a while, while your papa does his work. Is that going to be okay?"

Ana cocked her head, giving the question true weight. "I think so." Looking at Val, she fingered the plain neckline of the simple tunic she was wearing over a pair of shorts. "I like your *bufanda*."

Val looked down and realized the girl was referring to the black and silver fashion scarf draped casually around her throat. It was a cheap thing she'd gotten on some college spring-break trip, but it did a good enough job adding an element of class to an otherwise plain white T-shirt.

"*Bufanda*," Val repeated, fingering the frayed tassels. "My scarf. Thank you. And I like your shoes, Ana."

Ana's toes turned reflexively inward as if she could

somehow hide the faded, beat-up sneakers at the ends of her skinny legs. She cast Val a suspicious look.

"They look well-used," Val observed. "They look like they belong to a girl who goes on a lot of adventures."

There was a moment of tension as Ana tried to decide whether Val was making fun of her or not. Then her whole body relaxed and she gave Val a slow, secret smile that felt like an eggshell cracking somewhere behind Val's ribs. She'd won a little girl's favor and it felt as good as beating up a couple of bank robbers.

"You all have interesting clothes." Ana cast a furtive glance first to the other end of the patio, where Kat was lounging in his Hawaiian shirt and straw hat, then over her shoulder to Jacob. Ana leaned in a little closer to Val and lowered her voice. "But why doesn't his shirt fit right?"

Val glanced up. Jacob was leaning casually on the rail. The evening was warm and humid. He had taken off his professional button-down and was wearing a plain under-shirt that outlined every single one of his muscles.

Jacob turned his head away quickly, pretending not to pay attention to the conversation.

"That's a good question." Val dropped her tone, bringing Ana into some conspiracy. "I think he just likes to spend money on clothes that show off his muscles." She flexed her own bicep until the muscle bulged, kissed the swell, and dropped Ana a wink.

Ana giggled.

Behind them, Jacob coughed. "It's just a workout shirt."

Val dropped her voice into a false baritone. "It's just a workout shirt," she repeated, curling her arms into a mockery of a strongman pose.

Ana clapped her hands over her mouth to hold in a peal of laughter.

"All right," Jacob rolled his eyes and started toward the patio door. "You girls have your fun. I'm going to—"

The door slid open before he could reach it and Sofia Vargas poked her head into the evening. "Ana?" she called softly. "Why don't you bring our guests in and have them wash up, niña? It's time for supper."

**Villa**
**Isla de las Flores**
**Off the coast of Campeche, Mexico**
**Monday Evening**

Val stood in one of the villa's many bathrooms and felt compelled to address the elephants in the room. Specifically, the bronze elephants that served as custom pipe fittings for the double sink where she and Kat were washing their hands before supper.

"The place doesn't exactly scream 'man of the people who stays in budget hotels,'" she remarked under her breath.

Kat chuckled coarsely and nudged the handle on the faucet, cutting off the flow of hot water pouring from the elephant's trunk. He grabbed one of the monogrammed towels hanging by the door. "Don't you fret, Miss Daisy. Our Jorge isn't just pretending to be a hardscrabble man. See? 'Canek.'" He indicated the letters stitched on the towel in fine golden thread. "It's an indigenous surname. Sofia's family. Plenty of other members of the Mexican senate enjoy long holidays on private islands, but usually on the dime of some lobbyist or cartel boss. Jorge skipped the corruption and just married rich."

Val wouldn't deny that the news sent a trickle of relief down her spine. After accepting this low-paying job on the premise that a good fight was worth a pay cut, she wasn't sure what she would do if it turned out that her boss was living it up behind closed doors after all.

"Just as long as it's not some crime family," she muttered, taking the towel Kat passed to her.

"Nah," Kat assured her. He examined the row of crystal bulbs sitting beside the sink and picked one up to sniff the nozzle. He spritzed himself, filling the room with a cloud of rich, musky cologne that did not befit the portly man. "Come on, Miss Daisy. I wouldn't let you take a client like that without a heads-up. Have a little faith. Canek was an entrepreneur! *Refresco de Ora Ambar* was one of the early brands of soda to make it big in Mexico. Big enough to buy Sofia's grandpappy a small island and keep it staffed until the ice caps melt."

"Huh." Now tempted by the toilette offerings herself, Val picked up another bulb and flipped open the tiny copper lid. The rich scent of ripe fruit made her head spin. Reginleif leaned in close, savoring the aroma. "Never heard of it." Val set the bulb down. "We should pick some up while we're here."

"Good luck with that." Kat was wistful as he returned the hand towel to its hook and opened the restroom door. The hallway leading to the villa's dining room smelled like baking corn and roasting chili. "His son sold the recipe to

Coca-Cola and they discontinued the brand. Now all that's left of the family fortune is this island and the trust fund that keeps it running."

**Villa**
**Isla de las Flores**
**Off the coast of Campeche, Mexico**
**Monday Evening**

Every chair around the twelve-person dinner table was full. This wasn't just a meal for the new guests and hired help. A family dinner at Isla de las Flores included the old gardener, the two maids, the groundskeeper, and his son, as well as Ricardo, Sofia's longtime bodyguard and companion, and his apprentice, a curvaceous woman named Isabella. Once the old cook emerged from the kitchen carrying a basket of steaming fresh tortillas, she too settled into an empty seat between the maids.

"Abuelita." Jorge stood at the head of the table and raised a tiny glass of brandy to the old woman, smiling. "I would have crossed the world just for the food alone if I'd known you were making your famous mole."

The old woman grinned, showing a set of yellowing, slightly crooked dentures.

"But I am doubly blessed," Jorge went on, turning his little glass to each person seated at the table. His words had a tipsy brightness, though if it was born of booze or the simple joy of being around his family again, Val couldn't tell. "For the family and friends, as well as the food. I've had an exciting few days and nothing makes me happier than to come home and see all of you sitting at my table, eating together." He leaned down, planting a long kiss on Sofia's lips. Then he laughed and plunked into the seat next to her.

"Eat," he told the assembly. "Get to know our new guests, yeah? I'm leaving them behind with you when I go back to the mainland. I hope you don't fatten them up too much with your cooking while I'm gone, Abuelita."

Val, Jacob, and Kat were seated across from Ricardo and Isabella. As the dishes made their way around the table, Val studied the mismatched pair of bodyguards. Ricardo was an older, toughened man in his midsixties, still clinging to his thick gray mustache. Isabella couldn't have been older than Val herself. Her short hair was curled into tight ringlets that, coupled with her thick lips, gave her a pouty flapper-girl look. She had mismatched eyes of a sort Val had never seen: one dark and stormy, the other a rich brown the color of polished oak. Her appearance was striking in a way that might be great for an Instagram influencer, but Val couldn't help but wonder if the woman stood out a little too much for the bodyguard circuit.

Not that she or Jacob could say much to that, she supposed.

One of the maids passed a heavy crock full of brown stew to Jacob, who sniffed discreetly before politely dropping an entire tablespoon full onto his pile of plain rice. He passed the crock to Val, who asked Ricardo, "How long have you been working for the family?"

Ricardo leaned back in his chair, rubbing his mustache between his fingertips thoughtfully. "Don Canek hired me as a groundskeeper for the island when I was very young, so…just about fifty years, now."

Val spooned a generous ladle of stew onto her plate, silently scolding Jacob for turning his nose up at the rich, spicy scents of smoked chicken and cacao. "Fifty years taking care of one island?" As lovely as it was, Val thought she'd start to view Isla de las Flores as a verdant prison if she were forced to stay for more than half a year.

Ricardo shrugged and passed the basket of tortilla shells without taking any. He did not seem interested in eating with the family. "No. There was a fire in the villa back when I was nineteen or twenty, see. Nearly burned the whole place down with Señora Canek and baby Sofia inside. The Don was away on a business trip, and it was the morning after Cinco de Mayo. Most of the house staff was drunk, too hungover to notice the smoke. I was out trimming the trees when I saw it. Came running back in, all I could think was to make sure that lady and the little girl got out okay. Pulled the señora right from her bed at the crack of dawn." He chuckled. "She was spitting mad at me until she realized her curtains were on fire. We put the fire out, but when Don Canek returned, he fired the old bodyguard who was supposed to watch his family. Offered me the job instead, if I wanted it. Ever since then, wherever little Sofia goes, I go." He nodded, dipping his head in the direction of the elegant woman sitting beside Jorge at the head of the table. "Mostly that means living in Mexico City with the family while Jorge sits in government and Sofia does her charity work."

"So you're more a member of the family than an employee," Val suggested. Inside her head was a growing list of notes, details to cross-check when she had a few moments to herself. Her gut said that Ricardo was a loyal man down to his bones and not likely to sell his employers out to some cartel boss, but her gut had also told her that the Cardinals would win last year's World Series.

Ricardo nodded. "Sure. I'd say that. Spent more Christmases with little Ana than with my sisters, I'll tell you that much." He took Isabella's shoulder in a strong grip and shook her gently. "But I'm trying to reconnect in my old age, you know. Isabella here is my sister's daughter. A good kid, as much as she pretends to be a punk."

Isabella rolled her eyes, but her mouth was full of mole and she didn't bother trying to object.

"Fifty years." Val dabbed the corner of her mouth with a napkin. She was of two minds about the mole. In Val's opinion, it was on the list of top five stews she'd ever had. Reginleif, on the other hand, found the whole brown mess of it rather befuddling.

"*It tastes of chocolate and cinnamon,*" the ancient demigoddess concluded. "*But it is a meat dish? Perhaps the cook dropped one of those candy bars into the pot?*"

Val made a mental note to start feeding her co-pilot a wider variety of food. Having one picky eater on the team was bad enough.

Val continued with Ricardo. "In all that time, have you had to deal with, uh, outside security personnel much?"

Ricardo shook his head. "Not at all, until Jorge joined Evolución Social a few years ago. Even then, those guards were federal men, ones interested in protecting the senator himself from his enemies. Even in America, I think, government protection does not extend to the families of elected officials."

"Unless they're immediate relatives of the President or Vice," Jacob agreed. After having sniffed or sampled every dish passed to him, the poor man had piled his plate high with nothing but rice and a symbolic dab of refried beans.

*At least he's eating those with gusto,* Val despaired, praying the cook wouldn't notice. On her other side, Kat was happily assembling a homemade mole-and-bean burrito.

Ricardo nodded. "Ana and Sofia try to keep low public profiles." He hesitated. His gaze cut to the left, where Ana was talking animatedly to her father at the other end of the table. Then he leaned in, lowering his voice. "So this is the first time we've had people like yourselves on the island," he admitted. "Professionals. Jorge called last night and told me all about Fiesta Navidad. About the threats made against his family. He says it's likely that Tierra Roja knows the location of Isla de las Flores. Sofia knows too of course. There are no secrets between them. But they don't want to scare Ana with the details."

"Have you noticed any changes around the island?" Jacob asked. "Anything out of the ordinary?"

Ricardo hesitated.

"The boats." Isabella used a strip of tortilla to scoop a bite of beans into her mouth. She did not look up from her plate.

"Boats?" Val asked sharply.

"Hey now, hey." Ricardo pulled himself upright. Val followed his glance to the head of the table and saw Ana was watching them curiously from her seat beside Sofia.

"It's the holiday season," Ricardo went on boldly,

shaking out one of the cloth napkins and, at long last, dipping his fingers into the tortilla basket and reaching for the stew crock. "Fishing has been good this year. Of course, people like their pleasure cruises in these warm sapphire waters."

# CHAPTER ELEVEN

**Isla de las Flores**
**Off the coast of Campeche, Mexico**
**Monday Night**

With dinner concluded, the little Vargas family retreated into one of the villa's game rooms to play Ana's new favorite board game while Ricardo took Val, Kat, and Jacob into the island's security hub to talk shop. Isabella had wanted to follow her boss down into the office, but Ana had taken the young woman's hand and insisted they needed a fourth player. It was probably best to have at least one set of eyes on the family, anyway.

Canek might have come across his fortune honestly, as Kat claimed, but no rich man in early twentieth-century Mexico built his mansion without a wary eye for gangsters, rebels, insurgents, coups, crooks, or robbers. Tucked between the villa's wine cellar and billiards room was a security hub with a gun safe and emergency bunker. An antiquated monitor hung along one wall. The screen was split into nine windows, three of which showed grainy black-and-white footage from various points across the island. Five more feeds showed an inside view of each of the villa's exits. The last corner of the screen was dark.

Kat took one look at the setup and sucked his teeth. "Nothing a little TLC can't spruce up," he allowed when Val turned a sharp look on him. To her surprise, he shouldered his computer bag and turned to Ricardo. "Mind if I run a diagnostic?" His voice had an unusual edge of deference.

Ricardo nodded. "Go for it. All I ask is that you loop Isabella in on what you're doing. Bring her up to speed. I'm no good with all that electronic stuff but she's still young enough to learn."

Kat smiled stiffly and slid into the creaking office chair without giving Ricardo an answer. Val could practically hear the man trying to calculate how much he should charge to tutor the young woman.

"Jacob is going to escort Jorge back to the mainland in the morning," Val began. "He'll hand the senator over to his federal security detail and return to the island. Is there any other business we need him to handle while he's out on the mainland?"

"I'll tell you right now, Miss Daisy," Kat called from the corner of the office, where he was already elbow deep in wires and computer guts. Apparently, his idea of a *diagnostic* was a bit more hands-on than Val had anticipated. "We're going to need a half-dozen wireless transponders. I'll send the specs to Jake when I have a better idea of what we're working with. Ricky, hon, do you happen to have a bale of CAT-9 cable laying around anywhere? The interior cameras are going to need an update."

Ricardo's cheeks, already leathery and deeply tanned, turned a shade darker. "I'll, uh, ask Izzy. Campeche isn't a very big town, Mister Gato. Doesn't have more than a Wal-Mart or maybe a CompuZone. Are they going to have that stuff?"

Kat waved his fingers through the air without looking around. "Don't you worry about sourcing, hon. I'll rustle up a few independent dealers before the night is out. Oh, and we're going to want a cash budget. People like the ones I have in mind prefer to stay off the grid."

Ricardo scratched his stubbled chin and shrugged. "I'll send Hernando into town with you and the senator," he told Jacob. "He'll hit up the bank and make a withdrawal from the family account. You can use the money to get the supplies. But remember to get receipts, yeah? Sofia likes to keep the books straight."

Jacob nodded. "Boat's leaving at eight a.m." He glanced from Kat to Val to Ricardo. "Make sure you get the shopping list to me before then, and make sure they're arranged in order of importance. I don't want to be gone too long and I'm not overnighting on the mainland just to hunt down anybody's favorite brand of potato chips."

"I guess you'll have to pick up some of that Amigos Perdidos some other time." An old whiteboard hung on the wall behind her, and she uncapped a marker to wave an aimless dark line over the board before jotting notes for the assembled team to see. "Ricardo. You started to talk about the boats at dinner."

"Sí," the old man muttered.

"We're only a couple miles from the mainland," Jacob said. "I could see it from up on the patio. Maybe ten miles from the Campeche docks. Not exactly far off the beaten tourist or fishing paths."

Ricardo stroked the edges of his long mustache. Val watched the man, struggling to decide whether he looked more like a grizzled eighties action movie star or a plain-clothes Klingon from the vintage *Star Trek* era. "Boat traffic always increases this time of year," he explained. "But I would say, I have been here fifty years and I've never seen the waters around Isla de las Flores quite this busy. I thought little of it until last night's call from Jorge."

Val doodled a little boat on the board. "What kind of busy?"

Ricardo shrugged. "More speed boats and fishing boats, I would say. About the same number of sailboats as any other year. Some will circle within seventy, eighty meters of the island."

"Has anyone tried landing on it?" Jacob asked.

"Not since Sofia put signs up along the beaches two years back."

"Still, seventy or eighty meters is plenty close enough for people to scope out the island if they've got decent gear," Val mused. "Say El Águila knows Vargas is married to Sofia Canek. Vargas starts making trouble for his cartel in the last few years, so El Águila does some legwork. Finds out that this island has been Canek land for a few generations. Sends some of his boys out to scope the place and they happen to notice Sofia or even Ana on the beach or patio."

Ricardo nodded grimly. "The family spends their time evenly split between here and Mexico City, where Jorge works and Ana goes to school. Ana and her mama like to spend whole days on the beach."

Jacob nodded. "Plenty of time to get spotted by a patrolling boat."

Val added *boat scoping* to the whiteboard. "We can't really stop boats from getting too close to the island, so our first order of business then is to get Ana and Sofia inside if one wanders too close."

"They won't like that." Ricardo folded his arms. "But they will understand, I think."

"So we have four security personnel to cover the entire island and all nine residents for several weeks." Val frowned, thinking through the problem. "We should split into twelve-hour shifts. One American and one resident per team, so we can bring Ricardo and Izzy up to date on our methods and equipment, and they can show us the ins and outs of the island."

"Four security personnel?" Ricardo dipped his head to the corner of the room, where Kat was on his hands and knees examining the wiring behind the monitor. "He will not patrol?"

"He's, uh, not cleared for field work," Jacob answered.

"And he's not pawing at the gate to get himself shot," Kat called.

"We're...working on him," Val told Ricardo. "Mostly he handles the tech." She leaned back, pushing her hands over her head in a back-bending stretch. "Pinky's got to be alert for his field trip tomorrow, so he should get some sleep. I'll take the overnight." She glanced over to Ricardo. "Izzy strikes me as a night owl."

"Perhaps," Ricardo agreed. "But I'd like to be the first

one to show you around the island, señorita. I know it better than she does."

Jacob shifted his weight. "Are you sure? How much of the island are you really going to see at this time of day?"

Val shot Jacob a puzzled glance. She had perfectly excellent night vision, he knew that. But there was a knot of concern between his eyebrows, and to her surprise, he was regarding Ricardo warily.

Ricardo chuckled and shrugged. "Don't worry, my friend. I know this land better than I know the insides of my own eyelids. I won't let the señorita slip on any rocks and break her ankle."

That casual comment, born of deeply ingrained machismo and undercut with the faintest hint of cultural misogyny, might have irritated Val under other circumstances. Tonight, though, her mind was on something else: the hard set of Jacob's jaw as he studied Ricardo.

*"The bulls are squaring off,"* Reginleif delighted. *"Learn to enjoy the rivalry of strong men, Valkyrie. I daresay thou shall witness it oft enough."*

Val closed her eyes. Testosterone. Of course. Jacob and Ricardo worked for the same man and they might even think well of one another—no ire at all! they would insist —but there was still some subtle dance of *firm handshakes* and *look 'em dead in the eye* wherever two dominant men met.

If they were bulls taking the measure of one another, Reginleif was the damn matador between them shaking the red cape to see what would happen.

"Ricardo and I will go patrol the shore," she cut in, catching and holding Jacob's gray gaze. She gave him a knowing grin. She wanted to tell him, *There's no point in arguing about who in this room has the biggest balls when the correct answer is* neither of you. "Don't worry. I won't let the sharks swim off with him."

Ricardo chuckled. Jacob nodded, taking Val's promise as utterly sincere. "In that case, I'll go settle in to my room and grab a few hours of sleep. Don't forget to get me those shopping lists."

---

"The sky is clear tonight." Ricardo tightened his tactical vest across his broad chest. It was almost ten p.m. and they were preparing to go on their first perimeter sweep of the island. "But you will probably want to bring a flashlight anyway, yes?" He rummaged around in one of the storage lockers and pulled out a vest that was similar but faded and worn with age. He offered it to Val.

Val slung the vest over her shoulders but shook her head at the offered flashlight. "It's a full moon. Artificial light will mess with my night vision."

Ricardo shrugged, slotted a mini lamp into one of his vest pockets, and grabbed a wood-stocked rifle that had been propped against the back door. "In case the javelinas get rowdy," he explained. "I think one of the sows had a litter recently. It makes them aggressive."

Val followed him through the patio door and into the night. Scattered lamplights bathed the villa and surrounding garden in a soft golden glow, but the jungle pressing up against the walls was dense and black. Ricardo paused beside the locked gate and showed Val how to work the electronic lock before stepping out of the compound and leading her down a narrow but well-worn path through the underbrush.

Moonlight filtered down through the dense canopy in little trickles and streams, turning the jungle into a zebra mural of black and white vines, tree trunks gnarled and withered, grooved and smooth, broad and bushy leaves that came in every size and shape Val could imagine. The air was heavy with the scent of ripening fruit and damp earth and a thousand nameless insects buzzed through the trees, chirping and whirring beneath the scattered songs of night birds.

Tree roots jutted and spilled over the ground, and Val realized most people unfamiliar with this trail to the shoreline would be in real danger of breaking an ankle. She eyed Ricardo's back as they marched silently down to the shore, wondering why he hadn't insisted she bring a flashlight. *He* didn't know she had superhuman eyesight.

"Are there many trails like this across the island?" She kept her voice low above the background song of insects, but Ricardo's ears were as sharp as his eyes.

"Only a few are this well maintained." He grabbed a low-hanging branch and pushed it aside as he clambered down a stretch of slope. Once at the bottom, he twisted, holding the door open for Val, as it were.

Val dropped to his side, landing easily on her feet despite the uneven terrain. Ricardo blinked in surprise but shrugged and released the branch. It *thwapped* back into place and the man resumed his hike. "There is the gravel drive from the boathouse up to the villa, this path to the west beach, and another path that goes straight across the island to the weather station. Both of them meet up with the trail that follows the shoreline, but that one has gotten pretty overgrown since Don Canek died."

"Why the weather station?" Val asked. "The National Weather Service doesn't use it anymore. I checked. Does the family use it?"

Ricardo hesitated, swatting idly at a mosquito. Ahead and through the trees, moonlight shimmered against a great expanse of black water.

"I like to go there on my time off," he admitted. "It's my private space. To think."

Sweat glimmered against his skin. They passed out of the dense foliage and stepped onto a thin ribbon of beach that glimmered palely in the moonlight. The sky was on fire with stars.

Val closed her eyes, breathing deep of the salty air. In that moment she wished, more than anything, that Ricardo was far away from here. She wanted to strip off her clothes and go dancing in the surf. She wanted to fly.

"It has been too long since we have hunted by moonlight or bathed in the sea," Reginleif murmured.

Ricardo shouldered his rifle and strolled along the beach, tracking dark boot prints in the sand. Val hurried to catch up and saw him slip something small and metallic into the inner pocket of his vest. He cast her a guilty glance. The wind shifted and she caught a sniff of whiskey in the air. It wasn't professional to be drinking on the job, and his indiscretion should have made her wary. It was late, though, and she felt her blood moving with the waves, pulsing and flowing like it belonged to someone else.

She held out her hand. "Cough it up, hombre."

Ricardo coughed, and then his cough turned into a chuckle. He drew the flask from his pocket and passed it to her. "Ah, so you're *that* kind of girl."

"No idea what you mean." She unscrewed the cap, tossed back a swig of the world's smokiest booze, and handed it back to him. "Tell me what you know about El Águila."

"Eh?" Ricardo tucked the flask away once more.

"Hector Aurora. The nephew of Jorge's friend Cascobel. You know. The motherfucker threatening your family."

Ricardo's mustache twitched. The two of them passed from the sand onto a stretch of rocky shoreline where the stones were slick with algae. "I do some reading," he acknowledged. "I hear he's gone back and forth between Miami and Campeche state ever since he got into the family business. Now that Cascobel is in custody and the Fiesta Navidad attack went badly, I imagine he'll crawl back into one of his family's villas somewhere in the homeland.

"The Aurora family homesteads." Val frowned. "Where are those?"

Ricardo shrugged. "I'm sure you could go find videos of their houses on TikTok. These young gangsters, they live to show off their wealth. It's the whole point of the game to them. Rub their crimes in the faces of the old men who would see them in prison."

"Not exactly laying low."

Ricardo shook his head. "I wouldn't try to make a visit to any one of those homes even if I knew exactly where to find them, niña. These are dangerous men. El Águila, he'll be circling the wagons now. More brutal than ever, just to remind the police and the other cartels not to try messing with Tierra Roja."

"An injured beast is the most dangerous," Val agreed.

Ricardo grunted. They walked in relative silence for a while, slowly making their way around the perimeter of the little island. Ricardo paused at intervals to point out landmarks. Shining white buoys off in the surf, warning boats and swimmers of hidden tides. Little coves where particularly daring captains might try to anchor their boats well out of sight of the villa's tall windows. Twice, he directed Val's attention to game cameras hidden in the tree line and she paused to wave to Kat.

They made good time to the far end of the island, where Ricardo led her up a stretch of dingy beach and into a little one-room building beginning to succumb to the advancing jungle. Satellite dishes and antennae jutted from the roof, but most of them were cracked and crooked. Several of the windows were smashed.

The front door creaked and groaned as Ricardo pushed it open. Rather than reach for the light switch on the wall, he stepped into the gloomy darkness and fiddled with something on a nearby table. Harsh blue-white lantern light filled the room, revealing a clubhouse that any red-blooded teenager would kill to own.

Ricardo had made the abandoned weather station his home away from home. All of the weather equipment had been stripped out long ago, leaving the walls bare and patchy. The old man had redecorated with a hundred magazine pinups and old glamour-shot posters of Marilyn Monroe and Brittany Spears. A beat-up old camping cot lay in the corner beside a pile of well-loved blankets and a stack of tattered paperback books. On every other flat surface, every shelf and tabletop and empty stretch of desk, lay half-empty bottles of liquor and crumpled packs of cigarettes.

"You've got quite a collection here," Val observed. She'd seen worse bachelor pads, but she was impressed by the *restraint* suggested by all of those less-than-half-empty bottles. Ricardo was a connoisseur, not necessarily an alcoholic.

"I never drink when I'm alone on duty," he explained. "Even then, only a little. But I like my holidays. I like my days off. Can I get you a drink, niña?" He sauntered over to one particularly curvaceous bottle. "It's good tequila…"

Val glanced around the little hideout. Perhaps she had given the man the wrong impression when she asked for his whiskey. If she had been a normal human woman, she supposed she would have found the situation—being alone in the jungle with an armed and dangerous man keen on luring her down into that old army cot—deeply unnerving. For a fledgling Valkyrie, however, it was an interesting, if slightly sticky conundrum. She was going to have to work with this man for the next several weeks and couldn't afford to bruise his ego with a harsh rejection, but if she was less than firm he might take it as a sign of weakness. It wouldn't just reflect badly on her team. Ricardo was an old bruiser used to getting his way, and you could never underestimate the sense of bald entitlement some men harbored.

Then again, she had a hard time imagining the Vargas family would trust him with their daughter if he were an absolute shitstain of a human being.

If he'd been a decade or two younger, Val might have given in to the temptation to kick his ass for putting anyone in this situation. *Hey Regin, how do you let down an old battleax easy?*

Smoothly, the other woman slid to the forefront of her mind. When Val next spoke, it was with Reginleif's rich, amused voice. "A generous offer that I am afraid I must decline. Someone must stay vigilant. But if you wish to linger here for a spell while I continue the night watch, I shall not be upset."

Ricardo's mustache twitched into a disappointed curve, but he shrugged and pulled an empty shot glass from a cabinet. "If you're offering. You be careful out there in the darkness, though. Give a sharp whistle if you need help, okay?"

"Copy that." Val assumed control and slipped away from the old weather station, relieved. He shouldn't have asked, but at least he took the rejection in stride. As a bonus, now she had the night to herself.

"That was diplomatic of you," she told Reginleif as she walked away from the shore and slipped back into the jungle's humid embrace. As she walked, she shrugged off her vest and scarf.

Reginleif deferred, *"As you said, the man was overbold, but we must work with him for weeks yet to come."*

The night pressed in close, wrapping Val up in the song of insects. Leaves brushed gently at her face, tickling. She moved without thought, shedding first her shirt and then her boots and socks as she moved through the darkness. Her skin itched.

*"It is the moonlight,"* Reginleif murmured. *"It calls to us."*

Val found a small hollow beneath a half-rotted tree and stashed her boots. With a resigned sigh, she surrendered to Reginleif's aching impulses. She stripped down to her underwear, relishing the caress of the soft wind against her bare skin.

"We *did* tell Jacob we would check the island for any stowaways," she remembered as black horns curled out from her temples and nestled against her cheeks. Pulsing energy stretched out from her heart, pulsing beneath her skin as her limbs grew long and impossibly strong. Shaggy wings unfurled from her spine, flexing and testing the tropical night air.

Val crouched on the mossy ground, tasting the starlight.

"*Then what are we waiting for?*" Reginleif asked. "*Let us hunt.*"

# CHAPTER TWELVE

**Isla de las Flores**
**Off the coast of Campeche, Mexico**
**Late December**

The days slid past in sleepy luxury. Jorge returned to America to complete his diplomatic tour and prepare for Cascobel's trial in Mexico City. Jacob came back from the mainland with a cart of electronic doodads and thingamajigs and Kat spent the better part of their first week on the island running fresh cables and installing new security cameras in a frenetic bid to update the Vargas family's security infrastructure.

Val found that, in the end, she was grateful that the residents of Isla de las Flores ran on what mainlanders called *island time*. Ricardo and his niece were unprofessional, yes. Val's first shift with the old man had told her everything she needed to know about his vices. They swore around the family, they drank on duty, and they made off-color jokes that left Sofia laughing and flushing at the same time.

They were excellent marksmen and sharp-eyed sentries though, and they were wonderfully easygoing. Ricardo never made another pass at Val, instead treating her with a vague genial paternalism that might have offended her had the old man not lavished the same grandfatherly treatment on Izzy and Sofia. As long as he respected her input when it came to matters of villa security, she was content.

The four security personnel fell into a pattern of watches that was flexible and easily managed for such a small team, swapping shifts regularly so that Izzy could have this night off to watch the season finale of *The Great British Bake Off* or Jacob could take the little dinghy out onto the waters and go fishing with Sofia one sunny afternoon. Once Kat had the cameras set up—"as good as any off-the-shelf setup can be, down here in jaguar country"—he settled by the pool to enjoy a daiquiri, but Jacob pressed the man into service as a trainee security guard. Kat entered the rotation, allowing each of the full-time guards a shift off every couple of days.

Not that Val particularly wanted a shift off. Once she decided these strangers were a-ok, Ana Vargas turned into a delightful little firebrand of a girl who wanted to spend every waking minute on the seashore exploring tide pools and playing safari in the jungle. More than once, Val drew straws with Isabella to see which of them would join the little conquistadora on her adventures where they would go pick fresh crabs off the beach or spend the day observing the javelina piglets from a not-quite-safe distance.

Blue skies, sunny seas, warm days, and pleasantly chilly nights. Val could have forgotten it was the Christmas season if not for the little nativity scene the cook tended in the front foyer.

She left the villa at dawn with a picnic basket in one hand and a pistol strapped to her hip, and returned before sunset to a home-cooked meal of fish tacos and fried ice cream.

"It doesn't exactly feel like work," Val confessed after supper one evening. She lounged on the patio with Jacob as Sofia and Ana cuddled on the couch in the living room, watching a Spanish-dubbed version of Will Ferrell's *Elf* on the wall-spanning television.

Jacob shrugged and leaned back on the lounge chair, sipping his espresso. Val nursed a local Mexican craft beer. He was about to go on duty, and her shift was ending. "Don't feel guilty," he advised. "You've been working this job for less than a year and you've already seen more action and been shot more times than most contractors experience in their entire careers. We have *earned* a few months of easy work. You regularly put your life on the line to make about as much money as a senior manager at a Taco Bell."

"The job's not actually all that dangerous for me," she pointed out wryly.

Jacob dismissed her supernatural powers with a wave of the hand. "In this business, no news is good news."

Val sighed, thumbing the lip of her beer glass. She wanted to go back into the jungle and hunt some wild pigs. She wanted to swim out to the deep waters and find a dolphin to befriend. She wanted to fly to the mainland and track down some gangsters. She wanted to *move*, and the drive for action came from more than her lifelong restlessness. As long as she was busy protecting Ana from treacherous riptides and angry sows, she wasn't thinking about other things.

Her days were lovely. Her nights, not so much.

She realized she hadn't spoken in several minutes and professional habit forced her to turn and scan the shadowy living room. There. Ana and her mother, curled up together under a woven blanket, bathed in the blue-white glow of the screen.

"You've been kind of withdrawn," Jacob remarked abruptly.

Val winced and tossed back the last of her beer. She set the glass down with a firm snap and longed to wander into the kitchen for a refill. Anything to get out from beneath the weight of Jacob's stare.

"Is everything okay?" Jacob asked.

*Damn you and your keen emotional awareness, Jacob Pinkerton.*

She shrugged. "It's two days before Christmas. I guess I'm just a little homesick. A Zoom call with the family isn't quite the same as a hug from Grams, you know?"

She wasn't sure why she was deflecting like this. She'd been telling herself for days she needed to have a heart-to-heart with her partner. He was studying her all the more suspiciously.

"*Best rip out the thorn quickly,*" Reginleif prodded gently.

Val sighed. She was outnumbered. Somehow, the ancient war-goddess and the grizzled ex-special-forces soldier were bullying her into *sharing her feelings.*

"I had a flashback at Fiesta Navidad." The words fell like stones from her lips. "It was brief, but it threw me off. I was facing down all those paparazzi and for a couple of seconds, I forgot where I was. We're lucky Tierra Roja didn't try to shoot Jorge right then and there."

Slowly, Jacob set his tiny coffee cup onto the glass tabletop. He gave Val a long, considering look, and she fixed her attention on an empty spot in the living room. Training, college, common sense, hell, even Reginleif, told her there was no shame in this confession. Still, she couldn't meet his gaze.

"Was it the Breakwater building?"

Val started. It took her a moment to grasp Jacob's question. They'd been part of quite a bloody battle in New York not so long ago.

He must have seen the troubled, puzzled expression on her face. "There was a lot of lightning when we were up there on the roof. I thought all the camera flashes and noise might have triggered some memory of the storm."

Val surprised herself by laughing. "Babe." She reached across the table to touch his hand. "We are *Valkyrie*. We're a goddamned eighties hair metal band all up in this head. *Ride the Lightning, Eye of the Storm, War Pigs, Welcome to the Jungle*. Standing atop a skyscraper in the middle of a lightning storm makes our top-ten list of *good* memories."

Jacob's mouth twitched into a brief and uncertain smile. He said nothing, waiting.

"No." Val sat back slowly. "No. It was McCormack. The bunker."

Understanding dawned on Jacob's face. Val supposed he could guess what she would say next.

"It was all those fucking *candles* Cypher had laid out." Her fingers curled around her empty glass. Suddenly her face was hot, her throat tight. "It's bullshit. The camera flashes look *nothing* like candle flames but for a second, they *were* candle flames. It doesn't even make sense."

If Jacob had any reaction, she couldn't see it. All at once her vision was blurring with repressed fury. "It was the creepiest shit I ever saw in my life," she rasped, recalling that dark hole deep in the bowels of the earth. That dead place, that no-mans-land that Cypher Frost had turned into some bizarre shrine. A shrine to *her*.

"*We have never been fond of the deep places,*" Reginleif whispered. "*Our home is not with the draugr.*"

"He saw me," Val said. "He saw *us*, and he didn't have the decency to be scared or humble or anything. Hell, he was into it. He was *turned on*. He was right where he wanted to be. Some little fucking *mortal* with crooked teeth and a weak hand-shake, and I couldn't do a gods damned thing to him because he didn't want anything. He didn't want anything except—"

There was a muffled *snap* and sharp pain spilled over Val's palm. She looked down to see the shattered beer glass clutched in her fist. She and Jacob watched together, unmoving, as her blood trickled over the glittering shards.

*He doesn't jump to his feet*, some part of Val observed. *He doesn't try to bustle me off to the kitchen to wash the cuts and grab a towel to stop the bleeding like he would if it was Sofia or Isabella out here smashing the glassware.*

"All he wanted was me," Val finished. "Dead or alive or whatever, it didn't matter. All he wanted was me, so whatever I did, I was giving him what he wanted."

Crickets hummed their nightly serenade to the sky. In the living room, the television screen went dark as the movie rolled to the credits. Sofia and her daughter dozed beneath the heavy blanket.

"We can't win every fight, you know."

Val looked at her partner. His face was in deep shadow, unreadable.

"Sometimes…" He reached forward, gently resting his warm palm over her bleeding fingers. "We just lose. Even if we come out without any scars. It feels like it should be a victory, but it's not."

Val sniffed, wiping her eyes with the edge of her scarf. "Yeah. Yeah, I think that's what Reginleif's been trying to tell me." She tried to smile. "But what does she know, am I right?"

Jacob did not return her smile. She loved him for that.

"You don't come across people like Cypher Frost very often," he offered. "The really fucked up ones that don't fit into the usual boxes. He caught you off guard. He lured you down there alone and he injected you with ten times a lethal dose of Ambrosia. Now he's dead and you're alive and still, somehow, *you lost.*"

Val covered her eyes with her scarf and drew in a wavering, painful breath. "This is not exactly the pep talk I expected, man." It was as much a laugh as a sob.

"Yeah." His hand ran up to her wrist, which, though it wasn't bleeding, had gone cold. He squeezed. "This isn't the eighties, Val. We don't *stiff upper lip* and *bootstrap* our way out of PTSD anymore."

It was that one word, spoken aloud, that broke the dam inside Val. She leaned forward until her head was on her knees. She clutched her hands to her face, ignoring—or perhaps embracing—the sharp sting as minute glass shards bit deeper into her palms.

Jacob scooted around the table until he was sitting beside her. He put an arm over her shoulder and waited, silent and watchful, as she pressed her face into his side and cried. She might have worried that Sofia would wake up and come onto the porch and see her in this state. She might have worried that Ricardo would wander out of his room, ready to begin the night shift, and witness her unmade. She might have worried about the humiliation she would feel, about the desperate need to explain or justify or defend herself as one hysterical young woman who couldn't handle the pressures of the job.

She didn't worry about any of those things. Instead, she trusted that her partner would guard her. She trusted Jacob to turn away whatever questions and stares might come. He couldn't *fix* the angry sadness inside her, but for a little while, he could stand at the door and give her a safe place to grapple with it.

He wasn't entirely correct, of course, because there was something she hadn't told anybody about what happened in that tomb beneath the desert. She had told them about the fighting, about the dust in the air, and about the way her foe danced and swayed and laughed at her, teasing.

She hadn't told them that once he'd gotten those needles under her skin, once the Ambrosia had turned her blood into liquid gold, she had laughed, too. She had danced with him, she had loved him back until their feet grew heavy and they collapsed in the sand together. With her brain on fire and her pulse a song of ecstasy, she had wanted to die with Cypher Frost.

"*You were bewitched, little sister,*" Reginleif reminded her gently. "*There is no shame in it. Even the gods are not all invincible.*"

"I know," Val told her constant companion. "I know that. It's just...going to take me a little while to *believe* it."

Reginleif said no more, leaving Val to cry herself empty on Jacob's shoulder. In time, the television screen behind them turned itself off. A floodlight flicked on in the garden below as Ricardo stepped out for his midnight patrol, which he would spend chain-smoking a pack of cigarettes.

Val wiped her crusted face on her scarf and then put her palm on Jacob's cheek and turned his head. She kissed him, slow and soft—and bless his heart, he seemed happy enough to indulge her.

"But maybe put a pin in that thought," he murmured when she came up for air. He rubbed comforting circles across the small of her back. "Sleep on it. And then, uh, shoot me a text if it's still looking good in the morning."

Val chuckled weakly as she slid to her feet. The bleeding on her palms had stopped, but she needed to fetch a broom and sweep up the glass so nobody else would get hurt. "All right," she relented, tousling her fingers through his hair before sauntering into the villa. "I won't keep you from your work anymore. But I gotta say, Jacob, you look good every morning."

# CHAPTER THIRTEEN

**Isla de las Flores**
**Off the coast of Campeche, Mexico**
**Christmas Eve**

Jacob advised the lady of the house against taking a day trip to the mainland, but it was the day before Christmas and some traditions would not be snubbed.

"We must light the candle," Sofia insisted. She strode through the upper living room, fixing a pair of modest studs to her ears as the cook, that withered little abuelita, bustled around in search of her misplaced wallet. Izzy, Ana, Val, and the two maids, Lula and Estrella, sat at the breakfast table eating obnoxiously large cinnamon rolls. Holiday carols played softly through the speakers.

"At the San Miguel cathedral," Sofia pressed. "Every year, the day before Christmas. What are we fighting for, Mister Pinkerton, if not the right to light mama's candle without fear? It won't take long. We will skip the Midnight Mass if you are so insistent."

It was the most annoyed Val had ever seen the dark-haired woman. Word around the breakfast table was that Sofia had gotten an early-morning phone call from Jorge. The senator had completed his diplomatic tour and returned to their little flat in Mexico City without incident, but a screwup in the court system meant that he would be spending his holiday filing legal paperwork ahead of Cascobel's hotshot lawyers.

Now, sitting at the breakfast table with Ana, Val saw the tears threatening to spill out of Sofia's pretty dark eyes as she grappled with the lie in *I'll Be Home For Christmas*.

Jacob scrubbed his forehead with a little groan.

"I'll go with Sofia," Val proposed. Jacob had taken the night shift, and she was mostly to blame for the fact that he was running on no more than an hour of sleep. "We'll pop into town for a couple of hours and be back before sunset."

Ana's head shot up, all early-morning sleepiness dashed from her face. "We were going to hunt seashells today!"

"Naw." Izzy tossed back the last of her coffee and pushed herself upright, stretching out her thin shoulders. "You stay here and watch Ana. I'm dying for a stroll through town. I haven't been off this island in three stinking months."

Val glanced from Jacob to Izzy. Sophia and Abuelita stormed through the living room, tossing over couch cushions in their quest for the lost wallet.

"Izzy takes point," Jacob agreed tiredly. "I'll be her backup. I'll catch a nap on the boat ride over."

Val cast her partner a guilty look, which he dismissed with a casual shrug. *Worth it*, he mouthed when Izzy turned to grab her go-bag.

Feeling somewhat mollified, Val took the dirty dishes to the sink. Over in the living room, Abuelita found the missing wallet and held it aloft with a triumphant whoop.

"*Gracias a Dios,*" Sofia growled. "*Ahora salgamos de aquí antes de que grite.*"

Val didn't need to be fluent in Spanish to know that was their cue to get outta here.

"Come on, Ana." She touched the girl on the shoulder. "Let's hit the waves."


**Isla de las Flores**
**Off the coast of Campeche, Mexico**
**Christmas Eve**


They were sitting on the beach when the Vargas' speedboat pulled away from the dock and cut a sharp white line across the uneasy waters. It was an unusually chilly morning and Ana's face was hidden beneath the cowl of her dark green raincoat, but when the boat turned out to sea she put down her seashell field guide and watched until it became a little black dot and vanished on the horizon.

"Are you worried about your mom?" The thought startled Val into speaking.

Ana's slicker rolled and bunched as she shrugged. She dropped her head once more, squinting at the list of tiny Latin names in the book. Over the last few days of wading the shoals, she and Val had amassed a vast collection of seashells and coral scraps and ocean debris of every shape, size, and color. Now that the weather had taken a turn for the worse, they had decided to forgo more wading and finally take a good hard look at the loot.

Val thought Ana was going to let the question go unanswered, but to her surprise, the girl licked her lips and nodded. "A little bit."

Val waited. The waves rumbled low along the beach, cresting and splitting and dying again. This was not the tropical paradise that had greeted them on their first day at the villa. It was more akin to the moody, mist-clad shoreline from her dreams.

"*Only a great deal warmer,*" Reginleif interjected dryly. "*Complain all thou desirest, Valkyrie, but this place is downright balmy still.*"

"There was a problem with the legal filings yesterday." Ana picked up a surf-chewed clamshell and turned it over, running her fingers along the shimmering mother-of-pearl inlay. Over the last few days, Val had grown accustomed to Ana's heavy accent and hardly noticed it anymore.

"I heard Mom and Dad arguing about it," Ana confessed. "Mom doesn't trust the prosecutor. She's scared they're going to call a mistrial." She frowned, chewing her bottom lip. "That's the word, right? *Mistrial*? When they decide that the whole thing is a mess and they need to start over or let the bad guy go?"

Val let out a long breath. It was too easy to forget that Ana was more than some carefree kid enjoying her last year of freedom before puberty turned her world upside down.

"Well, they *might* start everything over," Val acknowledged cautiously. "But they're definitely not just going to let Cascobel walk free. He'll stay in prison for as long as it takes."

Ana cast Val a look of pure, clear-eyed doubt. It was a startling, depressing expression, one that belonged on a woman three times her age. That look said, *You're supposed to be the expert, but you don't know how things work down here.*

Val started over. "Sometimes," she admitted, "the bad guys do walk free. They escape or they twist the legal system to their advantage or they bribe the right officials. But I don't think that's going to happen this time. Your dad has devoted his career to making sure this is the most televised, scrutinized trial in Mexican history. Cascobel is going to have a very hard time slipping out of this trap when the whole world is watching."

Ana set the clamshell aside and picked a heavy spiral seashell from the pile. It was about the size of her closed fist, light tan on the outside and smooth pink silk on the inside. "The whole world except for us."

The kid had a point. Sofia was a gracious, permissive, and generous hostess, but she did have one firm rule. The villa had half a dozen big-screen TVs, and not one of them was ever tuned to a news channel. That was for their Mexico City life, Señora Vargas insisted. Isla de las Flores was supposed to be a place for peace. Here on the island, if you wanted to catch a glimpse of the ugly outside world according to the mainstream media, you had to do it with headphones on, in secret.

"What kind of shell is that?" Val pointed.

"*Strombus gigas Linne.*" Ana passed the thing over. It was heavier than it looked, and hard as a rock. "A Pink Conch, but it's not very big. Dad once found one thirty centimeters long."

"It looks plenty big to me." Val set the shell down gently. Ana had turned her attention to the broken shards of clam, sorting out the dingy scraps from the ones that glistened with mother-of-pearl. "What are you going to do with all those pieces?"

"Ricardo gave me some wire and old tools last summer. I'm going to wrap them and make charms for the senoras to wear on their bracelets so wherever they go, they have a little piece of the Isla with them."

Val nibbled her lip, watching the waves kiss the shore and recede. There was a grim heaviness to Ana's words as if she expected that at any moment, her señoras—Abuelita or Lula or Estrella or even Izzy—might step off the island and never be seen again.

"Your parents don't really talk to you about their work, do they?"

Ana shrugged. "I know how to use the internet. It makes them feel better, to think I don't know about Tierra Roja and El Águila and all the rest."

Val grimaced, though she understood. This place was serene and peaceful. Why would they want to spoil that for the child? Except Ana was perhaps older than her parents realized.

"They followed our car when we were leaving Mexico City." Ana examined a sand dollar the size of her palm and added it to the *save* pile. "There was a black car that drove behind us for a long time. Ricardo was driving the truck then, and mom was riding in the passenger seat, busy doing work on her phone. Ricardo changed lanes a lot. He didn't have to do that, but he did."

"When was this?" Val tried to sound as casual as Ana.

"Last month. When we were coming to stay at the Isla."

That would have been just before Jorge's raid on the Tierra Roja cartel in Miami.

*Tailed all the way from Mexico City*, Val thought grimly. *Ricardo didn't feel the need to mention it?*

She was drawn out of her stew by a sharp snapping sound. Ana had scooped up a fistful of the ugliest shell fragments and was crushing them in her little fist.

Val jerked forward, about to snatch up the girl's hand before she cut herself on the razor fragments, then forced herself to be still. The cuts on her own palm had healed, but Val remembered clearly the broken beer glass biting into her skin.

It was Ana's hand, and Val wasn't ready to tell the girl what she could or could not do with her own flesh. The kid would survive some superficial slashes.

Ana's face twisted into a knot of rage as she crunched the shells together and flung them down to become part of the sand bed. Little dark streaks of blood ran along the inside of her palm, mingling with the pale sand.

"El Águila is still free," Ana growled. "Cascobel is in prison but El Águila is still trying to kill my dad. Everybody says it's a victory but *they're still out there*." She looked up, probing at Val with dark and shining eyes. "Mom says she just wanted to come to the Isla early this year. She said she felt like getting out of the city and doing more gardening. But we *never* come to the Isla before *Dia de la Virgin de Guadalupe*." Her accent thickened as the words spilled out faster and faster. "Dad was back from a trip to Baja and we went out shopping together at the Reforma mall. Like a family. Mom and Dad and me and Ricardo. It was the day after Revolution Day and there were all kinds of extra little shops open in the mall, like a festival. It was supposed to be a party. It was supposed to be fun."

Ana paused for breath. Restless, she flicked her wrist and sent a rejected clamshell hurling into the waves. "I had too many conchas." Her hand fell across her belly, cradling the memory of pain. "It made me sick. I went to the bathroom and I puked. As I was coming out someone grabbed me from behind."

She looked down now and for the first time seemed to see the blood smeared across her palm. She plunked heavily onto the sand, and her seashell guide vanished beneath the flapping hem of her jacket.

"He was very big," Ana muttered. "He had a thick beard. He smelled like lulo fruit and his hand was hot. It hurt, where he grabbed my shoulder." She swallowed.

Val sat still, fighting the urge to offer the kid hollow comfort or wrap her up in a hug she hadn't asked for. The best thing she could do right now was to listen as Ana's story melted into a fragile string of mingled English and Spanish.

Silently, she thanked Jacob for reminding her what emotional support looked like.

"But then Papa and Ricardo ran up. *Hubo una lucha.* Papa punched him and Ricardo picked me up and carried me away like a *pequeña bebe.* Someone called the *policía,* but the big man got away. He's still out there, too. I look for him, on the websites where they show what gangsters have been arrested."

"Did your mom and dad ever talk to you about that?" Val asked softly.

Ana's shoulders twitched in a rough shrug. "Sí. Mama hugs. Mama cries. Papa promises to take better care, to watch closer. They argue about it when they think I'm not listening. Ricardo asks me why I didn't scream or fight back."

"There's a saying for that," Val suggested. "For how people react when something scares them very badly. It's called *Fight or Flight or Freeze.* A lot of people freeze up when bad things happen to them. Your reaction was very normal."

"But I should have run," Ana insisted. "Or I should have hit him. I know what the cartels do to the families of the people who fight them. And I would have just let him carry me off and kill me and send my ears back to Papa in a bloody little envelope." She hung her head, bowing beneath the weight of shame.

"Do you want your dad to stop hunting the cartels?" Val inquired.

Ana shook her head violently. "No. No! They are bad men. *Someone* needs to stand up to them, and Papa knows how. He can do it. I know he can." Self-loathing twisted her words until each one sounded like its own unique curse. "Not like me. Some scared little niña waiting for Papa to come save her from the bad man."

"There's nothing wrong with being a girl."

Ana looked up. Tears were shining in the corners of her eyes.

Val brushed the sand from her palms and pushed to her

feet. A black fury was brewing like a storm inside her, but she set it aside. In that moment, she couldn't wing off to the mainland to hunt down the lowlifes who taught children how to hate themselves. She couldn't corner Sofia and Jorge and give them a piece of her mind. She could only do one thing.

She held out her hand. "There's nothing wrong with being scared. Come with me, Ana. I'll show you what to do the next time someone tries to grab you."

**Isla de las Flores**
**Off the coast of Campeche, Mexico**
**Christmas Eve**

Neither wind nor rain nor the foibles of modern technology would stop Kat Mulaney from enjoying himself on Christmas Eve. He lounged in the villa's six-person hot tub, which was nestled in a private alcove in the pool yard. Green passion vines crawled along the walls beneath the strings of gently glowing tea lights.

An extra-frosty piña colada sat on the patio beside Kat. A laptop floated on a thick paddle board at the center of the gently burbling water, protected by a clear plastic tote box. On the screen, a fire burned merrily in a stone hearth. *Trans-Siberian Orchestra's* newest holiday album piped through the speakers deftly hidden behind clusters of scarlet passion flowers. Overhead, the stars glimmered brightly. Kat let out a long sigh. All in all, he'd had worse Christmases.

The pool yard doors slid open with a grinding noise.

Miss Daisy stepped out of the rec room and onto the pool deck wearing a black one-piece swimsuit that walked right on that fine line between athletic and sexy. Her hair was back in a messy bun. She carried a beach towel, two small bags decorated with curls of red and green ribbon, a bottle of chilled champagne, and three glass flutes.

Kat smiled and nudged his floating computer aside to make room for her in the tub. "Are we having a party, Miss Daisy?"

She set her things on the patio and sat with her ankles in the warm water with a pleasant shiver. "I think we're due for a small one, aren't we? The household is upstairs unwrapping presents. Sofia gave me the booze and insisted the three of us take a few hours to unwind."

"You look like you could go for a few hours of unwinding," Kat noted. "Got some bags under the eyes." Slyly, he added, "Did you not sleep well last night?"

Rather than rise to the bait, Miss Daisy sighed and shook her head. "I spent the afternoon doing emergency therapy for a twelve-year-old girl. She's been putting on a brave face for her parents but this whole cartel business is stressing her out."

"Ah. Lots of tissues, a few action movies, and a bucket of cookie dough ice cream, I'm guessing?"

Miss Daisy gave him a blank look. "I took her into the forest and taught her how to punch trees without breaking her knuckles."

Kat chortled and slurped up the last maraschino cherry from his glass.

"I have a lot of sympathy for Jorge and Sofia." Miss Daisy lowered her voice as if afraid someone might overhear. "It can't be easy, raising a family when there are hit men after you. But I don't think they're doing that girl any favors by trying to shelter her from it."

Kat shrugged. He was a content bachelor and could imagine raising a child no more than he could imagine running an ultra-marathon through the Sahara. "When the bill comes due for the senator, you be sure to tack on an extra fee for parenting advice, got it?"

Miss Daisy uncorked the champagne and started filling the flutes. "At any rate, it sounds like they'll be having a big traditional meal around midnight. We're invited to that."

"None for me, honey." Kat moved the third flute out of Val's reach and held up his piña colada glass. "I like my drinks to be colors God never intended."

Val chuckled but nodded. She looked more tired than he had ever seen her. Perhaps Miss Daisy was homesick, on top of worrying about the girl.

The patio door slid open once again and Jacob joined them. He wore nothing but swim trunks and a pair of flip-flops, giving the entire world a good view of the *USMC* tattoo etched onto his pecs, right beside his left nipple.

"Well, aren't you both a sight from a magazine ad." Kat sighed, looking down at the flabby body and pink Bermuda shorts he was hiding beneath the water. "I always figured it was better to look at pretty things than to be pretty oneself." He raised his glass in a mock toast as Jacob slid into the water next to Val. "You do the whole world a service every time you hit the gym, Pinkerton."

Jacob nodded, accepting the compliment without comment. Fatigue was etched into his face as well, but Kat figured that was from spending the day carrying Señora Vargas' shopping bags after pulling all-night sentry duty.

He'd also found time somewhere along the way to stop by Miss Daisy's room if the uplifted toilet seat in the bathroom she and Kat shared was any indication. An industrious man indeed.

Val picked up her two little gift bags and passed one to each of them. "It's not much." She sounded almost shy. "But we're all spending the holiday away from home and family and I wanted both of you to know how much I appreciate you. VALKYRIE hasn't exactly hit smooth sailing yet, but you're here. Your support means everything to me."

Kat set the decorative tissue paper aside, peered into the bag, and let out a coo of delight. "Oh, my stars, how perfectly *awful!*"

It was a painted tchotchke about the size of his open hand, a tableau of four cartoonish oysters sitting around a poker table playing a game of Conquian. The oysters wore tri-cornered pirate hats. The words *Laguna Beach, Campeche, Mexico,* were painted across the base of the statue.

Perhaps it was the piña coladas speaking, but it just might have been the most deliciously tacky souvenir he had ever seen.

"A crowning jewel for my collection." He grinned, setting the gift aside. "That is assuming we don't happen to find ourselves stranded at sea and need to use it as an emergency anchor. I'll put it on the shelf right next to the ashtray shaped like a toilet bowl that I picked up in Myrtle Beach."

Across the tub, Jacob pulled a small collection of pewter

figurines from his bag. Kat was puzzled by the gift until he remembered that Jacob enjoyed painting wargame miniatures in his free time.

"It's a custom set I found online." Miss Daisy blushed. "Some independent artist had a real nice Norse pantheon set."

Jacob chuckled, turning the finger-sized statues over in his hands. The details, Kat noted, were remarkable. He could make out the individual braids woven into the Vikings' beards. Among the figurines was a tall, fierce-looking man with a hooked staff and an eyepatch and a winged woman in full battle armor with her sword and shield at the ready. Jacob studied each figurine fondly but paid that one particular attention before setting the gift aside.

"Merry Christmas, y'all." Val downed her glass of champagne.

"We got you something, too." Jacob threw a meaningful glance at Kat, who nodded and reached around the nearest lounge chair.

"A group effort?" Val asked curiously.

Kat found what he was looking for and pulled a dark glass bottle out of the shadows. "It had to be. This stuff was *hard* to find. Pinkerton fronted the money. I pulled the strings."

He passed the bottle of Amigos Perdidos Reserve mead across the water to Val, who let out a gasp that bordered on a scream.

"Reserve? You found *the reserve?*"

She set the bottle safely away from the edge of the pool and threw her arms around Kat with a delighted squeal.

The water rocked and roiled, and he snatched his floating computer aside before she could knock the thing over in her excitement. As quickly as Val grabbed him, she let him go and turned to fling herself at Pinkerton.

She didn't fool around with a platonic hug. She took Jacob's face in both palms and assaulted him with an open-mouthed kiss that left Kat glancing at the clock on his monitor and muttering, "I guess the action figures aren't all he's getting for Christmas."

When Miss Daisy composed herself and climbed down from Jacob, she was bright-eyed and flushed with delight. "Sorry," she told Kat as she fumbled to refill the champagne glasses. "Is your computer okay?"

A little bit of water had splashed into the floating tote, but the gear was unharmed. "Of course, I wouldn't need to resort to such crudities if I had full access to the Viking stockpile," Kat lamented. "I know for a fact there are multiple underwater-capable tablets in Hawk's toy chest."

Val grinned. "Oh gosh. I hope we don't wind up needing to use a computer under water on this job. Things will have gone seriously awry."

"*Probably*," Kat begrudged. "*Probably* I don't *technically* need a diving computer or a surveillance drone or a remote-controlled submarine while we're down here. *Probably* I'll make do just fine with the MacBook here and the Radio Shack special, but Miss Daisy. Come on." He spread his arms in supplication. "Tell me we wouldn't have a delightful time playing with those toys. This is pure cruelty, is what it is. Nathaniel Hawker is dangling all the fun stuff in front of my face and then snatching it away."

Jacob smiled into his champagne glass. "I'm guessing you'd do the same thing if the roles were reversed."

Kat pursed his lips, eyeing the other man over his horn-rimmed glasses. "True," he admitted. "But if *I* did it, it would actually be funny."

Sinking into the water up to her neck, Val turned sideways to stretch herself out over the hot tub bench and rested her head on Jacob's broad shoulder. The fatigue had gone from her eyes and she had relaxed, ready to settle in for a night of friendly chatter. "What would you do differently?" she asked.

Kat sipped the last of his piña colada as he considered the question. "Nothing," he decided finally. "I'd just be the one laughing."

# CHAPTER FOURTEEN

**Isla de las Flores**
**Off the coast of Campeche, Mexico**
**Christmas Day**

Christmas Day brought the gift of rain and moody skies. In a way, it was nice to know that even in paradise, the weather could turn gloomy. The household stayed in. Ana and Izzy and the maids played board games while Ricardo and Abuelita and the groundskeeper chewed their way through a bottle of good tequila and Sofia paced around the living room in her silk bathrobe with her ear pressed to the phone, sending holiday greetings to extended family on the mainland. The leftovers came out at noon and everyone gathered in the kitchen for a meal of twice-baked empanadas.

Val, modestly hungover from a night of close cama-raderie, was halfway through the buffet line when she felt a small, calloused hand close around her wrist.

Ana stared up at her, eyes shining and restless. "Let's go

outside," she said in a low, fierce voice. "Let's go back up the hill."

Val hesitated, looking around the living room at the fire in the hearth spread beneath the antique nativity set, Sofia enjoying a latte and reading a romance novel, and Jacob and Ricardo in the corner discussing something no doubt fascinating in Spanish.

Val looked back at the girl. *You should spend this day with your family,* she wanted to say. *Don't leave your mama without you on Christmas,* she should have said.

*You need to give your hands time to heal,* she didn't say.

Instead, she slipped a husk-wrapped tamale into her messenger bag and led Ana out into the rain.

As they passed Jacob, he glanced up from his conversation to watch them go. He met Val's eye, and then he saw the rain spitting down onto the upper patio. He returned to his conversation. Rain and weather and the terrors of nature be damned. There was no safer place on the island than wherever Val was.

They climbed to the highest point on the island, a western cliff that towered a modest sixty feet above the beach. Ten years ago, Sofia's father had cleared a swath of forest about the size of a basketball court to serve as a landing pad. Somewhere along the way, Sofia had sold the family helicopter, but it would be several years still before the jungle fully reclaimed this stretch of grass. By the time Val and Ana stopped, they were both soaked to the bone.

"Mama would be furious if she knew I was outside in the rain." Ana laughed. Sometime in the last twenty-four hours, she had given up on the more formal, grown-upsounding *Mom* and *Dad,* but it did not feel like a surrender. Indeed, there was a new fire in the girl's face.

"Art thou a witch, Ana Vargas?" Reginleif teased. "Wouldst thou melt in the rain?"

They were neither Val nor Reginleif when they were out in the forest with Ana. They were both, slipping easily back and forth in smooth and unspoken coordination.

"She always said rain would make me sick." Ana grinned, wiping clods of mud from her knees as they reached the edge of the old landing pad.

"It might," Val acknowledged, who no longer believed in lying to children to make them feel better. "If you were out here for a very long time or stopped moving and started to freeze. But we'll be outta here long before it gets to that point."

At the edge of the clearing, a rubber tree about two feet in diameter grew. Yesterday, when Sofia had been away on the mainland, Val had taken a few throw pillows from one of the unused lounges in the basement game room and lashed them to the tree with half a roll of duct tape. By the time Ana had exhausted herself on this makeshift punching bag she had worn a hole through the center of one of the pillows and left it bleeding white batting down the tree trunk.

Now Val stuffed the guts back into the cushion and secured them by winding several more loops of tape around the tree.

"You remember what I said about making a fist?"

Ana was already standing with her legs spread wide and her knobby elbows out. She barely waited for Val to get out of the way before she lunged forward and sank her fist deep into the cushion with a wet, meaty *thwap*.

Valkyrie watched the little girl kick and hit and punch and scream out her wordless fury like it was a sacred rite of passage. When Ana stumbled she stepped forward, gently correcting the girl's stance. When Ana's knuckles grew sore and bruised, Val introduced her to the wonders of a good roundhouse kick.

"But be careful with kicking," she advised. "It's easy to lose your balance when you kick. Always use your fists first, if you can."

Ana spit out mud and hair and nodded and attacked the tree like it had kicked her dog, or tried to snatch her from a mall bathroom.

Time rolled onward, as steady and relentless as the waves against the base of the cliff. Val found herself standing by the edge, perhaps twenty yards from Ana, staring out to sea. The ocean might rumble and the sky might complain and continue spitting rain across Isla de las Flores, but there would be no proper storm today.

It made her a little wistful. She hadn't been lying when she told Jacob the storms were the good memories.

It made her restless.

"Kat thinks he's pinned El Águila to a couple of possible compounds on the mainland."

"*Aye*," Reginleif answered.

"That girl behind us is seventy pounds soaking wet."

"*She is learning to defend herself,*" Reginleif pointed out. "That *is what we are teaching her.*"

"She's learning how to punch trees. That's it. You know

what my jiu-jitsu teacher told me when I graduated to my first red belt?"

"*I might guess.*"

"Women take self-defense classes thinking they'll learn how to protect themselves on the streets. But for ninety-nine out of one hundred women that graduate from his class, if some man ever chases them into a dark alley, they're still going to lose that fight." Val plucked a twig off a nearby bush and rolled it restlessly through her fingers. "Because even women who are good athletes just don't have a man's upper body strength. Those self-defense classes aren't teaching the weak how to fight back. All they do is give girls enough self-confidence to run and scream instead of freezing when someone tries to grab them."

"*It is something.*"

Val set her jaw. Out of the corner of her eye, she saw Ana wipe her rain-soaked brow before assaulting the tree with a series of low, fast punches.

"It's not enough," Val protested. "It's a game of eternal defense, and *it's not enough.*"

"*You might shake your fist at the sky for a thousand years,*" Reginleif reasoned gently, "*And not catch a single drop of justice falling from the heavens.*"

Val snorted. "Isn't that what we're here for? To put a thumb on the scale? To go hunt down the assholes before they come stealing away our children in the night?"

"*Aye.*"

"Then I'm going after El Águila. Kat thinks he'll have a location for me by morning. I'm going after him."

"*Then our little sister will be safe?*" Reginleif asked.

Val's jaw snapped shut. The question was like a dagger to her heart.

"She'll be safer. She won't have to worry so much about getting grabbed during a damned Independence Day festival."

"*Until her father catches the ire of another drug lord,*" suggested the witch in Val's head.

"I'll talk to him. I'll convince him he has to take a step out of the limelight. He's doing good work but it's not worth his family's life."

"*Isn't it?*" Reginleif asked. "*Yon girlchild isn't begging her father to put down his spear, Valkyrie. Instead, she seeks to pick up her own, as vague and as unformed as her desire yet is. Jorge Vargas is a warrior of the modern era, and his battlefield is the courtroom.*"

"But he doesn't need to fight," Val insisted. "Not if I can do it for them. We're an army, Regin. We're a fucking superhero. We can go fighting in the jungles so people like Jorge and Sofia and Ana can sleep easy at night."

"*We are but one, and the world is vast. I would not presume to know Granddad's mind, but I suspect he did not bring me back into this world to be one savior for the entire human race. Protect what thou canst, Valkyrie, but if they wish to fight, thou must let them fight. Gods know, if they are any kin to thee at all, it would be foolish to try to stop them.*"

"Why are you doing this?" Val growled. "Before we got here you were practically begging me to go on the offensive and hunt down these cartels."

"*I have had time to reflect.*"

"Well…" Val snapped her twig and cast the broken

pieces into the sea far below. "You should reflect on something else."

The day was growing long, and though Val herself was not cold, she felt a chill threatening to creep into the muggy air. It was about time to get Ana home and into a warm bath. Val wouldn't mind another dip in the hot tub, either. Perhaps she would break the seal on that precious bottle of Perdidos Reserve if Jacob were in the mood to share it with her.

Life was short, after all. You had to live while the living was good.

She was about to turn her back to the beach when a glimmer on the rocks below caught her eye.

She turned her head, but the flash of light was gone. There was nothing beneath her but the cliffs running down to a stretch of dense underbrush and rocky shore. Uneasy waves rumbled and rolled over the rocks.

Val held her breath, staring into the foliage. It might have been nothing. A seagull streaking across her vision and winging off into the bushes, a trick of the shifting light, or a stray whitecap roaming across the water.

Or...it might have been *something*.

Val flicked on her ever-present earpiece as she went to rejoin Ana. "Pinkerton," she said under her breath as she flicked through the comms channels. "You read me?"

Jacob answered promptly, his voice sharp and alert. "I read. What is it?"

"I need you to head up to the old helicopter landing pad to meet me and Ana on the double." She leaned down and collected her messenger bag from where she'd left it in the shelter of a particularly dense bush.

"Trouble?" Jacob inquired.

"Just a tingle in the old, uh, spidey-senses."

"I'm on my way."

Val had to tap Ana on the shoulder to get the girl's attention. Steam was rolling off her bare skin and she was breathing hard. She had punched a respectable divot into the fresh pad taped to the tree, and though her shoulders sagged with fatigue, the look she turned on Val was fierce and a touch defiant.

"It's time to head back inside," Val said.

"I'm not ready."

"Thou might stand here battling dormant dryads for a thousand years and never feel ready," Reginleif pointed out. "The trees will be here on the morrow. Come, child. Thy body needs rest."

If Ana found Val's altered speech pattern strange, she said nothing. She dropped her bruised and calloused fists, nodded sulkily, and picked up the jacket she had cast onto a nearby boulder. Though the stew of clouds overhead hid the sun, by this point day had decidedly rolled over into early evening, and the air had changed. The sky no longer had that lazy, morose, drooling quality, nor did it carry the electric tang of pre-storm ozone that Val and Reginleif both found so alluring. Instead, it felt suddenly dark and alien, unfamiliar.

"What is this?" Val asked under her breath as they descended the narrow path back down to the villa. She trailed a few feet behind Ana, always keeping the kid at the center of her focus. The skin on the back of her neck prickled, but every time she glanced over her shoulder, she saw only the dense jungle pressing around them. "Just my anxiety?"

*"If it is, thy nerves are mine now as well,"* Reginleif answered. *"Nay. I suspect the wind has shifted. Norori turns his eye upon us and it is just as baleful as it ever was."*

"Norori," Val muttered. "The personification of the north wind. Is he real, Regin? The way you and Odin are real?"

*"Do not speak the Allfather's name so casually."* The rebuke came automatically and without rancor. *"Norori was all too real, back in the days of old."* Reginleif sounded uncertain. *"Though if he now sleeps as I once slept or if he rides the currents and streams once more, I do not know. But even if he only dreams, the winds remember their riders. And Norori does not remember us fondly."*

"Us!" Val sniffed. "This little spat of yours was way before my time. You mean *you.*" A blast of chilly unfamiliar wind rattled the canopy above them. Its cold fingers pressed down through the trees and crawled up Val's spine, and she saw goose flesh rise on Ana's bare shoulders. They turned a bend in the trail and had to slow as Val helped Ana climb over a knot of fallen trees. Now that she had given up the sparring, the child's exercises were catching up with her. Ana's arms were hot, and her muscles were weak and watery and trembling. Val had to lift her over the densest patch of underbrush.

"Real or not, sleeping or awake, Norori's got a bad attitude," Val muttered as another blast of wind rattled the trees. "What did you do to piss this guy off, anyway?"

*"It was nothing,"* Reginleif insisted. *"It was only a small matter of pride—ah, look. Jacob approaches."*

It looked as though Val had called him directly from a run on the treadmill. He wore sneakers, gym shorts that revealed the carved muscles of his calves, and an under-shirt that was at least two sizes too small for him. With the tactical vest hastily slung over his shoulders, he looked almost comical, like a pinup from a *Sexy Marines of the Southwest* fundraising calendar. He was jogging up the path in their direction. He caught Val's eye before his gaze slid to the girl between them.

"There you are, Ana," he said casually. "Sofia was starting to wonder where you guys had run off to."

"Why don't you take her inside," Val suggested. "I'm already out here and all wet. I might as well run a check of the perimeter."

Jacob nodded and took the baton. Val turned away from man and child and slid into the gathering shadows beneath the jungle canopy. She moved westward, pushing through the underbrush as she made her way to the shore-line. The vegetation snagged at her clothes, teasing her and biting her. She flung herself over upturned roots, squeezed between rough-barked trees, and plunged through thickets of broad, spade-shaped leaves that smelled of lemon and oozed skin-tingling sap. She felt bright and alert, filled with neither alarm nor dread but with the hot-blooded energy of a curious hunter taking wing, eager to learn what oddity had encroached on her domain.

In her mind's eye, she saw that one brief flash of light flickering over the rocks, over and over again. It could have been a gull or a white cap, or a flash of waning daylight catching off the lens of a sniper rifle. *Just a few minutes to go down there,* she told herself. *Poke around, make sure it's nothing.*

A distant snapping sound in the jungle could be a thousand things. An overripe fruit falling from a tree and splatting to the ground. The heads and tusks of little javelinas clashing as they squared off in some ritual rivalry. An old tree trunk, filled with rot, finally cracking and tumbling over. A twig snapping beneath the heel of some careless jungle denizen.

When it was followed by a muffled animal scream, the list of options narrowed instantly to a familiar and dreadful pinpoint. It was a single gunshot, partially muffled by the barrel of a silencer, and the terrified scream of a child.

Val did not bother trying to slow down. She was running full bore downhill when she heard the awful twin sounds behind her, and momentum was not her friend. She had a better friend, though, one that came instantly awake beneath her skin.

Valkyrie saw a low-hanging branch ahead and reached up, leaping to catch the wood in her palms. Her blood was on fire. Her heart was a drum. Gunfire. She had left her partner and the child *alone.*

Talons erupted from her fingertips, cutting deep gouges into the smooth wood as she sprang off her feet and pivoted. The thin fabric of her tee shirt ripped like tissue paper as great black wings tore free of her spine and beat at the humid air. With two heavy flaps, she burst free of the canopy in a shower of disturbed leaves and dewdrops. She hurtled through the air, heedless, racing toward the sheltered trail where she had left Jacob and Ana. The canopy stretched beneath her, and even Reginleif's sharp eyes could not penetrate down to the forest floor. She could only fly by landmark and instinct. She found the suggestion of a gap in the trees, a thin crack stretching from the top of the island down to the villa that hinted at a walking trail. The trees beneath her were still.

*Noise*, she begged silently. *Make more noise. Scream again, fire again, anything. We shouldn't have left them alone!*

She found the cluster of downed trees near where she had left Ana and Jacob and tucked her wings in a dive. Something moved against the ground, big and languid. Branches beat at her face and arms as she dropped like a stone through the canopy, too big to wing her way silently through the brush. She landed on the narrow trail with a thud, her wings slipping fluidly beneath her skin.

Jacob was struggling to his feet at the edge of the trail. He held a pistol in one hand and was trying to pull himself upright against a nearby tree with the other, looking around sluggishly. Blood poured from his scalp and painted a red curtain across his left eye. A steaming gash cut a line along his temple, blowing a hole through the top of his ear and tearing a ragged path through his hair. Gods willing, the bullet had only grazed off his skull.

Ana was nowhere to be seen.

Jacob saw Valkyrie and his lips moved, but the noise he made was an incoherent mumbling. He pointed a shaking finger to the left. She heard a distant rustling and muffled shouting through the trees in that direction.

She smacked her earpiece, opening an emergency line to Kat as she ducked her head and plunged into the foliage once more. "Code Gamma," she snarled into the little mic.

"Man down halfway up the trail to the helipad. Hostiles in the area."

She prayed that Kat remembered their drills. In that moment, it was all she could do for Jacob.

She burst through the trees and into a narrow clearing to find every parent's worst nightmare.

A man in deep gray camo was dragging little Ana Vargas through the forest. A hasty gag was tied around her face and he had an arm locked around her throat. He was more than twice her size and moved with the confidence of a man who had trained for combat in the jungle, but as she gasped and wheezed and gulped for air, the girl fought like a raging wildcat. Her face was white and the gag was bloodstained. Ana hissed and shrieked, flailing, mad with terror and rage. The man grabbed a fistful of her black hair, jerking her head this way and that as he dragged her stumbling, struggling form further from the path. She jerked and sank her pointy little elbow deep into his gut.

Valkyrie lunged forward, twisting her upper body at the last second. Her left wing snapped outward, exploding from her spine, and the slender edge of her phalanges snapped across the back of the man's head with a sound like a whip crack. He screamed and dropped Ana as his hands flew up to clutch his skull. The girl hit the wet ground hard and scrambled away.

The attacker recovered quickly and danced away before Valkyrie could twist and strike him with her other wing. He drew the pistol holstered on his hip and spun, firing two wild shots in her direction. The first bullet clipped a wing and blasted a quarter-sized hole through her primary feathers. The second hit closer to home.

Pain exploded through Valkyrie's shoulder. She screamed a high, wordless, animal scream that rattled the trees and silenced the insects. With hot blood pumping down her arm, she enveloped the man in a full-body tackle. It was a reckless, stupid move, one that would have left any of Valerie's past jiu-jitsu trainers shaking their heads in disgust, but with the added mass and striking power of her wings, it got the job done.

The attacker staggered under her assault and they slammed to the ground together, rolling and wrestling for supremacy. Valkyrie shrieked and sank her talons into his wrist. His hand popped open and the gun vanished, lost beneath them as they rolled down the slope. He punched, sinking his good fist into her shoulder and sending a fresh wave of blinding pain down her spine.

All sense had gone from her. She was wounded and they were locked together in an intimate and deadly dance, and all that mattered was that the struggling body beneath her, the flat-faced man with a mole under his left eye, *stop moving*.

Black horns sprouted from Valkyrie's skull and curled around her ears like closed fists. She drew her head back and then slammed it forward.

She felt the bones of his brow ridge crack. For a brief instant, he went rigid, his eyes clouding with pain and shock. And then his muscles slackened and he stilled, stunned.

Valkyrie sprang into a crouch. Blood spilled from her shoulder and dribbled onto the man's chest, where it steamed. She snatched the knife from her belt and held it over his face, ready to plunge it downward.

"*Take his ear,*" Reginleif whispered. "*In payment for Jacob's.*"

Valerie hit the brakes on that particular impulse before it could filter down into her aching arm. She crouched over the attacker, gasping for breath. The tumble had left them both filthy, caked with mud and decayed leaves.

"Who sent you?" The words came out in a hiss as her teeth grew long and sharp. "And who's with you?"

The light on the sheltered side of the island was dim and dying fast, but her eyes were keen. She saw his expression shift from shock back to awareness. His lips moved, but the words were barely a whisper.

"*Las...Las sombras...*"

She leaned in close, turning her head to better catch his words. "English," she cursed under her breath. "Dammit. *Habla inglés!*"

"*...siempre... están conmigo...*"

This wasn't going to do her any good. She was about to push to her feet when his head jerked to the side. His jaws snapped and his eyes bulged.

"Whoa!" She recoiled, startled out of her fury. His face had gone pallid, as if he were in the first throes of a seizure. "Hang on now—"

His neck snapped in the other direction. His mouth opened and then snapped shut with a crack like a snapping twig. Words gurgled in the back of his throat.

"*A madness has him,*" Reginleif said grimly. "*Give him peace, Valkyrie. There is no other way.*"

"He might snap out of it," Valerie argued. "We can't question a dead man!"

The breath had gone from her lungs. She stared in

horror at the jerking, twitching thing on the ground in front of her. His jaw opened and closed, his teeth snapping together like a wind-up monkey's toy cymbals.

*"están con...migo...!"*

His head exploded.

# CHAPTER FIFTEEN

**Villa basement suite**
**Isla de las Flores**
**Off the coast of Campeche, Mexico**
**Christmas night**

Once again, Val was sitting in a panic room with the client while other people secured the property.

"I tell you what, I would just *love* to have a good surveillance drone right about now." Kat sat at the security console, scrolling through the security camera feeds. He was wearing a yellow bathrobe, slippers, and an acne peel. On the screens in front of him, little grayscale images of Isabella and Ricardo stalked through the darkened jungle, combing the island for any more unwelcome guests.

"One of the nice new ones with sound dampeners and infrared. At least they'd take some of the pressure off Ricky and Izzy." Kat's complaining was more subdued than normal. Even he could read the room.

Sofia, Lula, and the groundskeeper huddled on a couch in the corner, anxiously combing clods of dirt and leaves from Ana's hair. Nerves, chill, fatigue, and residual panic left the girl shivering despite the thick blankets coiled around her like armor. On the other side of the room, the door to the little ensuite bathroom hung open. Jacob sat on the edge of the tub, allowing Abuelita to stitch shut the ragged hole in his ear.

As far as panic rooms went, the Vargas' converted basement suite was quite luxurious, but with Val's team in here along with the entire household, things were a bit cozy. Estrella sat cross-legged on the floor beside Val, silently dabbing blood from Val's shoulder with a damp cloth.

The bullet had been a through-and-through and the wound was sealing itself up at a rapid pace. At least she didn't have to explain the immaculate healing to her employers.

No, she had to explain the assassin with the exploding-fucking-head.

Val forced her attention to the young woman cleaning her wounds. The painkiller hadn't kicked in yet and her head was still throbbing. "You're taking this really well."

Estrella's shoulders rose in a tiny shrug. "I come from a poor village of avocado farmers," she murmured, as if this explained everything.

"Sweet mother of our lord and savior." Kat turned away from the bank of monitors. "You poor thing. I'm so sorry." Catching Val's questioning look, he added, "Oh, I'm surprised you haven't heard, Miss Daisy. The green *cojone* fruits are the new opium down here south of the border.

Ever since #AvacadoToast started trending up north and the price spiked to match, all these drug cartels have expanded into the trade."

"Jeeze." Val scrubbed her tired eyes. "They're fucking up the guacamole pipeline too? That's a bridge too far."

Nobody laughed.

The bathroom lights flicked off. Jacob and Abuelita had finished their rough surgery. Abuelita, busy as ever, bustled over to minister to the shell-shocked Sofia and Ana as Jacob joined Val and Kat in the far corner. The gauze wrapped around Jacob's skull was already turning pink with blood and he had a faraway look in his eyes that Val did not much like.

"I didn't see much," Jacob muttered. "He shot me from behind and grabbed Ana before I could—"

Val shook her head firmly. "Nope. Take a seat. You don't get to apologize for being shot in the back of the head."

He sat. On the security camera feed behind him, Ricardo and Izzy had reached the weather station at the far end of the island. Their blurry shapes moved slowly across the rocky shore, scanning for anything out of the ordinary. Kat was right—a drone would be useful right about now. She'd *love* to know how the fucker got onto Isla de las Flores.

In her mind's eye, she saw his jaw snapping, his eyes flying wide in the half-second before his head burst like an overripe melon hitting concrete at Mach two.

She waved Estrella away and brought Jacob and Kat in close for as private of a huddle as they were going to get. "I think it's time to consider a strategic retreat."

Kat winced but Jacob closed his eyes and nodded.

"We don't have enough staff to keep every inch of this island patrolled," Val went on. "There's no putting the toothpaste back in this tube. El Águila knows where Jorge's family is, and now he's proven he can slip an assassin out here under the radar. This place is no longer a fortress. It's a trap."

"We don't yet know this man was Tierra Roja," Kat noted. "We ought to take a good look at the body." He cast an uncomfortable glance at the dark patches of blood in Val's hair. She had changed shirts but she was still going to be combing chunks of skull and brain from her hair for a while. "I mean, what's left of it."

Val waved the concern away. "This guy was a professional. He's not going to have a signed Assassins-R-Us invoice in his front pocket." Though he could have said as much, for all she knew. He had said *something* in those seconds before the explosion, but it had been in a language Val did not speak, and after the pursuing excitement, she had no hope of recreating the syllables for someone else to translate.

"If he wasn't Tierra Roja, then he was sent by another cartel," she decided. "The exact *who* doesn't matter."

"Val's right," Jacob muttered. "This location is burned. We need to get the household moving. Pick a direction and drive. Stay ahead of the next guy they send over. They can't hurt what they can't find. They can't anticipate where the family will be if *we* don't know where the family will be."

"I think we should find a real doctor to check on Ana," Val added. "I'm worried about that swelling in her wrist, and what shock might do to her." *And Jacob*, she added silently. Her partner was tough, but he had lost a lot of blood and he shouldn't be up and walking around so soon after getting shot—and she felt this point bore repeating —*in the head*.

Kat glanced over his shoulder, mournfully taking in the security setup he had worked so hard to make his own. "From life on the beach to life on the run. Merry Christmas to me." He cheered up as a new thought occurred to him. "I know. I'll call Nate and have him help coordinate the evacuation. God only knows he's not doing anything special tonight." Buoyed by the prospect of a late evening driving jarl Hawk up a wall, he turned to his computers and got to work.

Val leaned in close to Jacob. "I'm going to go check out the body before the rats and insects get to him." She had come this far and stayed in the panic room this long to ensure Jacob, Ana, and the rest of the household were secure. "Then I'm going to join Izzy and Ric to finish the perimeter sweep. I double-checked the exterior cameras. Kat has every inch of this island's shore monitored, and no unauthorized boats have come by. I'm going to find out how that bastard got here even if I have to take this island apart with my bare hands."

"Just don't take too long." Jacob sucked in a steadying breath and sat upright, forcing his voice to be steady and strong. "I want everyone on the boat out of here by dawn. Is there coffee down here?"

Val left him to manage his self-medication and tapped Kat on the shoulder on her way out. "Keep a close eye on

Pinkerton. There's no way he doesn't have a concussion. Call me right away if he starts slurring or throwing up or anything."

Kat nodded, all business. "All right. You go on all alone into the assassin-plagued jungle, Miss Daisy. I'll stay here and protect the former Marine."

Val supposed she was going to have to come clean with Kat sooner rather than later.

One more thing stood between her and the jungle that hid the dead body and the answers she craved. That thing was a knobby-kneed twelve-year-old girl with mud on her shins and dark intensity in her eyes. Ana had extracted herself from her family's ministrations and was waiting for Val beside the reinforced panic room door.

"I hit him," the girl whispered fiercely. "I hit him back."

Val nodded. "I saw you get him good in the ribs. You should be proud."

Ana clutched her blanket around her shoulders and studied Val closely. "I saw you, too."

Val glanced over her shoulder and lowered her voice. "It's crowded in here, Ana. Stay with your family and do what Jacob says. You know I have to go back to work out there. We can talk about what you saw when everything is settled, okay?"

The girl hesitated. Val saw the turmoil on her face, horror mingled with anxiety and awe and dread. She was the same kid that had cried and confessed her frustration and self-hatred and her terror into Val's shoulder, only one day older. You could fit a whole lot of experience into one day. You could fit a whole war between drug lords and black-winged angels in a day.

Exhaustion made Ana's head sag. "Come back soon," she whispered.

Val ran her fingers fondly through Ana's dark hair before pushing open the panic-room door and stepping into the night.

**Isla de las Flores**
**Off the coast of Campeche, Mexico**
**Christmas night**

The clearing smelled like blood and death. Clouds had washed away the hope of moonlight or starlight and the whole island was cloaked in blackness so deep that even Reginleif could barely make out more than shapes and motion. Val had brought along an electric lantern that cast the trees in an eerie blue-white glow and gave the corpse a flat, unreal quality, like something from a horror-themed video game.

She set the lantern on the dirt and crouched, studying what remained of the assassin. From his neck down he was a collection of big, muscular limbs.

From the neck up he was a pile of red and pink mush.

"*Unnatural,*" Reginleif said uneasily.

Val forced herself to look at the ruined head. She'd heard stories about agents or fanatics who implanted suicide capsules in their teeth. Jacob had assured her that such things were real, if exceedingly rare. Remembering the way this assassin had gnashed his jaws together, she thought now that he had been trying to trigger a similar device, one that was a bit more extravagant than a dose of cyanide.

She tried to bring his face to mind but could remember little except the pain, the motion, and the fight as they locked arms and tumbled to the ground. Like his last words, his face was lost to her.

She touched the fabric of his seamless suit. It was smooth, poreless, and tough, like reinforced rubber that hung weirdly off his frame. No air circulation. It was one of the strangest things she had ever seen. A man wearing a suit like this could sweat out and die of heat exhaustion in a few hours, even on a relatively chilly day like today.

Holding her breath against the stink, she took him by the arm and rolled him onto his side. Some kind of mechanical device was fixed to the base of his neck, about the size of an old audio cassette tape. Judging from the smooth edges, it had survived the explosion intact, though it was crusted with gore. Val leaned in, squinting. Little mesh windows over the device obscured an array of tiny fans.

"It's a sealable diving suit," she realized. "Holy smokes." She glanced at the man's chest again, impressed despite her revulsion.

"*You suggest the man swam to the island?*" Reginleif sounded skeptical. "*We are leagues from land. Beowulf himself could not have braved that sea alone.*"

"Maybe he didn't swim all the way," Val muttered. "Maybe a boat dropped him off out in the open ocean."

A long slit ran against his hip, sealed with a strip of strong and tacky adhesive. She had to cut through the goo with a talon to get it open, and it was like unzipping the back of a ball gown. Aside from a pair of stained boxer shorts, the man was naked beneath his rubber suit. A bandolier of equipment was slung across his bare chest, where it was preserved not just from seawater, but from the earlier rain of blood and bone.

His skin was sallow, cold. Stubborn little beetles chewed around the edges of his neck and what remained of his chin, humming contentedly. The wind shifted and Val turned her head with a frown. Beneath the scent of blood and moss and gore that permeated the clearing, she caught a whiff of something light and sweet.

Bracing herself, she put her nose closer to the dead man's chest and sniffed. He stank from the rubber of his suit and his evacuated bowels, but something else was there as well.

"Did...Did he wear cologne out on a hit job?"

*"I have heard of stranger things than men who mind their grooming even when out on raids,"* Reginleif replied.

Val set the thought aside and picked through the assassin's meager belongings. A couple of granola bars, a tiny first-aid kit that included several water purification tablets, a coil of cable that was thin and very strong, two knives, a pair of slender night-vision goggles, and two small, waterproof cases of ammo. As she expected, the man carried no helpful cell phone, or personal journal, or logbook detailing his adventure to Isla de las Flores. What was the point in blowing up your whole damn head, after all, if not to protect your identity and the identity of your employer?

Val tucked the goggles into her pocket and flipped open the first ammo case. It was full of mid-sized rounds for the Glock he had used to shoot Jacob. The second case was heavier and contained two dozen explosive-tipped shells meant for a long-barreled rifle.

"Fabulous." She rose to her feet and waved her hands in front of her. The air was thick with insects of every sort, coming late to the feast. "He's got more crap stashed around the island."

---

**Isla de las Flores**
**Off the coast of Campeche, Mexico**
**Christmas night**

Isabella and her uncle picked their way slowly down the rocky western shore, pausing to scan every nook, cranny, and shadow before moving on. Ricardo wore an old set of night-vision goggles he'd dug up from the security office back in the villa. Izzy, who had better eyesight in the dark, was left to crawl along the rocks. So far they had found a discarded bag of trash washed up on the beach and a lost fishing net tangled around one of the Low Tide signs along the eastern shore. The trash bag had been full of empty soda cans and beer bottles, probably the discarded litter from some fishing charter.

Izzy carried it slung over her shoulder anyway. Some-times this island felt like a prison, but by God, it was *her* prison and she was going to keep it tidy.

They had almost completed their sweep of the coast-line. All that remained between them and the boathouse beneath the villa was a quarter-mile strip of narrow, rocky beach beneath sheer cliffs. The tide was high and they had to wade through the treacherous waters.

"I was so sure we'd find the squatter made himself at home in the weather station," her uncle muttered. "But nothing. No boat. No footprints. All my tequilas, right where I left them. No trace. He can't have been on the island long."

"No self-respecting cartel hitman would hole up in that little dump," Izzy grumbled. "*Dios mío, tío.* The place smells like the inside of a crusty gym sock."

"You are a woman," Ricardo shot back. "You don't understand."

"I understand why you can't get a girlfriend, after seeing how you keep your bachelor pad."

This seemed to sting the old man and he stayed silent, which was just as well for Izzy. She didn't want to be the second security guard ambushed and shot in the back of the head today.

When she heard a crack in the brush above them, she whirled with a gasp. She nearly slipped on the wet rocks but caught her balance, dropped the stupid bag of trash, and lifted her pistol against the darkness. In the shadows of the cliffs beside her, Ricardo froze with his old shotgun on his shoulder.

"At ease. It's Valerie." A figure slipped down from a dip in the cliffs and dropped onto the narrow sandbar a few yards from Izzy.

"You're out here alone?" Ricardo dropped his gun to his side. "After what happened earlier? Are you crazy, chica?"

Val ignored the question, picking her way over the

jagged rocks. "I went to check the body for clues. Didn't find much. You?"

Ricardo cursed under his breath. Izzy didn't see the point in getting worked up. What was done, was done. She shook her head and scooped up her bag of litter once more. "Shoreline is secure, as far as we can tell," she reported. "We were just heading back to the boathouse. We'll have to wait till morning to sweep the jungle, though. It's too dangerous to do it at night."

Valerie ignored the unspoken reproach in Izzy's words and joined the two in their sweep along the rocks. "We don't plan on being here in the morning. Jacob and Kat are making preparations to get everyone off the island."

The prospect of getting off the island, even under such difficult circumstances, cheered Izzy. Her uncle grunted.

They were near the entrance to the boathouse when Val held up a fist and called them to a halt. She pointed into the wet black maw of the manmade cavern. Inside, Izzy could almost make out the outline of Sofia's little hobby sailboat.

"Is it just me, or is that boat listing to the side?" Val asked.

Izzy shrugged. Ricardo frowned and took this as a good excuse to flick on his night-vision goggles. "Sí," he confirmed, surprised. "It's favoring the aft side. Some ballast must have rolled around."

Val wasn't listening. She unclipped the holster belt from around her waist, set her gun on a tall boulder, and waded into the ocean. When the water was up to her hips, she threw out her arms and dove, vanishing beneath the water.

"Loco chica," Ricardo repeated. Izzy stood on the rocks beside her uncle, staring at the dark waves. There was a riptide somewhere out there, and lord knew how well that white girl could swim.

"Get on the line and call Jacob," Izzy called to her uncle as she scrambled along the rocks toward the boathouse. "I'll fire up the Jet Ski. Let's fish that woman out of the water before she drowns."

A light flicked on in the boathouse, casting a long white glow across the restless waters. Ricardo yelped and snatched the night-vision goggles from his head.

"Y'all better get in here," Valerie shouted from inside the boathouse. "I found the freaking submarine."

**Boathouse**
**Isla de las Flores**
**Off the coast of Campeche, Mexico**
**Boxing Day morning, early**

"That..." Kat flicked a finger over his computer tablet, scrolling until he found what he was looking for. "Is a Duskany Premium one-person midrange submersible vehicle. Not exactly a submarine, Miss Daisy. More like an underwater scooter."

He had put on real, if mismatched, clothes and joined Val in the boathouse. Izzy and Ricardo had gone up to the villa to help Jacob and the groundskeeper pack the essentials for a spontaneous mainland getaway.

Val sat on a folded beach towel on the sheltered dock. She regarded the strange device bobbing in the water before her. It looked a bit like a quadcopter. Four sturdy propeller cases surrounded an airtight storage compartment big enough for a couple of beer coolers. It was not big enough to carry a person, nor was it meant to. A padded handle and harness strap were tucked between the adjustable propellers, where an enterprising scuba diver might grab on and let the vehicle tow him across open waters.

She had found the submersible resting on the rocks beneath Sofia's little sailboat, and it had taken a great deal of help from Reginleif to haul it to the surface and lash it to the docks with a spare length of rope. It wanted to sink.

Kat plunked onto the damp wood beside Val. "Let's see." He scrolled through the user manual. "It looks like you blow the ballast tank by—" He set the tablet hastily aside and leaned forward, dipping his sandaled feet into the water as he tugged the lashing. The submersible bobbed forward and *thunked* against the dock pillar. Kat dipped his fingers beneath the surface, feeling around one of the storage compartments. "Holding—and—twisting—the—"

A sea of bubbles formed around the submersible with a loud *whoosh*. Suddenly lighter, it bobbed upward to float beside the dock.

"There." Kat pointed to the center storage compartment, which was now safely above the water line. "Should be safe to open now. That's, uh, assuming it's not rigged to blow or anything." The corner of his mouth tugged into a frown.

Val shook her head, amazed and horrified. "Honestly, if that current hadn't pushed the sailboat up against it we might never have realized it was right here beneath our noses."

Still, she checked the seal on the storage compartment

for any obvious signs of tampering before flipping the latch. Kat leaned over her shoulder to watch.

There were four things in the airtight compartment, each of them wrapped in a heavy plastic bag for extra protection against any leaks. A spare battery cartridge for the submersible, a deluxe emergency medical kit, a bale of MREs, and a long rifle case.

"That is the suitcase of a man on a mission," Kat remarked.

Val opened the rifle case and sighed. "And that is a Barrett M95 sniper rifle."

"I'm going to venture a guess that our uninvited guest hasn't been on the island very long." Kat shifted his weight uneasily, making the old dock wood creak. "Unless he's been living off of guava fruit pilfered from the garden. Those MREs haven't been touched."

"It is Christmas," Val agreed, remembering the story of Ricardo's promotion from gardener to bodyguard. She pushed herself upright, slinging the rifle case up and over her shoulder. "I'll bet the plan was to hit the villa at night after everyone was sleeping and hungover from the holiday. He was scoping out the lay of the land when he crossed paths with Jacob and Ana and decided he couldn't pass up the chance to snatch Jorge's daughter." She shuddered, not allowing herself to think of what the dead man might have had in mind for Ana.

She turned to her tech guy. "*Please* tell me we have a fix on El Águila."

Kat's thick lips pressed into a line. "The clients just went through a traumatic experience and now we're talking about taking them out of their home and putting this show on the road, Miss Daisy. Is this the best time to be going off the reservation?"

Val's eyes narrowed. She was soaking wet. She was tired. She was hungry. She was pissed. "That's not a 'no.'"

Whatever Kat might have replied was drowned beneath the jingle of an incoming call. He glanced at his tablet and a look of relief washed over his face.

He opened the line before Val could press him further. "Hey there, Jake. Tell me you're calling with good news."

Jacob's voice crackled on the tablet's tiny speakers. "I just got off the line with Jorge. He says Tierra Roja is coming for him as we speak."

**Gulf of Mexico**
**Off the coast of Campeche, Mexico**
**Boxing Day, morning**

The Isla de las Flores fleet consisted of three motorized boats—five if you counted the Jet Ski—and Sofia's recreational sailboat. The two-man dinghy was too small to brave the open waters between the island and the mainland in the choppy hours before dawn, and so the entire Vargas household and their essential belongings had to cram into the cabin cruiser and a tiny fishing trawler. Val's team rode on the cabin cruiser with Ana, Sofia, and a few others while Ricardo and Izzy took the trawler.

Sofia had been born and raised on the waters and took easy command of their little boat, ordering the groundskeeper away from the wheel so she could calm her nerves by crashing boat and crew headfirst through wall after wall of seven-foot swell.

"Oh—oh lord."

Kat hung off the side of the deck, clutching the rail and dry heaving with every pitch and sway. He covered his mouth with his Panama hat and gave Val a baleful look. "Can you please talk to her, Miss Daisy?"

"The waters are what they are," Jacob answered, pitiless. "Slowing down would only mean it takes us longer to get to the mainland."

The deck bucked beneath them as the boat plunged into another trough. Cold salt water sprayed over the prow. Kat moaned. Val wished she had more than sympathy to offer him, but Jacob was correct. The situation had devolved and the sooner they could get to the mainland, the sooner they could figure out where the hell to go from here.

"Go over what Jorge told you again," Val called to her partner. They had to raise their voices to hear each other over the buzz of the engine, but the other option was to squeeze into the already overcrowded cabin with the maids and groundskeeper. Ana was at the wheel with her mother.

"Jorge didn't give me many details," Jacob answered. "But I've been trying to keep up with the pre-trial proceedings. There was a problem with the extradition process late last week."

"That's why Jorge couldn't make it home for Christmas," Val recalled. "He had to stay and ram some paperwork through the federal bureaucracy."

Jacob nodded and took a long pull from his can of Coke. There hadn't been time to brew coffee, and caffeine was caffeine. "There was a miscommunication with the US Marshals. Someone leaked the details of Cascobel's extradition, so for security reasons they scrapped the original plan to fly him directly into Mexico City. They're taking him to a private air strip outside of Toluca and driving him the rest of the way via armored transport."

Val closed her eyes and drew up her mental map of central Mexico. "We're looking at, what, a twenty-mile drive?"

"Much of it through lesser jungle roads." Jacob drained the last of the Coke and crushed the can against the rail with his big palm. He had livened up since the head injury, which Val was glad to see. "Jorge's been getting all of the usual anonymous threats, but the last-minute change of plans for Cascobel, combined with the high-end assassin coming after his family…"

"Means he needs backup." Val squeezed her eyes together and nodded reluctantly. "Defense. We're back to playing defense."

For a glorious twenty minutes, she had allowed herself to believe that taking the Vargas family to the mainland meant she might have a shot at putting El Águila in the ground once and for all. Getting out ahead of this loser's game.

"That is what the client hired us for," Kat called as the boat sliced across another swell and plunged into the water.

Val resisted the temptation to blow a raspberry. "You said you had El Águila pinned to three possible locations."

Kat held up a hand, turning his head away from Val and Jacob. He sucked in a few deep breaths, swallowed what might have been a mouthful of bile, and nodded. "Three different safehouses across Oaxaca state. But Miss Daisy, that's where the trail ends. I can't narrow his location down further unless he slips up somehow and we just don't have the people to check all those locations, much less *raid* them."

Val slammed her fist against the rail and stared over the moody waters. Kat was correct. They had to focus on getting Sofia and Ana to safety and giving Jorge the backup he needed.

Something flickered in the edge of her vision and she looked up. A bright blue scarf was tied to the little flagpole beside the captain's cabin. It was Ana's scarf, the one she most liked to wear when she and Val had gone out seashell hunting.

A thought occurred to Val. She turned away from her team and mounted the narrow staircase leading to the captain's cabin. The door was not locked and she poked her head into the phonebooth-sized chamber. Sofia stood at the prow, straight-backed and proud as she manned the wheel. Ana huddled beside her, studying the equipment gauges. She looked around when Val opened the door.

"Ana. You told me something strange about the man who tried to grab you at the mall. Do you remember? You said he smelled funny?"

"She doesn't need to talk about that." Sofia's head whipped around and she glared daggers at Val. There was rage on her face—a rage she couldn't turn against the cartels or the assassin or the sea itself, and so she turned it on Val. "We've had a hard enough night as it is without talking about that. Now go back down to the deck and stop scaring my daughter!"

Ana wiggled around the instrument panels and leaned toward Val. Her face was bright, her expression every bit as intense as her mother's.

"Lulo," she whispered, cupping her hands in front of her to indicate a fruit about the size of a baseball. "He smelled like *lulo*. Like—like an orange, yes? Only not an orange. I don't have the word for it."

"Close the door, Valerie," Sofia snapped. "We're done talking about this."

Val didn't argue. She had what she needed. She couldn't give Sofia peace of mind, but she could at least respect her wishes.

She returned to her crew on the deck, where Kat was mopping his sweaty face with baby wipes. "Citrus," she declared. "The assassin smelled like citrus."

"You stopped to sniff the dead body?" Kat balked.

"He was *reeking* of it, even over the smell of gore. Like he took a bath in some kind of citrus oil. Ana tells me that the man who tried to grab her back in the fall smelled like lulo. It's a kind of fruit."

"A pretty nasty kind," Jacob agreed. "Someone tried to get me to try some when I was in Ecuador. You don't find it much outside of this latitude."

"Are any of the Tierra Roja safehouses on fruit farms?" Val asked Kat.

"You'll have to check the notes on my computer," Kat groaned, cradling his head in his hands. "I'm sorry. I don't think so." He hesitated and for a moment Val thought he was about to puke again, but then his face lit up. "Although one location did share an address with an essential oil distillery."

It was something, but it wasn't enough. Not enough to justify leaving Ana or Jorge short-handed while she went winging off after a whim and a hope, reckless for revenge.

*"We are but one,"* Reginleif agreed. *"The time will come to hunt down the eagle, but that time is not now."*

Slowly, painfully, Val released the tight knot of fury that had coiled round her heart the instant she'd heard Ana's panicked scream echoing through the jungle.

"I'll go after him."

Val blinked. A fresh spray of saltwater sloshed across the back of the boat, and Kat slumped to the wet deck with a groan.

"I'll go to the safehouse," Jacob repeated. "If we're ever going to strike at El Águila, now is the time. His attention is on Jorge and Cascobel. He just sent an assassin to Isla de las Flores. He's trying to keep us all scrambling on defense. The last thing he expects right now is for someone to strike back."

Kat laughed shrilly, clutching his head. "Mad as a couple of hatters! Oh God, it's not just Miss Daisy, is it? You're *both* crazy. And here we thought Pinkerton and I would be the calming influence…" The boat rocked and he cut off with a *hurk*.

"Jacob?" Val reached forward, taking her partner by the arm. His flesh was hot, his muscles flexing as he glared down at the waters. "You're not serious, are you?"

He scratched at his temple, rustling the gauze taped across his skull wound. He cast Val as serious a look as she had ever seen on the man's face.

"When we make land, Ricardo is going to rent a private tour van and take the whole Vargas household on a little road trip." He spoke in a low growl, forcing Val to lean in close to catch his words. "Kat will stay with them. You catch the plane to Toluca and escort Jorge and Cascobel into the city. You can do that, right?"

"With our eyes closed," Val answered, too startled to do anything but speak the bald truth. At its core, her mission was to keep the senator alive. If El Águila sent an entire gangster army after Jorge, she could simply pick the poor man up and fly him to safety. He'd complain after he got over the shock, of course, but at least he'd be alive to do it.

"Then do it," Jacob told her serenely. "I'll go after El Águila while he's looking the other way. I owe him for the chunk he took out of my ear."

"But you're talking about storming an entire cartel safe-house *by yourself*." Val glanced at Kat, but the other man was too wrapped up in his misery to hear anything they had to say. "*You* can't afford to be as reckless as I am," she hissed. "*You're* still bleeding."

She expected Jacob to draw himself up, offended. She expected him to get angry, or perhaps resentful. It was a matter of time before they came to this sort of impasse, she supposed. He was a combat veteran, a decorated professional, and a dangerous man. He was big and beefy and as empathetic as he could be, and he was accustomed to calling the shots. Sooner or later, he was going to rankle at the implication that he wasn't as tough as the woman he'd trained. Any man with his background would. Certainly Val's brothers and father would.

Once again he surprised her by reaching into his pocket

and pulling out one of the ammo cases she'd pulled off the assassin's dead body. He flipped the lid, showing her the long, slender rounds all laying in a row.

"I'm not looking to make a scene. I'm just going to get in close, shoot the son of a bitch, and run like hell."

# CHAPTER SIXTEEN

**Outside of Alpha Travel Rentals**
**Campeche City, Mexico**
**Boxing Day morning**

The fifteen-person travel van had been painted by a jungle-mad graffiti artist on LSD, but it would get the job done.

"Gabriel will meet us at a provincial airport outside of Cancun this evening." Sofia pulled her shawl tighter around her shoulders as Ricardo, Izzy, and the groundskeeper tossed the household's luggage into the rental van's cargo compartment. "With a plane big enough to fly all of us across the country if need be. We'll spend the day on the move."

The morning was chilly and wet, and the Alpha Travel parking lot was empty save for a couple of brightly painted minivans available for hire. Jacob had already taken the company's ordinary-looking Wrangler and set out to the west, leaving Val alone to see that Kat and the Vargas household got safely on the road. Val didn't ask Sofia for the details of their travel plans. Professional, well-equipped assassins were out and about. The fewer people who knew their movement, the safer the household would be.

"Kat's a smart guy." Val gave Sofia a smile that was meant to be reassuring. At that moment, VALKYRIE's tech guru was noisily relieving the last of his seasickness in the Porta-John beside the rental center. "He'll keep you ahead of any more trouble and Ricardo and Izzy can handle any that manages to find you anyway."

A few yards off, Estrella, the younger of the two maids, was trying to put a bold spin on the day's events. "It's an adventure," she told Ana as the two of them helped Abuelita up the steps and into the van. "It will be your very first road trip, niña!"

Ana shrugged the woman's false cheer aside and sidled up to where Val and her mother were going over final arrangements.

"There won't be any cabs running at this time on a holiday," Sofia informed Val. "Your best bet would be to call an Uber to take you to the charter center."

"How far is it?"

Sofia looked over her shoulder and pointed down one of the broad streets of Campeche's tourist sector. At this time of morning, it was deserted. "About five kilometers up the highway, on the left down a dirt road. There will be big signs shaped like bush planes. I called Manuela. She's been flying tourists over these jungles and seas for decades. She'll get you to Toluca as soon as you arrive."

Val figured that she and Reginleif could run a 5k in about as much time as it would take a rideshare or taxi to show up. Besides, they had some anger issues to work out and right now the pavement was the only thing around she could pound.

She bid Sofia farewell and good luck, but over the last twenty-four hours, relations with the woman had soured. Val didn't take it personally. Nearly losing your daughter and being forced from your home in the small hours of the morning would do that to a person.

No, it was Ana she was worried about. The dark-eyed girl was waiting patiently and silently, beside her mother. Val was about to step away when Ana snatched her hand in a shockingly powerful grip. In the blink of an eye, Ana twitched her wrist, wiggling something off her arm and down onto Val's. It was a hemp and wire bracelet dotted with tiny glittering seashells.

"You'll come back after." Ana stared into Val's face, holding her fingers tightly. "To visit. Mama will pay for the flight if you don't have the money. But you *will* come to visit."

Val wondered how Sofia felt about the invitation.

"*Save her husband and her family and she shall certainly show her gratitude,*" Reginleif suggested dryly.

"I'll come to visit," Val agreed solemnly. "And you'll remember to text." She had given Ana her personal cell number on the ride over. She supposed she'd have to figure out if SMS worked the same internationally. She glanced down at the bracelet, with its tight, even knots and the bits of shell woven masterfully into the fiber. Ana had a knack for jewelry making.

"I'm sorry I don't have a Christmas present for you,

too," Val admitted, but Ana shook her head and threw her arms around Val in a brief and frantic hug.

"Just go save Papa," Ana whispered. "That will be good enough."

**On a two-lane highway**
**Oaxaca, Mexico**
**Boxing Day, late morning**

Where music was concerned, Jacob Pinkerton was a sucker for the classics. Credence and Led Zeppelin, Styx, and Guns N' Roses. A little bit of KISS if he was feeling feisty.

He pulled up none of those golden oldies as he drove his rented Jeep out of Campeche city. In the last few minutes of decent cell service before the jungle swallowed him whole, he downloaded an older album from a little-known European industrial neo-synth artist called BLD.

For the next two hours, he raced through the heart of the Mexican rain forest with nothing for company but ethereal, macerated, wordless vocals and snare drums slamming to match the beat of his pulse. He hadn't heard this album in almost seven years, and back then, after that ugly, long-ago job was finished, he had promised himself he would never listen to it again.

But there was this thing called *state-dependent memory*, and on this overcast morning he found himself in need of a particular state. A violent, inhuman, needle-sharp state that was above all else, controlled.

He'd been a Marine, once. For a while, he had been in special forces, on a career track to successful anonymity.

Because you don't make a name for yourself doing the kind of work the special forces needed done. You make a modest paycheck. You make regular appointments with your military therapist, the one with all the high clearances. You make up lies to tell your family, your parents, your fiancée about where you'd been and what you'd done and what nightmares kept you up in the small hours of the morning. You make a black place in your heart and fill it with reckless noise and you hide it behind a big steel door. And you never, ever open that door.

A line existed somewhere between *unsung hero* and *dead-eyed killing machine.* Jacob didn't know exactly where that line was, but he knew he had flirted with it when he was in the Marines, a cog in the great military-industrial machine. At Viking, he had watched a few less cautious— or more bloodthirsty—agents fall over that line, but he had never taken that fatal step himself. Yes, sometimes the work got messy, but as a Viking, he had a freedom denied to a Marine: the freedom to refuse a job. The freedom to tell his bosses when the job itself was bullshit, and anyone who took it would cross that hazy but oh-so-vital line. A Marine didn't have that discretion. A Marine had orders and regrets.

His fingers tapped against the steering wheel, moving with the beat of the music. He hummed wordlessly with the vocalist. He looked within, found the door he had shut when he'd become a Viking, and pulled it open.

---

In the military, call signs and nicknames were never as sexy as the movies made them out to be. There were no *Mavericks* or *T-Bones,* no *Sinbads* or *Merlins*, and a guy earned the moniker of *Zephyr* by virtue of his fabled flatulence.

They'd called him JJ, or Jacob Junior. Junior, because he was the largest member of the squad by three inches and twenty pounds, and that was what passed for a joke in the Marines. Once upon a time, it *had* been funny, though there were times when Jacob could not remember ever having laughed.

Venezuela had been in the middle of one of its regularly scheduled collapses. The common folk had grown tired of watching the rich and powerful grow richer and more powerful while they struggled to put beans on the table. The population went on strike, the bolivar collapsed, and the riots began. At the heart of it all was old Uncle Sam with his eye on the prize: the pipeline connecting the country's oil-rich waters to the refining plants in Texas.

This had been before the current round of sanctions and high-minded moralizing, back in the halcyon days of American interventionism. With one hand, the land of the free called for peace talks and brokered endless deals between the standing government and the rebel factions. With the other, it sent people like JJ Pinkerton to put a swift and certain end to every anarchist or socialist bastard who threatened its interests in the region.

Most of them *were* bastards. Opportunistic sons of bitches apt to raid and rape their way through little villages in the name of *revolucion!* who paused now and then to blow up a pipeline for street cred. Got to keep up appearances, after all. Got to look tough.

There had been times—not many, but probably enough to make his future negotiations with Saint Peter awkward —when Jacob enjoyed hunting down those targets and leaving their corpses to rot in the middle of that wretched jungle. He'd let himself become the deadly arm of the machine, and he had enjoyed it. He was good at it.

Give Junior a knife and a gun and let him get to work. Let not your heart be troubled.

It was a little before noon on the day after Christmas, and JJ Pinkerton was driving alone through the jungle once more. His pulse beat with raucous music and the four under-regulated, high-octane energy drinks he'd shotgunned on his way out of Campeche. He cranked up the volume until his head throbbed from more than the residual pain of the gunshot wound. The tip of his left ear was missing and would never grow back. The GPS mounted to the dashboard led him ever onward, into the heart of Oaxaca state. Trees pressed in close to the crumbling stretch of road, wet and verdant in the gray light of day.

Propped in the seat beside Jacob was a beautiful, fully-loaded Barrett M95 sniper rifle.

**On a private airstrip**
**Outside of Toluca, Mexico**
**Boxing Day, noon**

Toluca was near the heart of central Mexico, where mountains rose high and dry above valleys of dense vegetation. The airstrip where Jorge's team was to receive Cascobel was splashed across a hillside above the tree line, huddled close to the low-lying clouds blanketing the countryside.

Turbulence bucked Manuela's ancient de Havilland Beaver up and down and all around as the old bush pilot came in for a landing.

"*Norori,*" Reginleif growled as the cabin rattled around them. "*He vexes us still.*"

Val pressed her eyes shut, wondering if she was going to have to grab the pilot, tear free of the cabin, and bring them to a safe landing herself. Even her strong stomach was threatening to rebel under this stress. "Is this a real thing?" she demanded of Reginleif. "Like, do I need to summon up your old rival through some kind of crystal ball and hash out your differences?"

She never could quite tell which of Reginleif's superstitions were born of personal experience and which were as fantastical to her as bedtime tales of talking dogs and moving castles were to Val.

Before Reginleif could offer further clarification, the plane broke through a final cloud bank and touched down on the edge of a long dirt landing strip. Manuela, who had not so much as broken a sweat through the turbulence, grunted and wrestled with the yoke as the Beaver bounced its way to a halt beside the long steel warehouse that functioned as an airplane hangar. Down the slope, two black SUVs and an armored truck lurked near the tree line.

Beyond that, on the other side of a chain-link fence as

insubstantial and reassuring as a cobweb, was a flock of journalists and news vans.

"Son of a bitch," Val grumbled. So much for getting Cascobel out of here *under the radar.*

Val thanked Manuela for the unscheduled and highly unusual charter, snatched her gear bag from the back seat, and helped herself out of the plane before the engine had gone silent. They had touched ground not a moment too soon. As Val jogged her way down the slope to Jorge's little convoy, a small cargo plane broke its way through the low cloud cover and touched ground on the airstrip's other runway. The star-and-eagle crest of the US Marshals was painted across its tail. On the other side of the distant fence, the paparazzi raised their cameras and came to life, vying for glimpses of the famous criminal scheduled to slide out of that big metal bird.

Val sucked in a few steadying breaths. She was prepared for them this time. If she had to swim through that sea of flashing lights, they would not get the better of her.

Mateo Alvarez and Jorge Vargas stood beside the armored truck, deep in conversation with a brawny man with an AK held at the low ready. Jorge turned red-rimmed eyes on Val as she approached.

"Where is your partner?"

The coldness in his words left Val taken aback. Gone was the youthful, handsome man. Here was a bedraggled, worry-worn victim of too many sleepless nights. There was no hiding the resentful disappointment plastered across his exhausted face. He was drowning and had been counting on two security specialists coming out of that Beaver to buoy his scant forces, not one.

"He's still recovering." It was not a lie, but it wasn't the whole truth either, and it came easily to Val's lips. "He took a *bullet to the head* yesterday." She tried not to sound reproachful. "This isn't the right place for him."

Jorge looked struck, but unsurprised, and it took all of Val's remaining patience not to add, *And I'm all the freaking 'reinforcement' we need.*

"At least that's one more person looking after Sofia," Jorge muttered.

"Yeah," Val agreed.

*"We oughtn't lie to our liege, as temporary as he might be,"* Reginleif suggested uneasily.

Val didn't have the bandwidth to handle Reginleif's peculiarly forthright sense of *duty*.

"It's a fifty-kilometer drive to the federal prison in the city." Alvarez rubbed crud from his eyes, looking from the crowd of onlookers clustered by the gate to the airstrip. "So much for a quiet operation."

Val leaned in, lowering her voice. "Do we know who blabbed?"

Jorge shook his head. "We'll add it to our list of things to investigate once we get a moment to breathe."

Up the hill, the US Marshal jet rolled to a stop and two heavily armed men pushed a rolling staircase to the side of the plane.

"Alvarez and I will be in the lead car," Jorge told Val. "We want you in the trailing vehicle with two of the guards."

"Can't exactly protect you from three cars away," Val observed. She glanced at Alvarez, wondering how he felt about separating the senator from his paid bodyguard.

Jorge shook his head again. "I've been getting regular updates from the Marshals. Cascobel has always been a temperamental man. Mean, like the snake from his name. But they say he's been in good spirits these last few days. Even whistling some."

"He's planning something," Val guessed. "This transport is going to be his last chance to pull it off."

"If he escapes and starts to rebuild Tierra Roja, we will be in a worse position than when we started this war," Jorge agreed grimly. "Nothing will stop them from sending more assassins after me and my family. We'll be hunted for the rest of our lives."

Even the overly cautious Alvarez seemed resigned to this truth. "The best way to ensure Jorge's safety is to get that *puto* into custody."

Val adjusted the strap of her go-bag and studied the SUV in line behind the armored truck. She wondered if the two weather-worn *Policia Federale* keeping the front seats warm were on Tierra Roja's payroll. She supposed she was about to find out.

"Copy that," she told her employer. "Let's rock and roll. I'll see you in Mexico City."

# CHAPTER SEVENTEEN

**In the jungle**
**Oaxaca, Mexico**
**Boxing Day, noon**

The music stopped when Jacob pulled the Jeep into a thicket off the side of the highway and set out through the jungle on foot, but there was still plenty of noise in his head. It was the crack of the shot that had ripped off the tip of his ear and come within an inch of braining him. It was the wordless industrial beat. It was the hum of the insects and the buzz of his blood through his veins.

He pushed his way through the unrelenting trees, climbing over piles of treacherous roots and dropping to his belly to crawl beneath a tangle of thorn-covered vines. The air pressed in close, heavy with moisture and the fragrance of the forest. Sweat beaded off every inch of him and by the time he'd made it almost a mile into the trees, he was soaked and panting. When the gnats swarmed him, nipping bloody holes in his brows and ears, he smeared himself with mud. The old habits, the old tips and tricks of jungle warfare, came back easily.

He had abandoned the Jeep on the edge of a road that, according to his satellite phone and Kat's intel, ran parallel to the Tierra Roja compound at a distance of about five miles. When you were bushwhacking your way through underbrush like this, five miles might as well have been ten miles, but it was Jacob's best shot at approaching the compound from an unguarded angle. Besides, the further he pressed into the forest, the less he was Jacob and the more he became JJ, who was all too at home in the dirt. When the wind shifted, it washed him in the heavy scent of overripe fruit from the lulo and mango grove that supplied the oil distillery with its raw materials.

He came across the first fence a little before noon. It was a pathetic affair, three strings of barbed wire separating the wild spaces from the edge of the fruit farm. He stepped over it carefully, scanning the trees for any signs of game or security cameras. He found none. Those would likely be posted around the coca plants that were no doubt hidden among the mango trees.

The land sloped down to the west. There might be a few scattered outbuildings around the edge of this sheltered valley, but the main compound was almost certainly down in the bowl, where there would be a creek or river to serve as an emergency water supply. Shouldering his pack, Jacob slipped through the grove toward the central compound.

He would not call this sloppy forest of half-tamed fruit trees cultivated, but at least the day laborers had cleared away the worst of the underbrush, and the biggest hazards he had to navigate were the occasional piles of discarded, rotting fruit and the fly swarms that held vigil on them. Twice he thought he caught movement through the trees and changed his course, giving himself a wide berth around whatever other creatures shared the grove with him, be they man or javelina or jaguar.

He was less than sixty feet from the whitewashed compound wall before he saw the first human. He was a withered old man standing beneath a heavy bough, plucking the lulo with a long harvesting stick and dropping the fruit into the basket at his feet. Behind the old gardener, the door leading into the compound hung open. Jacob watched from a safe distance, contemplating his options. The air reeked of perfume and the sour tang of diesel. This place was a distillery indeed, and judging from the patches of coca plants he'd passed in the grove, he had no doubt it was the Tierra Roja safe house Kat had promised.

JJ Pinkerton probably would not have killed the old man standing between him and the compound door. But he wouldn't have hesitated to beat him over the head, knock him out, and dump his still-breathing body somewhere out of the way. Jacob, the man he was now, likely would have done the same if the old man were wearing a gun or if any gang tattoos decorated his leathery skin.

Instinct said the gardener was just an old dude looking to put food on the table, so Jacob lingered in the shadows and waited. When the old man's basket was heavy with fruit, he hauled it up onto his shoulder and carried it into the compound. The weathered wooden door flipped shut as the man kicked it behind him.

Still scanning the trees for cameras, Jacob slipped his pistol from its holster and jogged forward. He pressed his back to the wall and studied his surroundings.

The outer compound wall was twelve feet high and topped with barbed wire. None of the residents had been gracious enough to leave a ladder laying around the orchard, so Jacob slipped his way to the only door on this face of the wall and tested the knob. It twisted under his fingertips. The old gardener hadn't bothered to lock it behind him.

Jacob pressed his ear to the door and heard nothing. Holding his breath, he pushed the door open a crack. The space beyond was a muddy inner courtyard ringed by several maintenance sheds, one mid-sized steel warehouse that Jacob presumed housed the still, and a two-story adobe manse.

He stood in that cracked door for an eternity, watching the buildings. He caught a few glimpses of movement through the darkened mouth of the warehouse's freight door where the old gardener and some younger assistant fiddled with the machines. The windows on the second floor of the manse were reflective, but if he squinted, he could make out occasional movement in what he took to be an office.

Only two things indicated that this compound was El Águila's main safe house. The first was the utter lack of personnel in the distillery. The holiday was over, after all, and cartels like Tierra Roja didn't gain their fierce reputation by taking extended vacations. No, given the number of coca plants Jacob had counted out in the forest he would have expected dozens of armed guards patrolling this compound. If they weren't here, they were somewhere else, perhaps on the highway preparing to ambush Senator Vargas' convoy and free their dear leader.

The second hint that this was a cartel hideout was the hundreds of six-foot-tall gang signs, emblems, and mottos painted across the interior courtyard wall. Some up-and-coming graffiti artist had gone nuts, covering every inch of the surface in an epic mural of armed gangsters in a shootout with police, led by a ferocious screaming eagle and a hissing rattlesnake.

Jacob angled himself in the cracked doorway, slipped his phone from his pocket, and snapped a picture of the mural. Val would get a kick out of it.

He put his phone away and pulled a few small matte-black canisters from his belt. When the two men working the still had their backs turned, he darted across the court-yard to the base of the exterior staircase that led to the roof of the warehouse, pausing along the way to deposit one canister on the lip of an old rain barrel, one on the padded lounge inside the cabana, and the last one beside the manse's back patio door.

The stairs could get tricky. Jacob was a big guy, and he hadn't worn his moccasins out on this mission. The stair-case was made out of metal grates and rusty old nails. Rather than stomp up the flight with all the subtlety of a wild bull, he crouched and leapt to grab the rungs of the second-floor landing. He gasped and heaved, pulling himself up the metal struts hand over fist until he reached the edge of the warehouse roof. The climb left his deltoids screaming in rebellion, but it was quieter than trying to get up those rickety stairs.

He crouched below the gentle slope of the roofline, peering over the edge. From here he could see the front of the compound, where six cars were parked between the manse's front door and the wide security gate. Each of them was easily as valuable as the whole compound itself, and as immaculately clean as the courtyard was filthy. He noticed movement beside the gate and ducked, but the gate guard was lounging by the hedge, picking his teeth.

Jacob held his breath. He could camp out on the southern side of this roof for the next six hours, so long as nobody happened to stroll through the edge of the orchard and look up, but he wanted to do that as much as he wanted another bullet to the head. He chewed his lip, considering the layout of buildings and pathways beneath him. Down in the front courtyard, the manse's main double doors swung open and a babble of male voices spilled into the wet, fragrant air. Jacob cocked his head, picking meaning from the sea of Spanish. As best he could tell, the men were planning a party.

*"Hey, when you pass through town, remember to get that ham that Cascobel loves so much,"* one man suggested and laughed. *"Bet they don't get much of that in American prisons!"*

*"Yeah, and as long as you're going into town, pick up a carton of cigs for me, right? None of that filtered shit!"* came another younger, excitable voice.

*"Ah, shut your whore mouth, Nacho. You'll take the filters or you'll go explain to mama why you've got lung cancer at the age of thirty-two, you hear?"*

*"That's enough."*

The last voice was sharp and deep and brought a blanket of silence down on the courtyard. Jacob risked another glance over the roof. A gaggle of young men loitered between the cars, and at their center stood a tall, broad-shouldered figure wearing an immaculate tan suit. *"If any of you were worth the jizz in your mothers' mouths you'd be down on the highway with the others. This party isn't for you, niños. You better remember that."* He looked around the group, shaming the men into silence with a glare. He had, Jacob would admit, an epic beak of a schnoz.

It seemed that all the yammering mice shut their traps when El Águila had something to say.

## On a two-lane highway
## Outside of Toluca, Mexico
## Boxing Day, noon

Three vehicles wove their way across the hills and valleys of central Mexico. The first was a sleek sedan with black-tinted windows and an array of antennae worthy of any police cruiser. The second was an unmarked armored box truck, the sort one might find parked in front of the local grocery store on any given Friday morning. The final vehicle in the line was a bulky SUV branded with the star insignia of the Mexican federal police.

Four additional police cruisers had departed the private Toluca airstrip that morning, but they had split up and were riding far ahead of and behind the main convoy, running a mobile roadblock to prevent any overeager journalists, or worse, from interfering with this transport operation.

The two-lane road was utterly empty. This should have

made Val feel better, but it did not. When the procession dipped into a wooded valley, the trees pressed in all around them, cutting them off from the rest of the world and bringing her horizons down to a narrow swath of dense foliage that could be hiding just about any nasty surprise. At least up on the hilltops she could see the sky and the distant cruisers running ahead of the convoy. Down in the valleys they were all alone in the world.

Val rode alone in the back seat of the rear SUV. The two federal officers were in the front, one behind the wheel and the other trading constant updates with Jorge's car on his two-way radio. She had tried to make small talk, asking them how long they'd been on the force and what kinds of guns they were packing, but from the moment Alvarez had left her in their company these two men had ignored the young American woman in the back of the car. She tried not to take it personally. She suspected they didn't speak much English, anyway.

She should have grabbed her phone and done a quick check-in with Kat. Made sure the Vargas household hadn't encountered any more assassins or murderous hitchhikers or gun-toting gangsters on their road trip through the Yucatan Peninsula. She had promised Jorge that at least two members of her team were looking after Ana and Sofia, and Jacob probably had his hands full.

She couldn't bring herself to reach into her bag for her phone. The flat metal square of the armored truck filled the SUV's windshield, giving Val a clear view of the galvanized steel and the layers of locks and bolts holding the cargo door shut. Four more armed Mexican federales were behind that door, guarding one handcuffed man in an orange jumpsuit. Deep in this valley, the convoy was isolated. Set apart from the rest of the world. Vulnerable.

She expected the door of that armored truck to come flying open. She expected some of the federal agents to turn coat, take Cascobel's bribes, bust him free of the box, and come out with guns blazing. She expected gangsters with machine guns to come spilling out of the trees, using hand grenades and nail strips to bring the convoy to an unscheduled and permanent stop.

She did not expect the trees themselves to topple over and come crashing down on the convoy like massive wooden fists punching holes through flimsy aluminum cans.

# CHAPTER EIGHTEEN

**The Lulo Distillery**
**Tierra Roja safehouse**
**Oaxaca, Mexico**
**Boxing Day, noon**

Jacob slung the case off his back and went about the busy work of assembling a sniper rifle. Down in the front yard, El Águila was barking orders and abuses at his young minions, who took the browbeating with their heads hung and eyes downcast.

*It's a wonder he even wants to break his uncle out of prison at all,* Jacob mused as he double-checked the scope. *He certainly seems to enjoy giving orders.*

That was the problem with all of these South American outlaws, JJ Pinkerton would have said. They'll set the world on fire if it means saving face to their family or underlings. If he wants to maintain cred and rebuild his game, El Águila has to at least try to bust old uncle Rattlesnake out of the can. It's the whole culture of machismo gone rabid. And there's only one thing to do with a rabid dog.

Jacob shook his head. He was no longer the steel-eyed, self-righteous man who would assassinate a revolutionary terrorist in front of his family and leave his young children clutching their daddy's bullet-riddled chest. He wasn't sure what he was, but he knew he was better than that.

He was more grateful than he could say that El Águila didn't have any kids.

His ears perked at the sound of car engines roaring to life. He turned, peering over the roof to see most of the young gangsters cruising through the compound's security gate in their brightly colored Corvettes and souped-up Mustangs. He made no move as the dust settled in the front yard, the automatic gate slid shut, and the cars vanished into the jungle. He hadn't come here for them.

El Águila stood on the front porch, deep in conversation with his two remaining guards—two brawny young men with Ars slung across their backs.

Jacob became suddenly, intimately aware of his own pulse. It thudded to the beat of the music he had left back in the Jeep. It was full of noise and violence. He checked the position of the sun. It was about dead overhead and hiding behind a thick layer of yellowish clouds.

El Águila's back was to him. Nothing stood between Jacob and that man's fine black hair but eighty yards. A cakewalk.

Except the two guards were facing their boss, which meant the distillery roof was plainly within their line of sight. Jacob could do nothing but crouch and wait and hope, the way a crocodile hopes the antelope will lean down for a cool drink of water.

The next few seconds passed like agony. The day was cool but it felt as if the muted sun were trying to steam Jacob alive in his sweat-soaked clothes. His head pounded. He bit his tongue, clawing back a scream. *Move, you sons of bitches, you kid-stealing animals, you desperate, greedy, pathetic motherfuckers. Move!*

He wasn't here because El Águila had sent a man who shot him in the head. He wasn't here because part of his ear, his body, was gone and would never come back. He wasn't here because a hard-eyed colonel had sent him out to *take care of* a troublesome jungle rebel.

He was here to kill the man who had sent an assassin after a little girl and her harmless charity-dame mother.

When the two guards finally turned away to carry out some order of El Águila's, Jacob nearly exploded. Confident that a reflection off the rifle's lens cap wouldn't give him away, he twisted onto his belly and slid the barrel of the M95 over the roof ridge. He felt the seconds slipping away. He should have had his gun in place long before the targets were beginning to leave the area. Now he had to peer through the scope and take the lay of the yard in the span of a breath. His targeting was slow. Now El Águila was walking away, vanishing beneath the patio awning.

Jacob found the patio in his scope and placed El Águila's fine black combover right at the center of the hairline cross. He squeezed the trigger.

There hadn't been time to put in earplugs, either, and the snap and recoil of the gun left spots floating in his eyes and his ears full of a static hum. Gasping for breath he drew back, whipping the rifle back over the ridgeline. Down below, the two cartel guards turned to find their leader had succumbed to a sudden and acute case of lead poisoning. Jacob had no time to double-check his work. Through the scope, he had seen El Águila collapse, seen the dark liquid spraying out of him. It was good enough. It would have to be.

Feverishly, as if trapped in something half a dream and half a nightmare, Jacob leveled the sniper rifle once more, aiming it down into the backyard. Instinct and tortuous, thorough training courtesy of the USMC took over. With the angry shouts of the guards in his ears—*Call Tulio! Call Raul! It came from the west! Move!*—Jacob peered through the scope and found the water barrel and the little black device he had left on its lid. He squeezed the trigger.

The compact hand grenade detonated and the rain barrel exploded with a bone-deep rumble and a concussive blast that knocked loose bricks from the outer wall. Water and twisted bits of burning plastic rained down across the compound.

More screaming bubbled up from below, and now it was confused. Perhaps the bullet that killed El Águila had not come from the west. Perhaps it had come from the rear yard, and they were under a full attack.

"*¡Federales!*" someone screamed. "*¡Nosotros estamos bajo ataque!*"

Jacob smiled. You bet your ass the place was under attack.

He found the grenade peeking out from beneath the distant cabana and poof, just like that, the entire canvas tent lifted off the ground and flapped its burning wings through the air, falling toward the manse like an enraged phoenix. By now, the day laborers had spilled out of the oil distillery and were darting across the compound in a frenzy of panic and confusion. The guards, bless their hearts, were doing their damnedest to maintain order and rally a counteroffensive, but their charismatic leader had a hole in his cerebellum and some things were not meant to be.

Jacob sighted the last of his planted explosives. *Ants, say goodbye to your hill.*

When he squeezed the trigger this time, he blew a hole in the back of the manse big enough to drive a truck through.

He did not have time to pause and revel in the chaos that followed the final blast. Because of his careful placement of the bombs, he was confident that collateral injuries were minimal, but once the remaining guards got their heads screwed on straight and figured out they'd been lured by three big ol' distractions, they were going to be pissed.

Jacob set the rifle down. It was a lovely piece of machinery, but he didn't have the time to take it apart and it would slow down his retreat. Leaving the Barrett behind, he crawled to the edge of the roof and peered into the sheltered side yard between the warehouse and the compound wall. He had planned to sneak across the front yard and finagle his way through the gate. Such things were rarely locked from the inside. When he saw a filthy tarp sloppily tossed across an upturned wheelbarrow and the stepladder propped on its side against the warehouse, he had a better idea.

He crouched and dropped, dangling by his fingertips for a moment before falling the last six feet to the ground. Something darted in the corner of his vision and he drew in a sharp breath, pressing himself flat against the warehouse wall. In the backyard, one young day laborer had run to grab a water hose from the big rain cistern. Distantly, Jacob heard alarmed shouts of "*¡Incendio!*"

The panicking young man grabbed the hose and vanished once more without glancing in Jacob's direction.

When the coast was clear, Jacob shoved aside the random, rusted garden rakes and shovels propped against the wall until he could pull the rickety old stepladder free from its prison.

By now, the stench of smoke and burning rubber had joined with the ever-present aroma of lulo oil. If the guards had the sense God gave a boa constrictor, they'd be sweeping this sector of the compound any second now. He could almost smell them getting closer.

He propped the ladder against the compound wall and gathered the filthy tarp up in his fists, yanking it free from the wheelbarrow. It was ancient, musty, and crusted with mildew. It nearly dissolved in his fingertips, but it would get the job done. It would have to, because now he saw movement in the corner of his eye. One man with a machine gun, slowly sweeping the back face of the distillery.

Jacob scrambled up the ladder and heaved, throwing the tarp up and over the lines of barbed wire topping the compound wall. Had anyone noticed all of that flapping fabric? Turning around to check would be pointless. If they hadn't, he was in the clear. If they had, he was probably dead.

The half-rotted rungs of the old stepladder cracked and collapsed beneath Jacob's weight. He used the last of his leverage to jump before it could send him tumbling back to the earth. His arms snagged around the tangle of tarp and wire and brick. He kicked his legs, scrambling over the wall and flinging himself into the boughs of the mango tree growing against the compound. The branches left him with some nice bruises, and the oil of the mango tree bark would leave his skin tingling for days, but it was better than an uncontrolled drop twelve feet onto uneven ground.

Jacob glanced over his shoulder, saw that the guards had not yet turned their attention to the secluded little side yard, and stretched out his arm. He snagged the edge of the tarp in his fist and dropped out of the tree.

# CHAPTER NINETEEN

**In the back of the trailing SUV**
**On a two-lane highway**
**Outside of Toluca, Mexico**
**Boxing Day, noon**

It happened so quickly that Val did not have time to cover her face. The windshield exploded, filling the air with a rain of broken glass. The roof of the SUV collapsed inward and laid Val flat on her back, crushing her into the back seat. Her vision blurred. The wind was sucked from her lungs. Flying glass and snapped twigs stabbed at her exposed skin as the great sweetgum tree groaned and pressed downward. Something slender and hard pressed against her hips, heavy enough to cut off circulation to her feet.

Terror gripped Val by the throat. She was trapped. She heard screams and gunfire on the road around her. The two men in the front seat had gone silent. She could not turn her head to gauge the severity of their injuries, but in the pit of her stomach, she knew they were both dead.

She was dying, too. She could feel it. The felled tree must have weighed several thousand pounds, and all of that weight was pinning her in place, with broken limbs stabbed through her shoulder and belly. The bunker. It was just like the McCormack army bunker. She was helpless to do anything but lie here and let the world happen to her.

She gulped at the air, but every breath felt shallower than the last. She couldn't feel her toes. Her muscles twisted, growing long and tough as she scrabbled for Reginleif's strength, but all the strength in the world would be worthless if she couldn't get any leverage—

"*Breathe!*" Reginleif's command cut through the cloud of panic. Val gasped.

"*Hands first,*" Reginleif insisted, urgent now. "*Move thy hands. See? Thy left hand. It is free. It is all you need.*"

She was right. Val's left arm was down by the wheel well, bleeding and bruised and snug beneath the crushed driver's seat, but she could move it.

Val closed her eyes and let the talons sprout from her fingertips. She pushed all the sounds from her head. The cries of battle, the blast of gunfire, the screaming metal and buzzing motors and—gods, was that a *blowtorch* roar?—all slipped away, draining from the front of her mind.

Where there had been mindless panic and the memory of flickering candles, there was now room for Valkyrie.

**In the senator's car**
**On a two-lane highway**

**Outside of Toluca, Mexico**
**Boxing Day, noon**

Mateo Alvarez was on a call with that harpy from the news station when Tierra Roja sprang its final trap. When he saw the first tree come crashing down from the forest lining either side of the road, his initial thought was that this was one more stroke of bad luck on an already unlucky day.

The broad trunk of the rubber tree crashed across the highway not ten meters from the nose of the car and the driver screamed, slamming on the brakes. Tires wailed and rubber burned, and Mateo's next thought was, *We're going to get crushed between a fallen tree and an armored truck.*

Then the second tree collapsed out of the forest and crushed the nose of the car with enough force to bend the frame and lift the back wheels off the ground. The airbag exploded in the driver's face, knocking the man instantly unconscious. Mateo's phone flew out of his hand to be lost somewhere in the chaos. He twisted, looking over his shoulder to see an entire line of trees dropping out of the forest behind them, bringing down a rain of leaves and twigs. A great oak tree hit the body of the armored truck dead-center, but its reinforced steel barely dented beneath the blow. The trunk bounced, rolling off the side of the truck, and Mateo saw the smooth white circle of its precisely severed base.

Mateo wondered how long Tierra Roja's men had been down here in this valley, carefully selecting each trap tree and making the penultimate cuts into their thick trunks.

He grabbed Jorge by the shoulders and shoved, pressing

the other man's face roughly into the car seat as the first gangster stepped out of the freshly trimmed tree line. A red bandanna was wrapped around his face. He let out a deep *whoop* of joy and brandished a mid-sized electric chainsaw in one hand. In his other hand he gripped an automatic pistol, which he aimed at Jorge's ruined black car.

Mateo flung himself down in the well beside Jorge as the windows exploded in a hail of bullets and gunfire.

"Grab the radio," Jorge screamed. "Call the other cars to us!"

With the world's most awful disco spinning around his head, Mateo reached over the center console and pawed blindly until his fingers found the radio receiver. A bullet punched through the side of the car and grazed his leg as he handed the receiver back to Jorge. Pain shot up his spine but in this moment of surreal, panicked clarity, Mateo understood that there was no point in screaming. There might be a point in braving the storm of swirling glass, reaching into the glove box, and pulling out the loaded revolver that Jorge kept on standby.

Lights and shadows flickered around the ruined cab. There would be more cartel soldiers spilling from the forest, Mateo knew. They had gambled that the tree traps would stop the escort vehicles but leave the prize of the armored truck largely unharmed. That gamble had paid off, and if Mateo knew anything about Tierra Roja, it was that Cascobel and El Águila would want Jorge taken alive. They needed to make an example of him, after all.

"You *stay here*," Mateo screamed, shoving the revolver into his boss' trembling hands. He twisted, straining long-unused muscles to the max in his attempt to stay below the line of sight as he reached for the door.

"Where are you going?" Jorge cried. He looked so young. Like the son Mateo never had. Terrified, too, but terror was the only proper reaction a sensible man could have in a situation like this.

Mateo reached into his jacket and drew the pistol the feds had issued to him at the beginning of this suicide run. It was about the size of a postcard.

"I'm going to fight back," he told his young, naive, wonderful friend with a shrug. "Never fired a gun in my life but hey, if this isn't a good time to learn then I don't know what is." Before Jorge could protest, he shoved open the door and rolled out of the car. He dropped almost a meter to the ground and landed in a sea of smoke. Smoke from gunfire, from the felling of all those trees, from burning rubber, maybe from smoke bombs lobbed by overeager gangsters. Who could say? Even crouching, Mateo could barely make out the sticks and broken glass carpeting the road beneath him. The smoke was thicker at head level, so he remained near the ground.

He saw sparks flying through the haze further down the convoy and squinted. He could make out the truck's cab and the silhouettes of the two soldiers slumped dead against the dashboard.

Light flared from behind the armored truck, casting larger-than-life shadows against the smoke. Men with cutters and welders gathered back there. They had already cleared away some of the larger tree limbs blocking their access to the cargo bay and were chewing their way through Cascobel's metal cage. If they managed to pop that can before backup arrived, they were going to find four angry, well-armed *federales* waiting for them.

Bitterly, Mateo wished them well. The guards trapped in that box with Cascobel would surely be more suited to gunfighting than he was.

He looked to the left and right. By the grace of God, he hadn't been spotted. Staying low to the ground, he crept along the edge of the road, probing the smoke for the outline of the tailing SUV. When he spotted it, his heart sank. A felled sweetgum tree had snapped the vehicle nearly in half. It was a twisted ruin. If any of the passengers had survived, they were going to need immediate medical care.

A row of felled trees blocked the road for a long way in either direction. The trailing cruisers should be catching up to them any second now and the lead cruisers should have turned to fall back, but if the security escort wanted to get within a hundred meters of this disaster they were going to have to get out of their cars and navigate the felled trees on foot. For the gangsters, it would be like shooting fish in a barrel.

In the distance, someone fired off a round and Mateo nearly jumped out of his skin, but who it was or what they were aiming at would remain a smoke-shrouded mystery. A cheer went up from the torch-cutting crew. Some of the men lifted and revved their chainsaws. The smoke burned at Mateo's eyes and scratched his lungs, but he forced himself to watch as the men scrambled backward, pulling open the back door.

*Here it comes*, Mateo thought desperately. *The counterat-*

*tack. The rain of gunfire, the angry guards with their guns busting free and taking Tierra Roja by surprise.*

There was no epic shootout, though. Deep in his gut, Mateo supposed he had known there wouldn't be. These federal guards were suitably well-paid, but at the end of the day, they were civil servants just drawing a paycheck. No amount of money was going to induce them to fight an uphill gun battle against a cartel force three times their size. Especially not when a snake rode in that box with them, whispering threats against their families and promising them not just life but a handsome payout if they put their guns down and looked the other way.

Mateo was not surprised when what emerged from the back of that truck was one skinny old man in an orange jumpsuit. One gangster sliced through the old man's manacles with his cutting torch. Cascobel raised his fists above his head in triumph and a ragged cheer went up from the gathered men.

Mateo crept closer to the gathering. He held up his pistol. The smog was thick, but that orange jumpsuit made for a nicely visible target. Backup was still a long way off, Cascobel was seconds from vanishing into the forest to rebuild his cartel and undo years of agonizing work, and, well, Mateo had lived a good life. This would be a worthy capstone to his career.

He was about to take the shot when, beside him, the frame of the crushed SUV lurched and bucked. Metal screamed and wood groaned as the massive trunk of the sweetgum tree rocked and tilted. The celebrating gangsters turned and stared, transfixed.

There was a moment of deadly silence before the crown of the sweetgum tree exploded.

**On a two-lane highway**
**Outside of Toluca, Mexico**
**Boxing Day, afternoon**

Valkyrie's wings billowed open, snapping the branches that caged her inside the SUV. Wood splinters flew in all directions, spinning off to make little trails through the noxious smoke that carpeted the road. The air was thick, but her eyes were sharp. Oh yes, they were sharp. She saw the little men with their blowtorches and their chainsaws clustered around the back of the armored truck. She saw the man in orange standing at the center of the crowd. She doubted any of them were going to get a good look at *her*.

Gasping for breath, Valkyrie emerged from the crude sunroof, lashing and flapping and slapping her way free from the ruined tangle of wood and metal. She found her footing on the dented hood and grasped the end of the branch jutting from her gut. She pulled it free and felt an immediate release of painful pressure from somewhere around her kidneys.

She brandished her bloody spear. She arched her back, spreading her wings into the smoke until she was nothing but a massive black silhouette, an inhuman monster backlit by the glow of distant police lights. She opened her jaw wide and howled like a banshee, like a skinned cat, like a demon fresh from the deepest pits of hell. Her howl shook the leaves from the trees.

About half of the men dropped their weapons and broke, sprinting into the forest with screams of terror and cries of *"Bruja!"* and *"Santa Muerte!"* The core of hardened gangsters who remained raised their guns.

Valkyrie had managed to rip one other thing free of the tangled mess that had been the police SUV. She stooped and snatched it up in her talons, then folded her wings, shrinking from a larger-than-life target to one itty-bitty dot in a sea of smoke and shadows. The first round of bullets whizzed far over her head as she dropped from the nose of the SUV and lifted the machine gun.

The second round of bullets went in every conceivable direction as she emptied her magazine into their bodies. They bounced off the road and sank into the tree trunks. They clipped the armored car and ricocheted into the wild gray yonder. One of them slipped beneath Valkyrie's horns, cutting a red trail across her cheek and clipping a ragged chunk from her earlobe.

The gangsters who had not fled from her had all been huddled in a tight cluster, and by the time her magazine ran empty, they were all lying on the ground.

Valkyrie tossed the machine gun aside and drew her pistol. She heard the wail of sirens and shouting through a megaphone, but the security guards were still far away, all the way on the other side of the tree barricades.

The air reeked of burning rubber. Her lungs itched. Her eyes watered. The sooner she could get out of this hellhole, the happier she would be. Something twitched in the corner of her vision as she stalked toward the armored truck. It was Alvarez, the little man who had worried so deeply about Jorge's safety. He was huddled in the ditch beside the road with his hands over his ears. He held an adorable little pistol.

Valkyrie discovered she liked Mateo, after all.

Reginleif roused and swelled within her as she approached the field of fallen bodies.

"*This brings back memories,*" the older one whispered. "*Of our roots. Of our calling. Oh, the battle is over, little sister. All that remains is to choose.*"

The battle was over and the enemies were down, but not all were dead. Indeed, some of them had pulled through with relatively minor wounds, limb shots, and concussions that very well might heal.

*If.*

Her shadow passed over one man in a white T-shirt now stained gray and red. He stared at her over his bandanna, and even through the smoke, despite the swath of viscera spilling out of his lower guts, she saw the hatred glittering in his eyes. She saw his fingers twitch and tighten around the hilt of his gun.

She shot him in the head.

Two others tried. They played dead and waited for her to come close before they raised their arms against her. She killed them, too.

The remaining survivors closed their eyes when she passed. Those who had the strength yet to do so turned their faces from her. She left them to survive or succumb to their wounds as the fates decreed.

She reached the man at the center of the massacre, the man in orange. He was older by far than his followers. His hair was white and thin and pulled into a long braid. His mustache drooped along the lines of his jowls. His neck was wiry and lean, splattered with fading blue prison tattoos and gang insignia.

He had taken one bullet to the thigh, and no more. He was trying to crawl to one of his fallen rescuers, perhaps to snatch his cell phone, when she crouched beside him.

He froze, his mustache twitching as he sucked at the wretched air. "*Santa Muerte. Te he rezado toda mi vida. ¿Por qué me enciendes ahora?*"

Valkyrie licked her lips.

"*We have not the tongue,*" Reginleif admitted solemnly. "*But I have heard pleas like this before, and in all languages they are the same. He wishes to know what he has done to earn our wrath.*"

"You took your name after a venomous snake," Valkyrie told the man. "You ask *me* for mercy?"

Cascobel's brown eyes flew open. "English," he whispered, fascinated. "Gringa?" The terrified reverence slipped out of his voice, replaced with a wet cunning. "It's not too late, señora. I have money. More money than you could dream of. Treasures all across the country to make pirates weep, eh? Men throw themselves in front of bullets for me, you see. So come. Help me to my feet. We'll go from here together, before the federales come. I will make you rich. You will have everything your heart desires."

Valkyrie regarded this withered husk of a human being for a long moment. "Anything my heart desires?" She spoke slowly, peeling back her lips with every word. He saw her pointed teeth, and she saw the gooseflesh that ran down his neck.

"Sí." He swallowed a lump. "Whatever it is, I can make it happen for you."

"That is true," Valkyrie agreed. She held her hands out to him. She saw the spark of hope flare on his face before he saw the talons at the ends of her fingers.

"Because what I want…" She slipped her fingers around his scrawny neck. He twitched. He shook his head, he jerked, he tried to grab at her wrist, but in the end, he was feeble mortal flesh. "…is to see you dead."

She snapped his neck.

*"And so the silence falls,"* Reginleif murmured as Valkyrie slipped away and Valerie rose to her feet. Her body ached, from head to toe. Valkyrie might be able to heal from gut stabs faster than cheese will sweat in the sun, but some part of Valerie was still human, and the aches tended to stick around for a bit.

"And the vigils for the dead will begin. Or recovery, for the fortunate wounded."

Val stared down at the corpse in the orange jumpsuit. *So much violence,* she marveled. *And so much trouble. All for this old prison janitor?*

Behind her, the shouts of the security escorts were growing louder. Overhead, a helicopter circled the scene. The wind shifted, urging the smoke from the burning tires away from this massacre.

*"There is still the choice,"* Reginleif mused as Val turned and picked her way through the rubble. She had to find Jorge. She prayed he wasn't too badly hurt.

"The choice?" Val echoed.

*"Our task of old. Left to their own devices the dead fade into Niflheim, but in the old days, it was our responsibility to send the valiant to Valhalla instead. Among his people, this man Cascobel was a respected warrior."*

"You can't be serious."

Reginleif chuckled. *"Oh, I am not suggesting we sponsor his passage into Granddad's halls. I only reminisce."*

Val grunted and approached the lead car, which had taken a good beating from the deadfall trap. The frame was bent, and the back half had lifted a few feet off the ground. She saw the exploded airbag and the unmoving driver. Her heart sank, but then Jorge Vargas poked his head up from the back seat and gave her a sheepish wave.

"You reminisce all you want," Val told her ever-present co-pilot as she picked her way over the broken glass and offered her arm to the senator. "In the end, I don't give a fuck if his soul went to Niflheim or Valhalla or Never Never Land. All that matters to me is that it's not *here* anymore."

# CHAPTER TWENTY

**Interrogation Chamber**
**Policia Federales Headquarters**
**Mexico City**
**Boxing Day evening**

It was amazing what a near-death experience could do to a person. After a brush against the old reaper, many people froze up or shut down or dissolved, waiting for some more capable adult to step into the situation and make it right. It was that burst of terror Ana had described when spilling her guts to Val about the man in the mall. In the past year alone, Val had seen dozens of otherwise competent, mature, and level-headed people collapse under the weight of shock and trauma.

Not Jorge Vargas. If late nights of endless paperwork and bureaucratic bullshit had sucked the man's soul right out of his body, it was the sound of gunfire and screaming that brought it back with a vengeance. He tore through the prison, barking orders to the guards and commanding the federal officials with a vim and vigor Val had not seen since Fiesta Navidad. It was nearly seven p.m., seven hours after the shootout, before he got around to visiting Val.

The prison officials had given her use of a small interrogation cell and left her to her own devices, which in this case meant hopping on her computer and coordinating a reunion with Kat, following up with Jacob, and trying to decide how she was going to invoice Viking for this job. Strangely enough, the internet had little to say on what to charge a client for saving his ass from a gang shootout. Val was, to her chagrin, coming to terms with the fact that she was going to have to ask Charlie for a crash course on black ops invoicing and billing standards when the door opened and Jorge stepped into the cell. His face was bright, his eyes shining with the still-lingering thrill of a job well done.

"You're good, Valerie? Got everything you need? Alvarez ordered catering. It's down in the cafeteria. Why don't you come get yourself some carnitas?"

Val cracked her back in a deep stretch and gestured to the bags of junk food and bottles of Diet Coke beside her. "I just raided the vending machine a few minutes ago, but thanks."

Jorge stepped into the cell, shutting the door behind him. His face turned sober as he looked over Val's disheveled clothes. She had tossed a spare prison guard jacket over her shirt, but it didn't hide all of the blood stains and dirt smears. "You really saved my bacon today."

"Happy to do it, Jorge. That's what you paid us for."

Jorge checked his watch. "There's going to be a press conference in forty minutes. We're going to tell the press and the public how badly these gangsters failed to rescue their leader. We're going to remind the people that there are no heroes in the cartels."

"But there might be a few of them left in the Senate?" Val asked, arching an eyebrow playfully.

Jorge preened, but only a little bit. "Alvarez has pointed out that this will look good for my re-election campaign. But I'm only one man. The guards who fought El Águila's men today, they're as much the hero as I am. You're the hero. I want you to stand at the conference with me, Val. Show all those cameras that you don't have to be a senator or a policeman to stand up to the thugs."

Val tried to imagine the sea of lights and flashes that would greet her if she stood at that podium and accepted Jorge's praise on national television. All those black camera lenses, inhuman and yet still intimate, trying to peer right into her soul.

She gave Jorge a gracious smile that she hoped reflected a regret she did not feel. "We're undercover black ops agents, Senator," she lamented. "It'll be awfully hard to find jobs in the future if you go plastering our faces on Telemundo."

Jorge gave a rueful laugh. "Sí, sí, of course. No fame for Viking, then. Just a pat on the back and my eternal gratitude."

"Well, perhaps a bit more than that." Val reached into her bag and pulled out one of the business card mockups she'd had printed back in Manassas. It was a plain white square with the letters VALKYRIE printed on one side in old-fashioned typeset font and a ten-digit phone number on the back. Not as compelling or flashy as the all-black

Viking card Charlie had given Val on their first meeting, but Val rather liked the old-fashioned look of it. "If you know anybody who could use our services, have them call my team. Technically we're contractors for Viking. We take the jobs they can't or won't handle."

Jorge studied the card with a frown. "*Valquiría*," he read. Quick as a shark palming a spare ace, he slipped the card into his jacket pocket. "I won't forget. I promise."

After a knock on the door, Jacob poked his head into the room. He was as sweaty and dirt-smeared as Val, but he had no additional wounds, at least that Val could see. "Hola. I ran into Alvarez downstairs. He said I could find you two up here."

Val pushed up from her desk and threw her arms around him in a tight but brief embrace. He smelled like sweat and citrus oil.

"How's your head?" she murmured into his beefy shoulder.

"It's, um, fine. I'm feeling better, actually." He patted her head awkwardly.

Val turned to see Jorge watching them with a sly, knowing grin plastered across his face.

She flushed.

Jorge smoothly stepped over the unprofessional PDA. "So, no to the press conference. But certainly, you will come to the party tomorrow, sí?"

"Party?" Val asked.

"I missed Christmas with my family, señorita. But for a little while now, thanks to you, all is well. We're going to a little vacation rental near Puerta Vallarta. The whole household. Ana wants to see the shells of the Pacific and I want a good holiday with my family. You'll come, of course."

Val and Jacob exchanged glances. The last few weeks had been her fill of beachside vacations, and judging from the faraway, vaguely forlorn look on her partner's face, he felt the same way.

"Thank you, Jorge," she murmured. "But the job is done for now and there is still time for us to get back home and celebrate New Year's with our families."

Jorge's eyes lit up. "Oh, no!" He threw his arms wide. His perfect English developed a distinct accent as he grew excited. "No, no, never apologize. Family is everything, señorita. But you will come visit, sí? Spring break, maybe? Fishing is best in June, you know. *Mi casa es su casa.* We may not be able to pay you as well as some of your other clients, but you'll never want for a vacation spot, I promise you that."

Val grinned. For a moment, she allowed herself to imagine a quiet week at a sun-drenched villa with Jacob, with no gunfights on the horizon. "We'll definitely take you up on that. But right now, you need to get ready for your conference and we need to pack up. When you see Ana, would you give her a hug for me? And get her into some karate classes. I never got to tell her, but she's got a mean left hook."

"Oh! You can tell her that yourself." Jacob cracked the door to the cell and waved to the people waiting in the hall. The door flew open and Ana flung herself across the room, wrapping her father in a spindly embrace. Sofia followed, and the three of them dissolved into a long and tender group hug.

Val glanced into the hallway to see Kat sitting on one of the hard plastic chairs and Izzy leaning against the wall, scrolling through her smartphone. Kat gave her a wave and a tired smile. "Flight came in just a few minutes ago." He fanned his face dramatically. "Lord have mercy, that Gabriel is a real looker, isn't he?" He glanced into the interrogation cell, spotted Jorge, and then caught Val's eye and mouthed, *"Just like his brother."*

Val shook her head and turned back to the reunited family. Ana was beaming and babbling excited Spanish to her parents like a child half her age. Val felt a delicious pang in her chest at the sight of the girl's wide-eyed joy. The last two days had been a nightmare, but her fire still burned strong.

Val went to her go-bag and dug through the disorganized mess. When she found what she was looking for she sat on the edge of the desk and waited for Ana to notice her. The excitement of the family's reunion died to a simmer, and Ana spun to snatch up Val's hand in her warm fists. "You kept Papa safe."

"It wasn't just me." Val remembered the federal agent lying in the middle of the gravel road with dozens of holes punched through his chest. She would have to find his name and pour a drink for the dead. "There were others helping us, too. And your dad is very brave," she told Ana. "Just like his daughter."

Ana's cheeks darkened with that soul-deep embarrassment that was the signature of teenage girls across the globe.

Val opened her fingers and dropped three small steel cylinders into Ana's palm. "I want you to keep these."

Ana frowned at the gift. "Bullets?"

"They're spent shell casings." Val risked a glance up. Sofia was watching with her mouth pressed into a tight line, but she did not protest. "From the fight today. You made a Christmas gift for me. You took little random things and turned them into something beautiful. I want you to keep doing that. I want you to take karate lessons and learn how to shoot a gun to protect yourself, but more than that, I want you to keep making things and exploring those old ruins. Do you hear me? Your dad is fighting to build a world with more of these—" Val indicated the bracelet around her wrist "— and less of these." She closed Ana's fingers over the shell casings. "That's the most important fight."

Ana nodded, lost in thought as she rolled the empty shells through her fingers.

Val stood, lifting her gaze to Jorge and his wife. Sofia's wore a pained expression, and Val met it without apology. Her little girl was growing up. Sofia couldn't isolate her from the world forever.

"Gabriel is at the airstrip," Sofia explained quietly. "He will take you wherever you need to go, with our gratitude. We would love to host you again in happier times."

"In happier times," Val agreed. She shouldered her bag and turned to Jacob. "What do you think, Pinky? You ready to go home and argue about what kind of business we're going to run?"

Jacob rolled his eyes. "If your heart is set on a meadery, okay. We can talk about it."

Val took his arm with a grin, wondering how much this excellent man would let her get away with.

"*Valerie.*"

Val nearly jumped out of her skin. She was used to Reginleif piping up randomly to offer insights and commentary, but she could count on one hand the number of times the old demigoddess had called Val by her full name.

Jacob saw Val jerk and straightened, suddenly alert. She waved him down with an absent frown. "What is it, Regin?" Over the last few months, she had mastered the technique of shaping words with her tongue without making sounds that would leave others wondering who the hell she was talking to.

"*I had a thought,*" offered Val's ever-present co-pilot. "*Or suspicion is perhaps a better word. For the moment, we have an airplane at our disposal. Might we make a detour before returning to your home?*"

# CHAPTER TWENTY-ONE

**Outside of Lake Carlos State Park**
**Western Minnesota**
**Early morning, December 27th**

"How exactly are we going to explain this little 'detour' to Kat?"

Val nibbled her lip and stepped over a tree that had fallen across the trail. The dirt path was crusted with ice and her breath made heavy fog in the frigid air. "Kat took an elephant-sized dose of Benadryl when we took off," she told Jacob. "With any luck, he'll sleep like the dead until we haul his ass out of the plane back in Manassas, and he'll be too hungover to wonder why we're eight hours behind schedule."

The bigger question in Val's mind was how Reginleif was going to explain this 'little detour' to her and Jacob. She had packed her bag with Mexico in mind, and while she wasn't normally bothered by the cold, one could only climb through so many snowdrifts in jeans and a light rain jacket.

Gabriel, thankfully, hadn't asked questions when Val instructed him to keep the plane going north instead of turning east when they'd hit Arkansas. He was a private charter pilot, accustomed to indulging the whims of the upper crust. Val hoped that Sofia wouldn't raise an eyebrow at the extra flight time logged on the invoice. They were flying on her dime, after all. Tapping into the secret network of private airstrips and landing sites familiar to all private pilots, Gabriel had brought them down outside the sleepy town of Alexandria in the small hours of the morning. They'd had a harder time finding a rideshare to take them to the correct trailhead.

*"That is no fault of mine."* Reginleif sniffed as Val and Jacob skittered over another patch of ice on the hiking trail.

"Yeah, that's just what we need," Val answered. "Some ambitious bird-watchers snapping a shot of this fallen angel soaring over Minnesota on this lovely clear morning."

Jacob, who was hiking the trail beside Val, cast her a curious glance.

"Regin says we should have just flown out here."

Jacob scratched the stubble on his chin. His fingers were pink and swollen from the cold, but he was not the sort to complain. "Could you really carry me that far?"

Val laughed hard enough to rattle the icicles on the trees. "She says yes, and in the same breath she insists the wings aren't magic."

Jacob gave one of his rare chuckles.

"*I do not see the joke,*" Reginleif grumbled as they reached a sharp bend where the trail turned away from the creek they'd been following for the last half-mile. Val felt a sudden spark of excitement ignite within the other woman as she recognized some subtle landmark in the forest. "*Leave the path here, Valkyrie. Dost thou see yon ash tree grown out of the headstone at the waters' edge?*"

Val squinted into the underbrush. She'd never been good at trees. Down in Mexico, you could easily tell the trees apart by the shape of their leaves and the color of their flowers and fruits. Here, though, Val saw nothing but tangles of dark branches against snow.

"*Oh, how children forget the signs of the forest!*" Reginleif lamented. She nudged forward, slipping toward the front of Val's mind. "*It is a shame. This may not be quite the land of our birth, but it is a cousin, a found home. Allow me.*"

Val consented and Reginleif seeped into her blood, creeping out of the darkest parts of her to curl into horns and meld into muscles turning long and wiry. She kept the wings tucked against their spine, at least. If Val had to hike her way back to the trailhead with a ripped jacket or shirt on top of everything else, she was going to throw a fit.

Reginleif ran her tongue over her sharpened teeth. Jacob was ogling her.

"Aye?" she asked slyly. She had a deeper voice than Val, older and richer. "Thou lookest as if thou hast never seen a trueborn Valkyrie before, Jacob."

Jacob's ears were red from the cold, and they could not have turned any redder, as much as they might want to. "It's, um, still a pretty novel experience." He forced his gaze down to his tennis shoes. "Sorry. I guess it is rude to stare."

Reginleif laughed. It was a sound that jangled against the icicles like music. "Observe all thy wish, *friðill.* I have been known to stand for paintings."

She left Jacob to fidget and leapt off the path, springing into the snowdrifts that had collected at the edges of the trees. Somewhere in the back of her mind, Val wondered if Reginleif was truly resistant to frostbite, or if she was just good at ignoring the discomfort and would leave Val to deal with the aftermath.

"Cease thy complaining," Reginleif ordered cheerfully as they waded through a waist-high thicket. Light snow shook free of the branches, crusting their skin in its cold embrace. "See? We are here already."

She reached the base of an old tree jutting up between a pair of massive river boulders. Crouching in the snow, she scooped old layers of snow aside to reveal the edges of a stone tangled in the tree's upper roots. She dug through the frozen ground with iron-hard talons. "This is an ash tree. See the pattern of grooves in the bark. Remember it. Thou knowest the story?"

"*Yggdrasil is an ash tree,*" Val recalled. "*It's what connects all the realms of the universe.*"

"Aye, though in my youth we called it Mimameidr." Reginleif heaved, ripping the stone free from the dirt and the grasping roots that had coiled around it in the eons since its placement. It weighed at least a hundred pounds. She tossed it carelessly aside. "Granddad hung himself from the great tree for nine days."

"*The stories always said he did that as a sacrifice to himself,*" mused Val, sufficiently distracted from the cold and the grime by a mythological puzzle. *"Which, um, doesn't make a lot of sense to us modern-day scholars."*

Reginleif chuckled, peering into the dark hole beneath the ash tree. "Dear Allfather always did have his eccentricities. Aha!" She turned, stretching her arm deep into the hollow and groping around the roots. Her talons closed over a box of about ten inches to each side.

The roots had grown thick and long over the years. It took some twisting and finagling to pull the box free without damaging the tree. When she stood, cradling the little box to her chest, her arms were covered in clods of dirt. She shook the frozen, half-decayed leaves from her hair and sprang back to the path where Jacob was waiting. She receded as she did so, and the woman who found her footing on the gravel was Val once more.

Jacob frowned at her as if he'd been puzzling over some deep problem. "Hey, what does *friðill* mean?"

Val stared at him. Then she laughed and took his arm with her free hand, turning him back toward the trailhead. Her fingers were numb. Her tits were numb. She was clutching a filthy, half-rotted box to her chest. "It means *lover*."

"Oh." Jacob contemplated this addition to his vocabulary in silence for a moment before shaking the fuzz from his head and peering down at Val's treasure. "Is that what we came for?"

"Regin's going to have some serious explaining to do if it's not." Val cocked her head to the side, listening for a voice only she could hear. "And she's *still* not telling me what's in it. Come on. Let's get somewhere warm and have ourselves an unboxing."

**Charter jet cabin**
**En Route to Manassas**
**Early morning, December 27th**

Val and Jacob huddled around the tiny airplane table, peering down at the ancient wooden box. They were flying into the sunrise and Kat snored gently in the seat across the aisle. Val clutched a paper cup of steaming hot coffee between her tingling fingers.

Jacob ran his hands over the faces of the box. The wood was soft and half-rotted with age, but the metal hinges holding the lid to the base held strong.

"How do you open it?" A look of puzzled concentration crossed Jacob's face as he turned the box over. There was no latch, no hook or lock, just a thin seam separating the lid from the base. He slipped his fingernails into the crack and pried but nothing gave.

"Pull harder," Val suggested.

He eyed her, suspicious. "You're cool with me maybe breaking it? Isn't this a historical artifact or something?"

Val shrugged and sipped her coffee. Gabriel stocked the best beans she'd ever encountered on an airplane. She'd have to ask what brand he used.

Jacob gripped the box in both hands and pulled until his shoulder muscles popped out against his shirt. He grunted. He huffed and heaved and strained.

Val drank her coffee.

"I give up." Jacob set the box down and rubbed his wrists. "I'd pull out a crowbar, but I don't want to wake up sleeping beauty over there." He nodded in Kat's direction.

"So it's some kind of puzzle box?" he speculated. "What's the trick?"

Val drained her cup and set it aside. She placed a palm on either side of the box. "The trick is you have to be a Valkyrie to open it. Gaze upon it and wonder, Jacob Pinkerton. According to Reginleif, this is our first encounter with honest-to-gods, bona fide *magic*."

She placed her thumbs on the lid. As Reginleif had promised, the lid sprang open beneath her lightest touch.

Jacob shifted his weight. "I loosened it up for you," he grumbled.

"That's right." Val grinned. "It's a magic pickle jar. Couldn't have done it without you, Pinky."

When Reginleif saw the two small bundles of cloth nestled inside the enchanted chest, she breathed a sigh of relief. "*Oh, thank the Allfather and the Mistress of Luck. They're still here.*"

"Did you think they wouldn't be?" Gingerly, Val picked up one of the bundles. The historian within her wailed, demanding she put on some gloves before manhandling an artifact of unknown age or origin. The ancient demigoddess of battle didn't have time for that fussing. To Reginleif, these things weren't artifacts from a bygone era. They were personal treasures.

"*They were placed beneath the tree for safekeeping long, long ago,*" Reginleif admitted. "*And I know little of my sisters' whereabouts over these last few centuries. There was always a chance that one of them might have had need of them before us.*"

Val unwrapped the bundle as delicately as if it contained a robin's egg.

The statue was about nine inches long and heavy. It

depicted a woman clutching a long scepter in both hands, sitting astride a fat and ferocious sow.

"Freya," Val breathed, holding up the idol for Jacob to see. "Goddess of fertility and divination and magic."

Jacob folded his hands, waiting, in respectful silence, to be told what he should do with this information.

"*Crafted by the blessed hand of Brokkr himself.*" Reginleif sighed. "*Or, at least, the original was.*"

Val repeated Reginleif's words in a low voice so that Jacob could participate in this conversation.

"The original?" Val frowned, turning the statue over in her hands. Silver, she supposed, though heavier than she would have expected. Perhaps it had a lead core.

"*Aye, Brokkr crafted the mold and his apprentices cast the replicas from pure electrum.*"

Val yelped and nearly dropped the statue, startled by the words that had come from her own mouth. Jacob leaned in close, casting a nervous but unnecessary glance at Kat.

"Did you say electrum?" he whispered.

Val nodded, speechless.

"Shit," Jacob breathed. His gaze fell to the second bundle in the box. "She handed us a box quite literally full of silver and gold. The electrum alone must be worth a quarter of a million on the open market."

Val couldn't believe what she was hearing. "Are you freaking *crazy?* Jacob, we are literally holding artifacts crafted by non-human entities! Sure, the Historical Association won't buy that they were made by *dwarves*, but at the very least this proves that the early Norse civilization had access to advanced smelting, alloying, and casting techniques!" She placed the Freya statue back in the box beside its companion, suddenly acutely aware of the oils on her hands. Valkyrie be damned, Historian Val would have her say.

Jacob flicked the cloth on the second statue aside to reveal a wizened old man with a staff and an eye patch. He looked remarkably similar to the pewter miniature Val had gifted Jacob a few days ago.

"Odin!" Val clapped a hand over her mouth to hold in a delighted laugh. "Oh, they're *gorgeous*. And they were placed *together*! Do you know what this means?"

Jacob stared at Val and waited for her to go on. She wiggled in her seat, doing a nerdy happy-dance she hadn't done since she'd been accepted into grad school. "Historians have been waging the Freya/Frigga debate for *centuries*. Frigga, wife of Odin. Freya, goddess of magic. Are they two separate goddesses? Or are they the same entity and the name just split due to linguistic drift? But here she is, placed right here next to Wednesday in a position of shared divinity—"

"Val."

"—and we found them in *Minnesota!*" Val's voice crept up another octave, right into the *delighted frenzy* zone. "There's been talk of a lost Viking colony in Minnesota ever since a farmer discovered some runestones in Kensington in 1898, but nobody's ever dug up solid proof of its existence. If we can authenticate these artifacts as being of Nordic origin—"

Jacob reached across the table and grabbed Val's face between his palms. Her mouth snapped shut. She gave him a goofy, punch-drunk grin. Her mouth opened again and

Reginleif spoke with Val's tongue. "I think perhaps she misunderstands the purpose of this gift. These treasure caches were always meant to support a lost sister in her time of need. Gold, silver, and electrum lose no value across the ages. And they are, after all, hardly original works."

Val yanked control of her voice back from Reginleif with a gasp of horror. "You mean for us to *sell them?*" she hissed. "These belong in a museum!"

"I'm...going to refill my coffee." Jacob grabbed his cup and pushed away from the table. The cabin was tiny, however, and his idea of an escape from Val's split-brained meltdown took him six feet away from her. He whistled quietly as he fussed with the coffee machine.

"*They were made for this cause, little sister,*" Reginleif insisted. Their argument had retreated to within the confines of Val's skull. "*Carried across the world and buried specifically to serve as emergency funds in times of need. And thou art in need of funds, aye? My memory is hazy indeed. We are fortunate I was able to recall the location of this cache, and even more fortunate that it has not been depleted in the intervening years. It was meant for us. To fund thy cause.*"

Val shook her head hard enough to rattle her brains. "Then you should have smelted solid electrum ingots. Not gorgeous and ancient works of art that the world has never seen before. And you should have known that I wouldn't be cool with melting them down and selling them off!"

Reginleif sighed. "*Child. Recall, if you will, the strange little fetish you gifted yon sleeping man this holiday past.*"

Val glanced at Kat. He was wearing his sleep mask and a

nasal strip that reduced the volume of his snores by about ten percent.

"The desktop statue of the clams playing poker?" Val was baffled. "What about it?"

"*Now look again at yon Lady Luck's sow,*" Reginleif suggested. "*And see again her scepter.*"

Val glanced down at the Freya statue. Come to think of it, that hog was absurdly fat. And that scepter in her hands had a weirdly biological look to it—

"They're gag gifts." Val's words dropped like rocks onto the table as Jacob returned to his seat. The man leaned forward, squinting at Freya's scepter.

"Oh." He grinned. "I see. It's a—"

"Which," Val cut him off sharply, "I would argue, makes them all the more novel and historically interesting."

Jacob studied Val over the rim of his coffee cup. "Are you two still arguing?"

Val's shoulders slumped. "No. At least, not for now. We'll revisit the topic in a few days."

Hopefully she could think of a better way to get her fledgling business a much-needed cash injection by then. The historian inside her wouldn't survive selling these statues off to some vaguely perverted private collector.

"I'm surprised Odin and Freya are chill with being satirized like that," she grumbled.

"*Satirized?*" Reginleif asked. "*Why do you choose that word? Even the gods think cocks are funny. At least, all of the worthy ones do.*"

# EPILOGUE

**Basement Suite**
**Viking, Inc., Business Division**
**Manassas, VA**
**New Year's Eve, morning**

Val would have figured that melting down that lovely, ridiculous Freya statue would be one of the hardest things she'd ever done, but as it turned out, washing the money raised through the sale of nearly ten pounds of pure electrum was harder.

"The IRS always gets its pound of flesh, Miss Daisy," Kat assured her. "I have looked at the rules surrounding the legal claim of sunken treasure discovered in the Gulf of Mexico. Trust me when I say that this is easier."

The 'discovery of sunken treasure while scuba diving in Mexico' had been Val's idea. A good way to explain to Uncle Sam how VALKYRIE, a three-man operation with absolutely no history of cash flow, suddenly found itself invigorated with nearly a hundred thousand dollars.

Jacob had suggested that, when an auditor inevitably came around to investigate the source of their funds, they offer to off her cheating baby daddy. By the look on his face, he'd only been partially kidding.

It was Kat, that master of the gray market and freelancer extraordinaire, who eventually convinced them that even if they hadn't raided a World Heritage site to steal ancient artifacts, they still needed to legitimize the money, and that as soon as they'd upgraded their tech arsenal, they needed to hire an accountant.

The morning of New Year's Eve saw the founding three members of VALKYRIE sitting in a dank and chilly basement compiling a list of all the pawn shops in the greater DC Metro area.

"All right." Jacob sighed, straightening his stack of notes. "Let me make sure I've got this straight. We split the electrum and sell it off to different pawn shops across the state, in individual quantities too small to trigger IRS investigations. Once that's done, we have a whole big pile of money that we still can't explain to the IRS."

Kat nodded. "So one of you fine folk heads to the riverboats with a couple thousand dollars just burning a hole in your hot little pockets. Casinos aren't known for tracking or documenting the money that pays for chips. You gamble a little bit, cash out, and then voilà, you've got yourself a nice big bag of legal casino winnings. We still have to report that income and pay the associated taxes, of course, but at least it will look like a legitimate source of funds."

Jacob scrubbed some early-morning grit from his eyes. "Somebody explain to me why we can't just say we found the statues on my family's homestead or something and that makes them legally ours to do with as we please?"

"Because I would rather die than go on official record saying I was involved with the destruction of historically significant oddities," Val hissed. "Do you have any idea what that would do to my chances of ever getting into a postdoc program?"

"I didn't realize that was still a desired career path for you," Jacob shot back dryly. "Considering…" He made a vague gesture to the basement around them, specifically indicating all the guns hidden in the armory on the other side of the center wall.

"I like to keep my options open." Val's cheeks reddened. "You know, for like….when I'm old and arthritic and need to take a desk job."

Jacob's eyebrows rose to his hairline. "I simply cannot imagine you riding a desk."

Val buried her face in the Gambling 101 instruction sheet Kat had printed out for her.

"Only after she's grown tired of riding everything else, I imagine," Kat put in archly, returning to his computer. "You know that one of these days you're going to have to explain to your information specialist where you got those little statues, don't you?"

Val and Jacob exchanged uncomfortable glances.

"Oh, no, don't mind me," Kat twittered. "I'm only one of the nosiest and most capable hackers in the world. I'll never get a bug up my ass and tear people's private lives apart trying to figure out where my business partners are getting the goods or how one of them manages to vanish off some of the most sophisticated surveillance equipment the world has ever known when the mood strikes her."

Val leaned back, rubbing her neck uneasily. "Kat…"

"I like them too much to invade their privacy quite that much," Kat went on. "But my goodness, after a while, all the secrets might just start to hurt my feelings. I'd start to wonder what I even took that ninety percent pay cut for."

"Kat," Val broke in impatiently. "I'm magic, okay? It's fucking magic and I can't explain it."

Kat blinked at her above the thick rims of his glasses.

"Not yet, at least," she muttered, looking away. "I'm not ready yet. Just give me some time. I'll come clean with you when I'm ready. I promise."

For a minute, the only sound in the basement was the hum of the furnace and the whir of the space heater.

"That might buy you some time, Miss Daisy," Kat allowed finally. "If you can guarantee that you'll spill the beans to me before Hawk cracks your odd little nut." He met her sharp look with a sheepish grin. "That's my price, honey. The satisfaction of having a secret that man desperately wants."

"You're a strange human being." Val sighed. "But I've got your back." With mock solemnity, she raised her right hand and placed her left over her heart. "I vow to you that as long as it is within my power, I shall spill my secrets to you before Nathaniel Hawker figures them out for himself."

"*Take no oaths lightly*," Reginleif warned.

"I'm serious," Val told her partner silently. "Kat's right, he's too smart and valuable to keep in the dark forever."

As far as Kat was concerned, the matter seemed closed

for now. He returned to his computer screen as Val and Jacob made plans for their great Pawn Shop Capers.

"So you'll hit the shops south of the border." Val leaned in close to her partner. "And I'll canvas everything that's open in DC on New Year's Eve. Then tonight we'll hit up the riverboat." She grinned up at him, eyes shining. "I hear they throw one hell of a ball-drop rager."

"Don't go too crazy." Jacob straightened his notes and tucked them into his jacket pocket. "I don't want to have to drag your hungover butt to your family's picnic tomorrow."

Val leaned her head against his shoulder. She felt bubbly inside. Giddy in a way she hadn't experienced since she'd found her first high school sweetheart.

*Careful, Kearie,* she told herself wryly. *Or you might develop feelings for the sexy, old-souled Marine you've been casually sleeping with for the past four months.*

Val was wondering if that would be the worst thing in the world when Kat let out a startled little yelp.

"Lord have mercy on my sodomite soul!"

Val nearly jumped out of her chair.

"Miss Daisy!" Kat was suddenly afire with excitement. "You remember what you told me about the bad egg who came after Miss Ana on the island?"

"What about him?" Val's mind tumbled back over the blur of events on Christmas afternoon. "The smell of lulo oil?"

Kat waved that away with an impatient flap of the wrist. "No. You mentioned he was wearing a hood, didn't you?"

Val winced. "Honestly, I don't remember much about

everything above the neck, before…" She mimicked an explosion with her fingers.

"But you did say that. I remember it clearly."

"Okay?" Val shrugged. "But it wasn't over his face when he attacked. It was probably the head part of his weird diving suit."

"Are you sure about that?" Kat whipped his laptop around to reveal a collage of photographs and hazy surveillance camera captures. Each image featured a dark-suited figure wearing a face-obscuring black shroud. There were blurry pale splotches over the shroud, as if someone had dabbed the vaguest likeness of a human face onto the cloth with white paint.

"This sneaky little lickspittle has been flitting around the underworld for almost twenty years," Kat breathed. "Assassins-for-hire. Over thirty confirmed kills with hundreds of other suspected victims all the way from Georgia to Timbuktu. They call them the Revenant."

Val stared at the odd half-formed face dabbed onto that black cloth. It did not look exactly like a skull, but close enough to justify the alias. Deep inside her, Reginleif stirred uneasily. The old Valkyrie had always been leery of teasing the undead.

"Kat, the odds that El Águila hired a world-famous assassin to—" She cut off, staring at the bulky black watch coiled around the figure's wrist in one of the larger images. She frowned. By this time, Ricardo had surely shoveled the dead man's corpse over the rail of a fishing boat, but she wondered if he had kept any of his gear. Because there had been an unusually bulky watch around the assassin's wrist.

"Maybe," she concluded, uncertain. She remembered

his submersible vehicle and the well-maintained sniper rifle. "He was packing some pretty specialized and expensive gear."

"Here's to hoping it was the same son of a bitch," Jacob suggested. "That's one less bastard creeping around trying to nab little girls."

"I would say the same thing." Kat reached for his computer again. "But nothing is ever that simple, is it?" He pulled up an article from an eastern European news site and ran the page through an English translator.

"*Christmas Day Massacre,*" the headline read. "*Minister for Internal Affairs Slaughtered at Family Gathering.*" And the sub-header: "*Security Cameras Confirm Witness Reports of Assassin in Skull Mask.* "

"Unless we have any reason to suspect this man can teleport or fly halfway across the world in under six hours..." Kat shot Val a meaningful look. She shook her head. She might have been magic, but she didn't know anything about that kind of magic. "Then it looks like we might have stumbled on a little cabal of killers for hire."

Val let out a long, slow breath. "Or the guy on Isla de las Flores was unrelated and the resemblance is superficial. Occam's razor and all that."

Jacob had whipped out his phone and was running searches of his own. He shook his head, pensive. "Nah. There are too many kills attributed to the Revenant for it to be one person. First one was back in the eighties." He shot Val a glance. "Which would have made the man on the island at least sixty years old."

Val shifted her weight. All of her giddy good cheer was threatening to drain away and leave her with an empty pit of hard-eyed hunger. Not that she disliked her drive to seek out and put a stop to that kind of dickwad. She just didn't want it to get in the way of her New Year's plans.

"Okay," she conceded quietly. "Given the age and kill count of Mister Revenant, I guess a cabal of masked assassins does seem likely."

"Given the fact that you left one of their number rotting on the jungle floor…" Jacob slipped his phone away, rose to his feet, and cracked his knuckles. The day was young and it was time to hit the pavement. "I'd wager that you just pissed them off something fierce."

# AUTHOR NOTES

## WRITTEN FEBRUARY 14, 2023

Thank you for not only reading this book but these author notes as well!

**It's Valentine's Day**

And you hold in your hand a romance, right? I mean, yeah, it has guns...and blood...and a little bit of cursing. Okay, Ryan Reynolds got away with calling Deadpool a romance, so why can't I?

(Maybe because I'm not nearly as photogenic and charismatic as Ryan? Could be. Probably. Most likely.)

Anyway, there is love in the air and shenanigans afoot.

**My Dad**

If you have read the Pain and Agony Series (see below), you know that my father (who hasn't read in, like, ten years) started reading my *Pain and Agony* series because "it's something without monsters and creatures and magic."

In short, almost all my other books.

*Pain and Agony* was a good old feel-good eighties buddy-buddy kick-ass adventure series, and it's right up his alley. He's read three books so far.

*Chooser of the Slain* MIGHT be able to get him to connect with the story because I didn't do much on the mythological front until the very end of the book. I've been considering suggesting he try the series, but I've decided (I think) to hold off until he makes it through the *Pain and Agony* series.

If he does, ONE of my parents (I have three) will have read my books. I wasn't looking for any of my parents to read anything, so it's like finding a twenty-dollar bill in a coat pocket the first time you wear a coat for the winter season.

A gift.

If you enjoy the feel of this series and don't mind a book without magic, paranormal, or science fiction, you might enjoy it. I'm sure I've suggested it before, but my father got me thinking about it again. There's a link at the bottom.

## AI

For those that follow my conversations, you know I'm dealing with the AI stuff in our industry. My short (very) update is that I'm still working like a one-armed wallpaper hanger, and I don't have a clue what's coming in the future. I wish I did.

## STORIUSFM

Want to try some audiobooks for free? Hate to download apps? Try www.StoriusFM.com and see if we have anything you might like. We are building the "Fiction 24/7" Internet Radio Station, and I hope to have more books and more fun heading your way soon.

*Chat with you in the next book.*

Ad Aeternitatem,

Michael Anderle

MORE STORIES with Michael newsletter HERE: https://
michael.beehiiv.com/

Link to the Pain and Agony series listed above

From Book 1:

**Those who killed their partners will wish they had
never been born.**

**Pain is a burned ex-mercenary. Agony is a burned
ex-cop.**

Together, they might just find out who did it.

*The only problem? They can't stand each other.*

**Trust apparently doesn't come easily between a
black-ops mercenary and an ex-police detective.**

What could make it worse for her?

*He doesn't like using guns.*

**Will Pain and Agony dodge the criminals who are**

**trying to take them out and avoid killing each other in the process?**

Will the criminals be able to handle the two of them together?

_Read PAIN AND AGONY_ and enjoy the exploits of two people who might become friends.

# CONNECT WITH THE AUTHOR

## **Connect with Michael Anderle**

Website: http://lmbpn.com

Email List: http://lmbpn.com/email/

https://www.facebook.com/LMBPNPublishing

https://twitter.com/MichaelAnderle

https://www.instagram.com/lmbpn_publishing/

https://www.bookbub.com/authors/michael-anderle

# BOOKS BY MICHAEL ANDERLE